AGENT OUT

Check out this thrilling new series:

FEARLESS® FBI

FEARLESS FBI

AGENT OUT

Francine Pascal

SIMON PULSE
New York   London   Toronto   Sydney

First Simon Pulse edition March 2006

Copyright © 2006 by Francine Pascal

SIMON PULSE
An imprint of Simon & Schuster Children's Publishing Division
1230 Avenue of the Americas, New York, NY 10020

 Produced by Alloy Entertainment
151 West 26th Street
New York, NY 10001

Printed in the United States of America
10 9 8 7 6 5 4 3 2 1

Library of Congress Control Number: 2005933401
ISBN-13: 978-0-689-87823-7
ISBN-10: 0-689-87823-0

AGENT OUT

Gaia

Time Stamp: 2:30 a.m.

[*Recorder on*] Agent Gaia Moore recording. I can't give a case number because this case does not exist—not as far as the FBI is concerned. They think Catherine is already dead. Apparently they're prepared to let her name just fade away on some inactive missing persons list for the next twenty years without lifting another finger, but with all due respect to you, Agent Malloy, I think that's a crock. You have no idea what's happened to Catherine, and neither do I. One abandoned laptop and some blood on a lost duffel bag doesn't tell you anything. You can't just declare her dead and be done with it—she deserves more than that. Catherine and I have pulled each other through every single day of this training. She never once lost faith in me, and I am not about to lose faith in her. She is more than my friend, she's my *partner*, and I doubt very much, sir, that you could write off your partner as easily as the bureau has written off Agent Sanders. I think that's lousy police work—lazy and shortsighted—and I think I can do better. I'm stating that for the record here, in the hopes that you and the rest of the bureau will understand my motives.

Eventually you're all going to see why I had to do it this way—sneaking off base in the middle of the night to find her. I admit I feel a little foolish. I feel like I'm seventeen years old again—sneaking out on my foster parents to dodge some ridiculous curfew. I swore to myself that I'd never be a rebellious teenage cliché again, but there you have it: I am what I am. I know how unprofessional this is, believe me. I would have loved nothing more than to pursue this investigation *with* your permission, sir; you just weren't inclined to offer it.

You've probably already declared me AWOL. Someone must have noticed that I'm not in my bed and I'm nowhere to be found on the whole Quantico base. I wouldn't be surprised if you'd already started proceedings for my termination, but all I can say is . . . I'm doing what I think is right. I'm doing what I need to do. If you knew more about my past, you'd understand. [*Pause*] What am I saying? You're the FBI—you probably know everything about my past. So maybe someone on some disciplinary committee who hears this recording will consider my history and show me some mercy. Maybe *you'll* understand, Malloy. . . . I'm just not going to write off another friend. I can't. And I don't see the point of having this badge or this gun if I can't even help my own partner. I don't care how hopeless you all think it is. I couldn't care less. [*Recorder off*]

Time Stamp: 2:48 a.m.

[*Recorder on*] I don't know why my foot is still on the gas. I don't even know why I'm going in this direction. My eyes keep drifting out the driver's side window—looking for signs of her body in the gravel on the side of the highway. That's what I've been reduced to here. I know it's irrational and naive, and I should be ashamed to call myself FBI, but that's what I'm doing. A dog would have a better chance of finding her like this. I need more to go on. I need *something* to go on. Jesus, I feel like such an amateur talking into this thing. You trained me to take audio notes in an investigation, so that's what I'm doing. You say it will keep my thoughts organized. You say it will help me flush out the right clue. Like this recorder is going to help me find her out here in the dark on this completely abandoned highway. I don't think so. I don't even need a machine to help me keep track of clues. I don't forget things. Ever. You can call it a photographic memory, but it's more complicated than that. You might have noticed, Agent Malloy . . . I'm not like the other trainees. [*Pause*] Note to self: erase that last part.

The point is, I'm not really using this recorder to take notes on this case. I'm using this recorder because it's the only partner I've got right now. I need someone to talk to while I look for her . . . even if that someone is me. I'm alone out here. And I mean that in every sense of the word. [*Pause*]

A message for Will . . . Will, I'm sorry. I'm sorry I stood you up for dinner—I was busy emptying my bank account at an ATM machine, but I know that's just a lame excuse. But more than that, I'm sorry if you think I don't listen enough. I know you didn't want to me to do this, but . . . Look, most of all I'm sorry for leaving the lollipop case right in the middle of the investigation. I'm sorry for leaving it all in your hands. I hope Malloy doesn't come down on you too hard. I hope you don't feel like I've abandoned you or abandoned the case or the victims or anything like that. We will solve that case, Will. We'll find the killer, I'm *sure* of it. Just give me a little time. If you can carry the case for just a few days . . . I'll be back. I swear I will. And I'll bring Catherine with me. [*Recorder off*]

The sun had risen, but Gaia hardly noticed. Somewhere along the way the sky had shifted from moonlit black to ugly amber to its current shade of ash white. How long had she been driving now? The miles of gas stations and convenience stores had all melted into one big peripheral blur. Her eyes stung like hell from exhaustion, and the harsh glare of the late morning haze was only making it worse. She could practically hear her body pleading for an hour of sleep, but rest was out of the question. All that mattered now were the worn-out street signs overhead.

She hunched farther over the steering wheel, squinting up through the dusty windshield of Catherine's Nissan Altima to decipher the faded names. Palmer Street . . . Mortimer Street . . . Winslow Road . . . But no Cherry Lane.

Where the hell is 1309 Cherry Lane?

The unfamiliar address had been rattling in her brain for three hours now—ever since Lyle had whispered it nervously to her over the phone. She could still hear his nasal voice cracking with anxiety. . . .

"I shouldn't be doing this, Gaia. You know I shouldn't be doing this. Malloy was just in here asking questions. He's pissed, Gaia. You know you're in serious—"

"I know that, Lyle. I know. The trace. Could you trace the origin of the signal or not?"

"Hold on."

"Lyle, do not *put me on hold!"*

"Just hold on, okay? I have to check the doors. They're searching the whole complex for you, you know."

6

She knew she'd put Lyle in an unfair position. After all, he was just a spindly little FBI lab tech—it's not like she wanted to make him an accomplice to her unauthorized investigation. But around seven in the morning, somewhere in the middle of Richmond, Gaia had come to terms with reality. Her *only* legitimate lead was back at that computer lab in Quantico. There was no other choice but to call Lyle on his personal cell and pray he'd already reported to the lab—which, thank God, he had.

All she had going for her was that cryptic computer program Catherine had left behind. Gaia had found the program still running on Catherine's computer after she'd disappeared. Gaia assumed it was the high-powered search engine Catherine had been boasting about—a little piece of software she'd created that was supposed to cross-reference all the evidence in the lollipop case and spit back potential suspects. But once Will and Gaia examined Catherine's computer more closely, they realized that her program was collecting a *very different* kind of information. Her turbocharged search engine had found something that it had clearly not been meant to find—namely, an index of Latin American addresses that looked an awful lot like terrorist sleeper cells.

This bizarre discovery had left Gaia and Will in a near catatonic state of puzzlement. But that was just the beginning of the strangeness. Not only was Catherine's program gathering this explosive information, but someone, it seemed, was *still* accessing the information in her absence. According to Lyle, even though Catherine had disappeared days before, someone had been using her program as recently as twenty-four hours ago.

Could that someone be Catherine? Could she be out there

somewhere trying to access her own computer? Could someone be forcing her to access it? Or what if it was someone else entirely? Some nameless, faceless asshole who'd already gotten rid of Catherine and was trying to nab the information for himself? These questions were the only thing keeping Gaia's eyes glued open and focused on the road ahead.

Will had asked Lyle if there was any way to trace the access. Lyle said he would try, but trying wasn't good enough. Gaia knew she'd have to push Lyle to get the info she needed—even if it meant taking advantage of his rather obvious crush on her. So with just the right combination of dominance and flirtation, she'd finally managed to coax poor Lyle past his initial anxiety until he'd coughed up an address.

"Baltimore, okay? The program was accessed from a telephone modem in Baltimore. The Verizon map pinpoints the signal at Cherry Lane near Ditmar Street. The exact address is 1309 Cherry Lane. Someone in that house was logged onto Catherine's computer in the last twenty-four hours."

"You're a genius, Lyle. You seriously are a goddamn genius. I don't know how to thank you for this."

"Well, maybe when you get back, we could go out for some—?"

"I've got to go, Lyle. We never had this conversation, okay?"

"You're damn right, we never had this conversation. I could be fired just for talking to—"

Click.

And so here she was, searching in vain for Cherry Lane. She would have asked Lyle to map out a route for her, but she knew she'd kept him on the phone too long as it was. Another thirty seconds and the bureau would have been tracing Lyle's call, personal cell or not—and she wouldn't risk getting him in any more trouble. She'd have to find Cherry Lane the old-fashioned way.

Once she'd made it into Baltimore, she asked for directions at a gas station, but the "attendant" with the faded faux-Nike Just Do Her T-shirt hadn't been much help. She could only make out every other word he said. All she'd been able to gather was that Cherry Lane was a few miles south and a number of blocks west. But the other half of his unintelligible directions were a seemingly endless repetition of the words "left," "right," "old church," and "Old MacDonald's," which, Gaia was reasonably sure, was not an old man's farm, but rather the term this man used to describe his favorite dining establishment. Eventually she did find her way to Ditmar Street, but Ditmar seemed to go on forever. . . .

"Jesus," she breathed through nearly closed lips, surveying the row of crumbling houses up ahead. There was no denying it: America could be one ugly-ass eyesore of a country. It seemed the city council had taken a meeting and decided to give up altogether on the outskirts of Baltimore. Each little house looked more forgotten than the last, from the broken, soot-covered windows to the rusted-out aluminum siding, and to the tattered stars and stripes hanging tenuously over the piles of bricks that stood in for porch steps. This sure as hell wasn't the lush backwoods of Quantico, Virginia. It wasn't the pristine sunny streets of California or even the rich, historical filth of New York City. No, this was something else entirely.

This was Absolute Nowhere, USA. Suburban degradation in all its glory.

Please don't let her be in one of these houses, Gaia thought, slowing the car to cruising speed. *Maybe Lyle has no idea what he's talking about.*

She was so distracted by the urban sprawl that she nearly passed right by the magic words. She quickly slammed on the brakes and backed it up a few yards. All her exhaustion drained away once she saw the faded white letters on the rusty blue sign overhead:

Cherry Lane.

It's about freaking time, she thought, slamming her foot down on the gas. The tires skidded with a deafening screech as she turned the sharp corner and picked up the pace, eyeing every numbered address that hadn't fallen off its facade. And finally, her marathon drive had come to an end. The nine might have slipped its hinge to become a six, but the rotting house before her was most definitely none other than 1309.

She pulled over to the side of the road and turned off the transmission. The engine sputtered with a long sigh—she could almost feel the Altima thanking her for the much needed rest.

She sat there for a moment in silence, examining the house from inside the car. Just as expected, it was not a pretty sight. The warped, hospital blue siding had that eerie generic flavor of a house that didn't want to be noticed. The porch door was boarded up with a thick slab of wood and couched in too much shadow to see clearly. The rest of the porch was bare, with the exception of a filthy black barbecue grill that a family of spiders had long since made their home. There was no front lawn to speak of—just a makeshift little garbage collection on a patch of black dirt. Anyone with a conventional genetic code would have taken one look at this place, locked all the car doors, and called for backup. But Gaia's genes were far from conventional. She could already feel a hungry buzz in her chest where the fear should have been. She was aching to kick through that knotty plank-of-wood door, but she thought better of it. She'd learned her lesson at Quantico about rash behavior, and she had no intention of repeating her mistakes.

Gaia might have gone AWOL, but that was the *only* thing about this investigation that would not be squeaky clean. Authorized or not, she was going to conduct this search like the professional she was. She would bring Catherine back, and she'd do it by the book, and Malloy and the rest of them would have nothing left to say but "thank you" and "you have our deepest apologies for underestimating you both." She had already acquired a wealth of knowledge at Quantico—probably more than she even knew—and now was the time to put it all into practice. This time she'd be going without the "training wheels"—without the supervision of Bishop or Malloy or Crane, without the unearned respect that the town seemed to afford its trainees, and most of all . . . without Catherine or Will by her side. This was her show now and hers alone. And she had no intention of screwing it up.

She made sure her badge was strapped to her belt, and then she pulled her gun from the glove compartment, ignoring the slight hitch in her chest that still accompanied a firearm. Her traumatic history with guns was becoming a little more manageable with each passing day of training. She checked the cartridge and then secured the gun in the holster under her black jacket. She took one last deep breath and then climbed out of the car, slamming the door behind her and locking it with the key chain remote.

Her approach was quick and deliberate: through the garbage-strewn "lawn," up the creaky wooden steps of the empty porch, and straight to the boarded-up door. She gave the door three stiff knocks and then stepped closer to listen for movement. Nothing. Four more knocks yielded the same result. Pure unadulterated silence.

She stepped over to the window and tried to peer through the one pane of glass that hadn't turned completely opaque with dirt, but all she could see was darkness. The mailbox was nameless, empty, and gathering dust.

This house was positively dead. Just an abandoned hospital blue box in the middle of nowhere. Standing there on the creaky porch, Gaia finally took a moment to ask herself the obvious question:

What the hell could this decrepit shack on the outskirts of Baltimore possibly have to do with Catherine Sanders?

She stood there puzzled for another few seconds, but her inertia made her twitch with frustration. She hadn't come all this way for a dead end. She needed more information. She needed to know the deal with this house. Did someone actually live here? Had anyone *ever* lived here? She scanned the adjacent houses for neighbors, but each place looked deader than the last. And then finally, a few houses down and across the street, she saw the first signs of life on Cherry Lane.

There was a diner. Moscone's. Old and dilapidated to be sure, but open for business. And old was good. Someone in there had to know something about this house. Whatever freak had lived here must have stopped in at least once or twice for a cup of coffee and a slice of pie.

There were still a few irrefutable facts in this life, and Gaia had yet to see this one disproved: it didn't matter if it was Moscone's in the crap section of Baltimore or Cozy Soup 'n' Burger in the heart of downtown New York. At one point or another, everyone needed a cup of coffee and a slice of pie.

UNFORCED AND CASUAL

As Gaia moved toward the diner, the *stillness* hit her again. It was so painfully quiet on this wide, deserted street. The asphalt was cracked and stained, and a paper cup was rolling in the dark gutter near a broken iron drain cover. *Moscone's Diner* was hand-painted over a dark metal door with dirty glass inlays. A white do-it-yourself sign with attached black letters in the window read: LUNCH SPECIAL SOUP AND SANDWICH $3.95 FREE COFFEE 12–2. Gaia stepped deliberately forward and pushed on the diner's door, rattling the overhead bell as it swung inward.

The smell of cooking grease entered Gaia's nostrils immediately. By comparison, the Greek diners in Manhattan, where she'd scarfed down chocolate milk shakes most of her life, smelled like four-star restaurants. Ignoring the smell, still holding the door open, Gaia waited for her eyes to adjust to the gloom.

Everyone was looking at her.

Control the scene, Agent Crane had told them all in one of his training lectures. Gaia could hear his harsh voice as if he was standing right in front of her, glaring at the FBI class. *Most people have never seen an FBI agent. When they do, they'll want to trust you,* want *to believe in you. So don't make it hard for them.*

Control the scene.

The diner was about half full. There were booths against the big picture windows—they had leather benches repaired with tape and Formica tables with metal edges. All of them were occupied. An elderly couple in windbreakers with identical bowls of soup sat closest to the door. The man was twisted around in his chair so that he could get a better view of the alien blond thing that had just walked in.

In front of her was a long, low lunch counter. The wall behind it was covered in metal sheets with stacks of miniature cereal boxes against it. A dark-haired man in a clean white T-shirt was frozen in the act of wiping the counter. The chrome stools were occupied by big men—they looked like truckers—with beards and dark caps pulled over their eyes. In the far back of the diner, next to what had to be a bathroom door, a thin, unshaven middle-aged man in a dark suit and tie sat motionless at a table, a steaming cup of coffee in front of him, watching her.

Well? Gaia told herself angrily. *You've got their attention. That's step one. Now do something with it.*

A waitress was standing in the middle of the diner, the weak fluorescent overhead light reflecting in her yellow hair. She was not a young woman. Her eyes were heavily mascaraed, and her hands were wrinkled and covered in rings. She was frozen in the act of writing on an order pad. The young woman at the table in front of her had a small dog in a pink plastic bag. Even the dog was staring at Gaia.

"Hi," Gaia said, giving what she hoped was a disarming smile. With her left hand she'd already flipped out her badge. "Have you got a second, ma'am? FBI."

Everyone in the diner had a second. You could have heard a pin drop.

That sounded weird, Gaia told herself. But this was very different from Virginia. In Quantico, even in the town proper, people were used to the presence of the FBI. When Gaia, Catherine, Will or whoever walked into a place, people looked up, mildly curious, and went back to whatever they were doing. "Just those government kids," people would tell each other. Suddenly Gaia felt very far away from home.

Had she sounded weird? She couldn't tell. She was supposed to say her name, followed by "FBI," while holding out her badge. It was routine. But somehow in this silent, dark restaurant, with the deserted, bare street out the dirty plate glass window, it was different. This was the real world—and her instincts had told her to be unforced and casual.

And don't worry about it, Gaia told herself angrily. She had enough to worry about without this completely unwelcome attack of self-consciousness. It didn't matter if she sounded weird—the important thing was her investigation, how she "controlled the scene."

"Help you with something?" the waitress drawled. Up close, Gaia could see the deep lines in her face and smell the tobacco smoke on her breath. She didn't sound *disrespectful,* exactly. She just wasn't going to give that much deference to a twenty-year-old girl with a mess of unwashed blond hair tied up in a scraggly ponytail—FBI or no.

"If you wouldn't mind," Gaia went on, reaching into her pocket to pull out Catherine's photo. "Could you take a good look at this picture, please? Have you ever seen this woman?"

15

The waitress tore her eyes away from the inside of Gaia's jacket—she must have caught a glimpse of her gun—and turned back to the snapshot Gaia was holding out. It wasn't that great a picture—Lyle had found it on the network and quickly printed it out for her before she left. It was a low-resolution digital snapshot of Catherine, taken during the Quantico admissions process. It couldn't be more than six months old, but to Gaia's eyes, Catherine looked years younger. Her hair was already trimmed in the trademark pixie cut (copied from Special Agent Jennifer Bishop), and the smile she gave the camera was innocent and engaging.

"Arf! Arf!" The little dog in the seated woman's pink plastic bag suddenly exploded into a barking fit, its marble black eyes fixed on Gaia. The sound was deafening.

"Waffles, hush," the woman told her dog. "Sorry, ma'am."

"That's okay," Gaia said, smiling at her. The *ma'am* reassured her—she had control of the room. She hadn't flinched—people might have noticed that. Gaia held the photograph out again.

As the waitress peered skeptically at the snapshot, Gaia tried to stay focused. But it was hard. She couldn't shake the thoughts of Catherine from her head. She *had* to know where Catherine was now—whether she was still smiling or whether she was trembling and pale, locked in a cold basement room somewhere.

Or dead, Gaia told herself. *Don't forget Malloy's theory.*

"Sorry." The waitress shook her head.

"Are you sure?" Gaia raised her eyebrows. "Ever? Anywhere? Take your time—look at the picture as long as you want."

"I could look at it all day—it won't change the fact that I never seen this girl," the waitress blandly insisted.

The thin man in the black suit was watching her. His eyes

seemed to light up in the darkness from the back of the diner. His narrow tie was clipped to his shirt, and his collar was freshly starched. The salt-and-pepper hair reminded Gaia suddenly of her father, for reasons she didn't quite understand—the man looked nothing like her father. But his calm stare was different from the looks of the other patrons—he was coolly appraising her, as if he saw this kind of thing every day and was ready to tell her what she was doing wrong.

"This is a federal investigation," Gaia said loudly, looking around the room. Fourteen pairs of eyes stared back. Her voice echoed against the walls, sounding high-pitched and young. "I'm looking for a missing person—a young woman my age, with short black hair and glasses. Her name is Catherine Sanders."

Who are you kidding? Gaia told herself. *They can see right through you. Because this* isn't *a "federal investigation"; it's a private wild-goose chase.*

"Waffles," the woman with the pink bag scolded her dog again. The dog had erupted into another frenzied spasm of barking.

"Let me see that photo." the man behind the counter said meekly. Gaia walked over, her heels clicking on the linoleum, and held out the snapshot. The counterman leaned over, squinting critically as he stared at the picture.

"She could look different," Gaia told him. "She could have different hair, or she could have lost her glasses."

Or she could be dead, that same voice repeated maddeningly in her head. The blood-streaked duffel bag snapped into focus in her imagination.

"Sorry, ma'am," the counterman said finally, standing back upright. "Can't help you."

"Do you know who lives across the street?"

One of the men at the counter looked over at her. Gaia caught his eye, and the burly man held her steady gaze. Behind him, out the window, the sagging facade of the house faced the street like an empty mask.

"You, sir?" Gaia stepped forward. "Do you know whose house that is?'

"Who wants to know?"

"I told you," Gaia said, stepping closer to the man. "I'm a federal agent. If you know who lives over there, I want you to—"

"Little girl like you? I don't believe it," the man said. From up close, his breath smelled of pepper and coffee. He was staring at Gaia, his teeth shining, his unshaven face twisted into a smirk. "Why don't you run home to your mama and leave us alone?"

Gaia reached out and grabbed the man's wrist. Slowly she started bending it downward. The man tried to pull away—looking very surprised when he wasn't able to.

"You interrupted me," Gaia said, leaning closer. "Please don't do that again."

"Let go—"

Gaia held up the photograph. "I want to know if you've seen this woman," she said calmly. "Why don't you take a nice long look and tell me if you recognize her?"

"Let go of my arm!" the man yelled. He was squirming in his seat, but Gaia was holding him at a particular angle so that he couldn't move. "Let me go, damn it!"

"You're not looking," Gaia said, moving the picture closer to his face. "Tell me if the woman in this pic—"

"No! No! I've never seen her!" the man yelled. Everyone in the diner was watching. "I don't know who she is!"

"None of us know," the elderly man in the window booth called out. "Now leave Jimmy alone and let us eat our lunch."

Gaia looked over at the man who'd spoken. He was ladling a spoonful of soup toward his craggy mouth, unconcerned. It was almost like a signal—the clinking of silverware resumed. It was as if the old man had given everyone permission to ignore Gaia.

At the back of the restaurant the thin man in the black suit watched her curiously. It was almost as if he was waiting to see what she'd do next—how good her training or her instincts were. She quickly moved her eyes away from his and gazed around again at the diner customers.

They don't know anything.

Gaia was suddenly sure of it. They hadn't seen Catherine and they didn't know who lived across the street—if anyone did. They weren't hiding anything; they just didn't know the answers to her questions. Nodding once, although nobody was watching anymore, Gaia moved toward the door. The bell rang again weakly as she walked back out into the still Baltimore air.

a perfect target

THE SHADOWS BEHIND THE HOUSE

Gaia could feel eyes on the back of her neck as she came back out to the sidewalk. She didn't turn around, but she was pretty sure the waitress and the other diner patrons were still watching her.

And the man in the suit.

Gaia wasn't sure what it was about that man that had caught her attention. And she wasn't about to go back for another look. She'd had just about enough of Moscone's Diner and its singularly unhelpful patrons. And all that man had done was sit in the shadows and watch her. Nothing so unusual in that.

Except that she knew better. One thing Gaia had learned from even the rudimentary amount of FBI training she'd had was that you had to pay attention to your instincts. Not *trust* them necessarily (in fact, that could be a terrible mistake) but at least be aware of them. And something about the tall, gaunt man in the diner was sticking with her. *Blue eyes,* she told herself. *Close-cropped salt-and-pepper hair. Not a military cut—a little longer. Needed a shave. Clothes have seen better days—suit a bit wrinkled, white shirt yellowing a bit.*

Anything else?

Like Dad, Gaia realized. The thought gave her a strange pang. She hadn't seen her father since her Stanford graduation—since that unforgettable afternoon when this whole crazy thing had started, the day she'd taken a high dive off a campus roof and saved three hundred people from ten pounds of exploding C-4 plastique. *The guy in the diner reminds me of my father, that's all. Dad, if things had never gone his way—if he'd fallen down on his luck and never quite bounced back.*

That was all.

Standing beneath the bleak white sky, Gaia gazed back at the house across the street. It was her next stop, obviously. Her only choice was to go back and give the place a much more thorough search.

Unfortunately, nothing had changed in the few minutes she'd been across the street. The door was still shut tight, and the house was still silent and unmoving.

So is Catherine in there or not?

Craning her neck, Gaia looked straight overhead. Squinting into the sky, she could see the rusted-out wires running from a nearby phone pole and over to an ancient-looking metal box attached right beneath the house's cracked eaves.

The telephone line.

That's got to be it, she told herself. *That's got to be the line that leads to the mystery modem.* She still couldn't quite believe it, but Lyle had sounded so sure.

Facing the creaky porch steps again, Gaia was very conscious of wasting time. She kept fighting off images of Catherine bound and gagged somewhere in the darkness behind that door, waiting for her to stop playing games and come get her. Looking at the front door's rusty doorknob, she knew she could break the door down with one good shove, but there was a little problem of fed-

21

eral law—the law that said she couldn't enter this house without an invitation or a search warrant. And a search warrant was flat-out impossible—it meant a judge, and a hearing, and actual FBI authorization, none of which she had. And it meant *time*—at least a day's delay. It was out of the question.

She glanced back over her shoulder. The reflections in the diner window made it impossible to see whether she was being watched—and at this point the last thing she needed was some-one calling the bureau and checking up on her. *A young blond woman was just here,* Gaia imagined the waitress saying into the phone. *Claimed to be FBI—waved a badge but didn't seem to know what she was doing. Then she went across the street and broke into that house.*

Casually, as if she was taking a scenic walk, Gaia strolled to the left, heading across the dirt yard and around the side of the house. Her footsteps sank into the soft ground as she walked. Brushing a stray strand of hair away from her face, she sneaked a glance back at the diner and the sidewalk. Nothing. Nobody around. She kept going and, once she was out of view of the street, she reached under her jacket and pulled out her gun.

The weeds got higher as she moved into the shadows behind the house. She could smell the stink of garbage getting stronger. Without looking down, she could tell she was walking on old beer cans and God knows what else in those tall weeds. The garbage smell grew stronger still, and Gaia could see why. Black plastic trash bags were strewn everywhere.

She tried not to think about what could be hidden in this dis-gusting backyard. It would take a team of five agents most of an afternoon to go through a place like this, carefully bagging and tagging everything and collecting chemical and forensic evidence. Gaia remembered a story Agent Crane had told them about an innocent-looking Idaho housewife who'd had two bodies buried in the icy ground behind her trailer home.

She finally sidled up to the back door, holding her gun straight out. She tried to stick to procedure, looking around for all her "danger spots"—the spots where she was vulnerable to an attack. There was a laundry line strung with bedsheets over a fence behind her—no sniper spots, no danger areas. Good. The other direction, she saw dark overhanging trees and more garbage bags—fine. No danger areas. Raising the gun, she reached with her left hand and rapped on the door.

"Hello?" she called out. "Anybody home?"

Nothing. Her own reflection looked back at her from the cracked glass of the door. She rapped again more loudly

Her shadow on the door suddenly deepened—a cloud bank had shifted and the sky had darkened. Somewhere in that brief gust of wind, as Gaia held her breath, she swore she'd heard the faintest voice coming from inside the house. *Catherine?* No—it was a male voice. Very indistinct, and very far away. Probably the television.

Now she was using every ounce of her will to fight off the impulse to break in.

Late at night, in their dorm room, Gaia and Catherine had gone through all the books, memorizing the guidelines for criminal investigation and the rules of evidence. Catherine's memory was impeccable—nearly as good as Gaia's—so they'd made fast work of it. *A federal agent may not enter upon private property,* Gaia recited to herself now, *unless sufficient evidence exists that a criminal act or acts or the reckless endangerment of civilians is in process within said property, such that the agent's intervention is necessary to prevent such crime from occurring or concluding.*

The blurred, faint male voice kept talking inside the house. She could hear it for sure now. It sounded very much like a television—the rapid-fire delivery of a commercial announcer. Now she could hear a female voice, too, and background music. Definitely a television.

But it could *be a crime in progress,* she convinced herself. *It could be.*

"Here goes," she muttered, sighing heavily. With the complete knowledge that she was crossing a line that she couldn't uncross, Gaia pulled back and slammed her shoulder into the door.

With a tremendous crack, the door lock fell to the ground and the door swung inward. It gave so quickly that Gaia nearly lost her balance, stumbling forward into the darkness. She kept her grip on the gun, immediately whipping her body to one side, out of the bright doorway where she knew she presented a perfect target.

THE GUN YOU COULDN'T SEE

The smell hit her first—a rank kitchen aroma of stale air, dirty dishes, rotting pizza boxes, and accumulated garbage. As her eyes adjusted, Gaia began to see dimly through the blackness. Dust motes danced in the light from the doorway. Glancing at the door itself, Gaia saw that there would be no way to hide the obvious fact that she'd broken in. The entire edge of the wooden door frame was splintered apart, with shards of splintered wood sticking out in all directions.

I heard a sound, Gaia imagined herself telling a judge and jury. *I heard voices—I heard a threatening male voice. I thought I could hear my friend. I knew my friend was in danger.*

"Anybody home?" Gaia called out.

No answer. As her eyes continued to adjust, Gaia could see a calendar tacked to the peeling wallpaper above the filthy old-fashioned sink. It was a wildlife calendar. It showed a dark green photograph of a wooded glade, where a single yellow-eyed owl gazed out at the camera. Gaia flicked her head back and forth, checking the room's entrances. There was a narrow, closed door that was probably a broom closet. Moving cat-like toward it, Gaia leveled the gun at the door, took a deep breath, and kicked it open. Two long-handled mops leaned on a wall in the gloom within.

To Gaia's left, a doorway led into another room. Now she could hear the murky voices more clearly, but it was still impossible to make out what they were saying.

"Hello?" Gaia called out. "FBI," she added—more to herself than to anyone else.

If there *was* anyone else. Pivoting through the kitchen door, gun raised, Gaia entered a narrow living room with a low ceiling and shag carpeting. A weak light shone through the blinds to the left and right—the blinds she'd been unable to peer through moments before. More cardboard pizza boxes littered the floor. Gaia kicked them out of the way as she walked.

The smell was worse. *Somebody* has *been here,* Gaia realized. *Recently—that's what the smell means. Pizza and dirty dishes from a week ago at most; probably more recent.*

She suddenly noticed the name on the delivery bills that were taped to the pizza boxes. JAMES ROSSITER.

25

Suddenly a muffled male voice called out, *"Time to bet it all!"*

The voice had her raising the gun and whipping her head back and forth, her blond hair flying as she tried to localize its source. *"Join host Bobby Shoshone and twelve thousand dollars in cash prizes on everybody's favorite steeplechase game after these messages!"*

A television. Gaia winced, trying to restrain a sneeze caused by the dust. The voices *had* been coming from a TV. But now, from inside the house, Gaia finally realized the sound was coming from *beneath* her—from underground.

Finally she noticed the detail she'd missed. In front of her, between two fraying fabric wall coverings, was another closed door—and down at its extreme bottom edge she could see a thread of bright yellow light. There was no question—the television sound had come from there.

Basement, Gaia realized. *Someone's in the basement. Rossiter or someone else.*

Catherine.

Gaia knew how to walk silently. She moved toward the door, gun held to one side, staring at the thin line of light along the filthy shag carpeting. In her mind, Gaia was already calculating her move—how to open the door and get through it.

Going through a door is maybe the most important skill an FBI agent has to possess, Special Agent Jennifer Bishop had lectured the trainees. *It can literally mean life or death.* Bishop knew what she was talking about. She went on in graphic detail that day, telling scare stories of top-notch agents who'd been cut down in their prime because they didn't know how to get through a door or had done it wrong just once and gotten a bullet in the face.

Gaia had concentrated very hard on those training exercises. All the martial arts skills in the world couldn't save you from the gun you couldn't see.

Jake, Gaia thought sadly. *Jake found that out.*

She angrily shook the image from her head—which, she was realizing, was becoming easier to do as the months and years went by. She stopped thinking about her dead boyfriend and the bullets in his chest and reached forward to open the door, swinging it open and diving through it. She swung her body back and forth to cover all the angles and crouched at the head of the stairs, the gun held straight out in front of her.

She was in a small, sooty alleyway looking down a flight of narrow wooden stairs. The stairs led down into the darkness, and the television sound was much louder. She could hear the frenzied applause of the studio audience, no doubt welcoming Bobby Shoshone and his twelve thousand dollars in cash prizes.

"Catherine?" Gaia called out. Her voice echoed in the stale air. Her shoes creaked on the wooden steps as she descended. The gun didn't waver—she could hold its muzzle steady, like Bishop had taught them. She glanced quickly backward as she moved.

"Whoever's down there," Gaia called out, reaching the doorway at the foot of the basement stairs, "this is the FBI. Throw down your weapons and put your hands up."

All according to the book, but there was no response. The shouting of the television crowd continued.

Either nobody's there, Gaia thought, *or I'm going to get a big surprise when I turn the corner.*

Being fearless was often synonymous with a lack of good

judgment, so Gaia brazenly turned the corner without a second thought. She covered the room with the gun, left, right, center, before she even recognized what she was seeing. She knew some trainees who couldn't manage to keep their eyes open when they did this—the fear made them wince and shut their eyes, and, as Bishop told them, they were as good as dead. But not Gaia. Her eyes were wide open now.

THIS TWILIGHT ZONE HOUSE

The basement was dark, wide, and badly lit. The ceiling was obscured by hanging pipes. Some of them were leaking. The floor was dark gray cement, covered in dust. The dust revealed several sets of footprints, and Gaia forced herself to stay in one place, midway through the doorway, so she wouldn't smudge the footprints before she could read them.

A large worktable stood near the center of the cluttered room. A large, humming fluorescent light hung above it from a pair of new-looking chains. The table, Gaia realized, was made from an old Ping-Pong table whose net had been removed. The table was swept clean, its pale green surface reflecting the harsh light. A small portable television stood in the corner of the table, showing a flickering, blurry image of the famous Mr. Shoshone, holding a microphone and joking with his studio audience. As she came into the room, Gaia reached over, covering her fingers with her sleeve, and flicked off the TV.

The silence was shocking. Now she could hear the clicks and hums of the house's heating pipes and the ticking of a small digital clock on the worktable. She couldn't hear anything else. She kept the gun drawn.

Opposite the worktable was an old-fashioned wooden desk. It was covered in papers and loose-leaf binders. A large, fairly new computer monitor stood in the center of the desk behind a computer keyboard and a mouse.

The computer, Gaia saw, was connected to a phone line that looked recently installed. A fresh new phone cable ran up the wall, stapled every two feet, and disappeared into a hole in the ceiling. Gaia knew the procedure to test the line for a phone number ID, but she already knew what the number was. This was the computer that had accessed Catherine's program. There was no doubt about it.

At that moment, however, the computer was turned off. Its screen was dead black, a dark glass eye.

Gaia looked at the worktable. Her eyes grazed along its smooth hardboard surface. There was nothing to see but little snips of wire, each about an inch long, in different colors. No big deal—but there was something about the image that nagged at her: those snips and that digital clock near the stained cement wall somehow looked familiar.

"Whatever you see, file it away," Agent Crane had lectured back in Quantico. "It doesn't have to make sense or be important. If you don't understand what it means, just file it away in your mind—and keep those mental files organized because you never know what you'll need to know later on. It's impossible to predict which detail will crack the case."

Gaia doggedly filed away the multicolored wire snips—and suddenly she forgot all about the worktable and its contents.

29

Now that she had moved near the center of the room, she saw something she'd missed before.

Behind the desk, in the shadows against the wall, was a cot—a low-slung, canvas-and-steel camp cot, the kind you'd find at an army/navy surplus store. The cot was covered in a dark, plaid wool blanket that didn't look particularly clean. As she got closer to the cot, she saw that the blanket was turned down, revealing surprisingly clean-looking white sheets and a white cotton pillow.

Carefully, making sure not to touch anything, Gaia leaned her face close to the pillow and took a deep breath. She wrinkled her nose in advance at the rank smell of the room, which seemed to penetrate everywhere. But through the stale air and the decaying aromas of pine cleanser and old food, there was another smell.

Shampoo, Gaia realized. Suddenly her eyes were nearly watering. It wasn't just the pungent, citrus aroma of the Neutrogena hair care product. It was the fact that it was so familiar. It was a smell she'd know anywhere. That was the thing about smells—she never forgot them, even years later, even if she thought she had. Her mother's spicy lilac perfume or the faint smell of Tide and ivory soap on Ed Fargo's shirt collars—when she smelled them again, the years melted away like fog and she was back in time, just like that. And, this was a much more vivid and recent smell. It wasn't hard for her to remember her roommate's shampoo—she had smelled it every day.

Snap out of it, Gaia told herself angrily. *Don't cry.*

But it was a near thing. She could feel her eyes stinging as her face moved toward the Neutrogena-scented bed—and she saw, distinctly, two short black hairs on the pillow.

Catherine.

It was all true then. She had been here—in this filthy basement, in this twilight zone house on this random Baltimore street, miles from Quantico or anything else.

When? When were you here, Catherine? And where the hell did you go?

Gaia forced herself to blink back the tears as she stood up, brushing her hair from her face. Had James Rossiter held her here, terrified, screaming fruitlessly in this dark basement? Had Catherine awakened in the middle of the night, blind with fear as she remembered where she was? Did she cry into this white pillow, wondering what would happen to her?

And what *did* happen to her?

Come on, come on, Gaia told herself impatiently. *Be professional. You're FBI—don't forget it.*

But she didn't *feel* professional right then. Her throat was aching and her eyes were stinging with the lingering smell of the shampoo. How many times had she lounged on her dorm bed on a Sunday morning, the one day they could relax and not worry about calisthenics and training drills, flipping through a magazine while Catherine sailed into the room in a towel, her face looking naked without its tortoiseshell glasses, her wet hair brushed back in black rivulets from her pretty face, filling the room with that Neutrogena smell? *Come on, Moore,* she'd say, her toothbrush dangling from her mouth and distorting her voice. *I think it's pancakes today. You're coming with me. A twenty-year-old girl cannot live on Froot Loops alone.*

Gaia stood motionless in the center of the basement, her hand gripping the Walther automatic, gazing down at the cheap, narrow cot, holding back tears. If she had been in a better mood, she might have allowed herself a moment of pride at successfully getting this far into the investigation. But she felt too helpless. *What investigation?* Gaia told herself angrily. The duffel bag with the blood, Lyle's phone trace, this address—she had no idea what it all meant.

I may not be able to save her, Gaia realized. *She may already be dead.*

No. Gaia firmly shook her head. She was going to find Catherine, and she was going to save her. There was absolutely no question about it. She just had to pull herself together and start thinking like a field agent.

Tearing her eyes away from the cot, Gaia stared at the desk. She wondered if she should risk turning on the computer. Some machines had passwords or detectors that protected them from prying eyes—Gaia had heard stories from her instructors about criminal data that were lost forever because some overzealous agent had flipped computers on, causing them to self-erase. If this was a legitimate investigation, Gaia would already be on a police radio, demanding that an electronics team come recover the computer and bring it to the crime lab's digital investigation center. But she couldn't do anything like that now. She was on her own.

Gaia wasn't sure what to do about the computer—it was the strongest link to Catherine and, maybe, the key to what she had been brought here for.

her vision was now totally black, flooding with iridescent shooting stars

RECEDING AWAY LIKE A DREAM

Later, Gaia tried to forgive herself for the mistake she made in that moment. After all, she was confused and distracted. She was staring at the bed, focusing on the two black hairs, trying to get all her thoughts in order. And to be fair, all her "crime scene" rhythms were thrown off. In all the crime scenes she'd visited (in her short career with the FBI), she'd known what to do. You got the forensic machinery moving. You cleared the area, you canvassed the witnesses, you collected the evidence. You contacted the crime lab, you began profiling, you put out descriptions and APBs if you needed to. But all of that involved having the force of the bureau behind you. And Gaia was completely on her own. She didn't even have envelopes to collect the hairs and fingerprints she could see in front of her.

So, maybe Gaia could be forgiven for letting her guard down—for facing away from an open door, for missing footsteps on the living room floor over her head, for not catching the careful, silent

33

tread on the wooden steps behind her. It was precisely the sort of lapse she'd been trained not to make, and afterward Gaia had plenty of opportunities to curse herself for getting caught up in her thoughts.

The blow crashed into her lower back with such sheer brute force that Gaia lost her balance completely as well as losing her grip on the Walther. Her breath was driven completely out of her body as the gun twirled neatly from her fingers and dropped to the cement floor like a stone. She lost her footing, her shoes slipping in the dust. She toppled to the floor like a fallen statue, a searing pain spreading through her back like fire. *"Oompf,"* she grunted as her face smashed into the edge of the cot, which flipped over. Her ears rang as a tremendous weight landed on top of her. With her head pressed to the floor, she could see a sudden kicking movement to one side and heard the unmistakable *thump* of her gun being kicked across the floor and out of view. As the weight on her back increased, a stinking, fetid smell washed over her head.

"Well, hi there," a rasping male voice whispered in her ear. "Welcome. Won't you come in?"

Gaia gasped for air. She couldn't breathe—the weight on her back was tremendous. The man—James Rossiter, she had to assume—had to be lying full on top of her, with his hands now wrapped around her neck. She could feel his whiskers scraping against her cheek as he leaned closer. "By all means, jus' walk right in and make yourself at home."

With a tremendous effort Gaia strained her back muscles, her hair tossing as she bucked and twisted, trying to get free. It was no use. She might as well have been bolted to the floor. Now her

34

vision was filling with spots. Her need for oxygen was becoming more and more urgent with every passing second.

"*Who are you?*" Rossiter—if it was he—screamed in her ear. "What the hell are you doing in my house? I told you to get out of here and take your stupid questions with you, but you *didn't listen.*"

The diner across the street, Gaia realized weakly, remembering the scruffy-looking man who'd given her attitude a half hour before. *That was Rossiter.* She could finally put a face to the voice in her ear. She remembered the sneer with which the man had regarded her badge and the enormous bulk he carried that had seemed to spill off the edges of the diner stool he'd occupied.

Gaia was losing consciousness. There was no question about it. Her vision was now totally black, flooding with iridescent shooting stars—she was trying to will it all away like she'd been able to do when the exhaustion from the fighting wasn't that severe. Rossiter's heavy breathing, the pain in her back, and the feel of the man's overwhelming weight holding her down against the cold cement—all these sensations were receding away like a dream. She was blacking out.

Sorry, Catherine, she thought weakly. *Some rescue—I didn't get very far, did I?*

The pinpoints of light kept swirling against the darkness—and suddenly Gaia felt a surge and a thump, and she could breathe.

What the hell?

The weight was off her. Faintly, as if it was all happening far in the distance, Gaia heard another thump. Her head still felt light. She was drinking in great gulps of oxygen. Her strength and her vision were returning, but slowly. She felt another surge of spinal pain as she tried to roll over onto her back. She couldn't make it—she was still too weak. Now her head was clearing, and there was a ringing in her ears, but she could begin to make sense of what she was hearing. Behind and above her, the sounds were unmistakable: an intense fistfight.

"Get up!" an unfamiliar male voice was yelling at her. The voice was interrupted by more scuffling and punching sounds—and Gaia felt another sharp pain, this time in her lower leg, as a foot in a heavy work boot slammed into her shin. "Get up! Quick!"

Talking to me, she realized. Her strength was returning. Wincing against the spasm of pain in her back, Gaia turned herself over.

Two men were fighting. They were right there—nearly on top of her. It was like watching a boxing match from beneath the ring. Their movements were silhouetted by the blinding fluorescent lamp that hung over the worktable.

Gaia recognized James Rossiter—he was the burly, unshaven hulk on the right, his sweatshirted arms pinwheeling through the air as he tried to fight off the other man.

And to her surprise, Gaia realized that she recognized the other man, too.

It was the thin, older man in the neat black suit, from the diner. The one who had reminded her, for a moment, of her father. His face was pulled into a tight grimace as he jabbed a series of karate kicks on Rossiter's shoulders and arms. His necktie was swinging in circles as he bobbed and weaved. His black leather dress shoes squeaked on the dusty floor.

There was no question about it—the newcomer had been trained to fight. As she weakly pulled herself up off the floor, bracing herself on the cot, Gaia watched as the man in the black suit began to win the fight. It was impressive—from the floor Rossiter seemed as big as a truck—and he was barely pulling it off. The man in the suit ducked his head, and Gaia heard the *swoosh* of air as James Rossiter's beefy fist swung over the suited man's head, clanging into the hanging lamp and causing it to swing crazily on its chains.

"Stand back!" the black-suited man yelled out at Gaia. He was incredibly fast—as he ducked, his upper body surged forward and he drove his flattened hand upward into Rossiter's chin. Blood spurted from the bigger man's mouth and nose. Rossiter stumbled backward, hitting the desk. The computer monitor slid to the floor and exploded with a bright flash of light, filling the air with an acrid electrical smell.

Rossiter's eyes rolled up. He slipped back against the desk again, swayed, and toppled to the floor.

Gaia stood next to the man in the black suit, looking down at James Rossiter. She firmly resisted the urge to kick him in the face. As angry as she was, she knew that a great deal of her anger was shame. This man should *never* have gotten the better of her.

"What did you touch?"

"What?" Gaia looked over, surprised at the question.

Beside her, the man in the black suit had already gotten his breath back. He was adjusting his clothing, tucking his drab tie back into his jacket. His eyes avoided hers—he was gazing around at his immediate surroundings, peering keenly at the

37

floor, the worktable, the desk, the cot. Gaia suddenly realized he was looking for his own fingerprints.

"What did you touch?" the man repeated. He had a guttural, deep voice that was not unpleasant—he sounded almost theatrical, like a seasoned actor. His unshaven face had Nordic features and high cheekbones. His weather-beaten eyes were blue. As the man reached to wipe off the edge of the table, he finally looked at Gaia. "Did you touch anything? Come on, think fast—we've got to move."

Gaia was so surprised that she didn't stop to question what the man was saying. "I didn't touch anything," she told him. "You're interfering with a crime scene, sir."

The man laughed humorlessly. "Tell me about it," he said, smirking. He had finished with the table—he was looking down at Rossiter now, trying to gauge his condition. "It's just a minor concussion—he'll wake up soon. Let's go."

"Wait," Gaia said firmly. "Mister, I don't know who you are or what you think you're doing, but I'm an agent with the Federal B—"

"Stop," the man said sharply. Now he was looking right at her. "We don't have time. I saw the door upstairs—you broke in." The man pointed at the bulky body on the floor, which was already starting to move. "I'm sure he called the cops before he came downstairs. You want to spend the rest of the day in a jail cell?"

Gaia looked back at the stranger. She didn't say anything. She didn't start arguing because everything the man said was true.

"No," Gaia told him. "No, I don't want that."

"Then let's not hang around here," the man said quickly. He was brushing the dust from his suit as he stepped over James

Rossiter's legs and moved toward the basement door. "Come on—we've got about five minutes before the cops get here."

"Listen, you want to tell me who you—"

"Come *on*," the man snapped over his shoulder impatiently. "We'll take your car. *Believe* me, you don't want to stay here."

And that was the truth. Gaia stepped over to retrieve her gun and then vaulted forward, following the man in the black suit out of the basement. Behind her James Rossiter moaned and stirred on his cold basement floor, his mouth and nose still dripping blood, lit in crazy light patterns as the fluorescent light kept swinging overhead. Gaia took one last look and turned to run up the stairs.

MYSTERIOUSLY SAVED

Sirens, Gaia thought. She wasn't sure, but it seemed like she could hear sirens in the street behind them. She was back in her car, ignoring the fading pain in her back as she gripped the wheel, trying to pay attention to the traffic. Her Walther was back in its shoulder holster, pressing uncomfortably against her rib cage.

A lot of good that did, she thought.

"You hear that?" the man in the passenger seat said. He was twisted around, peering behind them through the Altima's rear window. "I told you. He called 911, gave an intruder alert, and then surprised you. The station house is ten blocks away—the cops' arrival time is less than five minutes once the call is—"

"Wait a second," Gaia said tersely, flicking her hair away from her cheekbone as she turned her eyes on him. She was in no mood for this. "Just shut up for one second and tell me who you *are* and what this—"

"Shhh," the man said, raising a finger. He was squinting, seeming to concentrate on listening to the sirens. Gaia gazed forward along the car's hood, navigating the sparsely populated, seedy residential streets. "Follow the signs to the interstate. Don't speed—drive normally."

Well, that's obvious, Gaia thought ruefully. *That's what you do when you're fleeing a crime scene—especially when you're the criminals.*

Somehow everything had gone hopelessly wrong, and her pursuit of her missing friend had turned into—what? What was happening now? In the space of a half hour she had become a fugitive from the police, guilty of breaking and entering. Not to mention how close she'd come to being strangled for it—before being mysteriously saved.

The sirens slowed and stopped behind them. The man seemed to visibly relax.

"Good," he said, turning back around and facing forward. Gaia saw that he'd injured his hand during the fight—he was nursing it with his fingers. "We've got plenty of time now. They'll question him, question the diner patrons, question the waitress—it's going to be at least an hour before anyone remembers your car. By then we'll be miles away." He glanced over at her. "You're welcome, by the way."

Gaia glanced at the man and saw that he was smiling. The smile crinkled his eyes agreeably—in another context, she realized, he was a man whom a woman would be happy to meet in a hotel bar for a blind date—if you took away the stubble, the bruises, and the black suit that had seen better days. Up close, the resemblance to her father was more striking, yet more elusive. It wasn't that he *looked* like her father, exactly. He was a decade too young to begin with, despite the graying hair. It was the way he moved, the way he carried himself—and the precise, lethal way that he had fought. Gaia realized that he probably could have killed Rossiter if he wanted to.

"Thank you," Gaia said.

The man nodded crisply and then inclined his head, indicating that she should turn her attention back to the highway. Gaia did, just in time—a Plymouth SUV honked angrily as she darted out of its path.

They were moving toward the interstate highway, according to the signs. Now Gaia could see telephone lines, billboards, fast-food restaurants, four-lane traffic, and other signs of civilization. Gaia was far from calm. Her driving was still shaky, and behind her, she kept thinking, was a cot with two black hairs and the only clue she'd found about her missing friend and partner.

"Start talking," Gaia said. "Now."

"My name is Winston Marsh," the man told her. "I'm a private investigator. I'd like you to just try to stay calm and listen to what I have to say. Will you do that?"

"No promises."

Marsh frowned, pushing the corners of his mouth down. He didn't look unpleased. "Fair enough. Like I said, I'm a private detective, but I'm also ex-FBI."

"FBI—" Gaia's eyes narrowed suspiciously. "And you *happened* to be sitting in the, what, the Moscone Diner this afternoon? Come on—that's ridiculous."

"Of course it's ridiculous." Marsh's voice was resonant, even if he sounded like he'd smoked his fair share of cigarettes. The blue-green light from the windshield's antiglare strip shone on his prominent cheekbones. "I guess you've been with the bureau long enough to know there's no such thing as coincidence."

"What—you were tracking *me*?" Gaia squinted skeptically. "And I never saw you?"

"Impossible, right?" Marsh smirked, still gazing forward at the road like a rifleman lining up a complicated shot. He turned his head and squinted his blue eyes at her. "Nobody ever gets the jump on you, despite what I've seen after knowing you five minutes. No, I'm not tracking you. This isn't *about* you, Gaia. It's about your friend. It's about Catherine Sanders."

Gaia slammed the brakes. The tires screeched as the car lurched to a halt. Luckily she was in the rightmost lane and there was nobody immediately behind her, although a woman in a bright red Honda honked very angrily as she sped past.

Gaia had turned around in her seat and was glaring at Marsh. Maddeningly, he didn't look remotely frightened or intimidated. He was leaning casually in the car seat, a smile playing over his face as he gazed calmly back at her. He hadn't even flinched.

And why should he? Gaia thought ruefully. *He's seen me get my gun taken away and my ass kicked—it's not like I seem dangerous or anything.*

"Keep driving," Marsh said lightly, gesturing forward with one hand. "We've got some time now—I know a place nearby where we can talk. We've got a lot of ground to cover."

"Why should I trust you?"

"Because it's logical," Marsh said levelly, staring calmly out at

42

the Baltimore street. "Right now you need help. It's obvious. The fact is, you're confused and tired and you don't know what to do next."

All true, Gaia thought.

"Look, I know you're concerned about *time*," Marsh told her earnestly. "But think it through: no matter what kind of field agent you are, you must realize that the smart move right now is to listen to what I have to say."

Gaia thought about it. She couldn't come up with a counter-argument.

"I'm a *detective*, all right?" Marsh added earnestly. Up close, across the front seat of the car, Gaia could see the deepening wrinkles around his sharp blue eyes. "I find missing people—it's what I *do*. It's why I was hired to find Catherine. We're doing the same thing, Gaia. Right now you need my help—and I need yours."

"You were *hired* to find her?"

"Want to hear more?" Marsh pointed out the windshield again. "Start driving."

Will

Only a day since she vanished.

Only a day since the last time I saw Gaia Moore—saw her perfect blue eyes and heard her charming New York voice. New York by way of California, and if that isn't a fine vintage of wine, I don't know what is.

Our crack team of investigators—the unstoppable foursome of Taylor, Lau, Sanders, and Moore—has dwindled down to two. Just two depressed FBI trainees who, in the course of just a few days, have gone from getting envious stares and high fives over their Hogan's Alley victory (not to mention a lot of ribbing in the men's dorm about being partnered with the two prettiest women in Quantico) to this.

Now in the cafeteria, on the athletics field, I can see them looking at us. Carefully tearing their eyes away and then whispering when they think Kim and I can't hear.

That's them, the other trainees are saying. *They're the ones.*

. . . missing partners . . .

. . . some kind of manhunt . . .

. . . serial killers . . .

I can't pretend that I mind being talked about. Otherwise my life would be close to unbearable. I mean, I'm no stranger to getting a lot of attention. Growing up back in South Carolina, that was the story from the very beginning. On the football field, on the track field, in the classroom. Smiling at girls and watching them react. Getting them to smile back even if they thought they didn't want to. Getting them to glance at me a second or third time, even though they knew better.

But this is different. Now we've got notoriety. And not the good kind, either. The kind that can taint you for a long time. I can picture myself getting out of here and going back home— getting a posting in an FBI field office south of the Mason-Dixon line—and still getting those stares and hearing the whispers.

. . . failed at an important case . . .

. . . something wrong with his Quantico team . . .

. . . undisciplined, irregular . . .

. . . don't want to partner with him . . .

No, thank you. That's not what I signed up for. I came to Quantico for one reason only—to be the best damn FBI trainee anyone had ever seen. Easy, right? Just be better than everyone else. I've been doing that since I was ten, when Uncle Casper took me to that ball game and I saw my first major-league home run and realized what excellence was. I figure there's no point to doing anything if you're not going to force yourself to be the best.

Of course a stunning blond girl—from New York City, no less—turned all that around the first day. What do you do when someone's just better than you at everything—and to make matters worse, she's really cute?

Fall in love with her, I guess. At least, that was my brilliant solution.

And now she's gone.

Kim's sad, too. I can see it in his eyes—the way he looks tired all the time—like something's weighing him down. Things have gone bad here. And I don't know what to do about it. For Kim, Catherine was almost like a sister; I think he misses her more than Gaia. Misses Catherine's jokes, and her easy manner, and her brilliance.

Catherine may be gone. She may be—she may be dead. Kim knows it, of course. I think Gaia knew that, too. But if anyone can find her, can bring her home, Gaia's got a chance at it. I just can't think of anything more difficult for one girl alone to do. I mean, it's a big world to search.

Why did Gaia have to do what she did? Why be so stubborn as to go for the big heroic gesture—the solitary quest or whatever you want to call it? Does Gaia just need to be alone, like she keeps suggesting? Is it in her nature?

I don't think so. If I could have her back in front of me for just another couple of minutes, that's what I would tell her. You don't need to be alone, Miss Moore—that's a fact. And maybe someday you'll believe it. I might even have been the one to convince you, if we hadn't left things the way we did. That's probably all my fault, too.

Anyway, I hope she's all right.

I hope they both are.

NEARLY INSULTING

Kim Lau didn't enjoy being summoned to the chief's office.

The problem was, you couldn't predict anything. Kim had a knack for figuring out what was on people's minds—for reading their gestures and their faces. But when you got a text message telling you to come to the top floor of the Quantico admin building and report to Special Agent Brian Malloy's office, there was no way to interpret it. There was nothing to go on—just words on a cell phone screen, telling you what to do.

The Virginia sun was bright and warm as Kim walked across the FBI quadrangle toward the gleaming glass facade of admin. Kim was beginning to perspire in the heat, but not too much. It was under control.

He could see the tall figure of Will Taylor over by the dorm building, walking to meet him. So Will had gotten the summons, too. That wasn't surprising. He could tell that they were being watched. These days they always were. It was part of their Quantico lives now. In the bomb-training and antiterrorism classrooms, on the shooting range, in the cafeteria—everyone was looking at them. Kim was incredibly sensitive to it. It appalled him how badly people hid what they were doing. It was nearly insulting every time. Nearly, but not quite.

Sometimes Kim had an irrational impulse to stand up suddenly in the cafeteria, spread his arms, and yell out to the assembled trainees with their plastic trays and their vitamin supplements and their protein shakes and turkey sandwiches. *It's all true, folks!* he imagined yelling. *We got partnered up with the weird girl—the one from New York. We almost got expelled, and*

47

then she won the game for us . . . and she and the girl with the glasses got promoted to full agents and assigned to a real serial killer hunt—except it went nowhere, and now one of them is missing and the other one's AWOL and nobody knows what to do with us. It's all true, so stare all you want! Stare at the black sheep and be glad it's not you.

He never did it, of course. He never even came close. But he could tell from Will Taylor's chiseled face that Will was reading his mind. *Don't give them the satisfaction. Just smile.*

"Hey," Will said absently.

"Hey. Where were you?"

"Working out. You?"

"Library," Kim said as they approached the security desk— Will flashed his entry badge, got waved through, and waited for Kim to show his trainee pass to the guard and sign in. Even the Quantico security personnel were watching them, Kim realized ruefully. "You know what this is about?"

"No idea."

On the way up in the elevator, fingering the temporary pass the guard had handed over, Kim realized again how nervous he was. Security in this building was as tight as it got anywhere on the Quantico base, and the extra procedures with passes and electric gates didn't exactly have a calming effect. And Brian Malloy was a very mysterious man. Decades in the FBI had made him into the human equivalent of one of those tribal masks you saw in anthropological museums—the carved wooden masks designed to remind worshipers of the immobile, untouchable faces of the gods.

"Anything happening with the case?" Kim asked Will.

"What?" Will glanced over, the harsh elevator lighting shining in his blond crew cut. He seemed puzzled—and then he laughed derisively. Clearly the lollipop case was the furthest thing from Will's mind. "Don't even ask me about that."

"Nothing, huh?"

Will shook his head. "Permanently stuck at square one."

He misses her, Kim realized sadly. *He doesn't want me to see it, but he really, really misses her.*

The elevator door bonged softly and slid open, and Kim and Will unconsciously straightened their backs as they strode out into the carpeted hallway, past the enormous Federal Bureau of Investigation seal on the wall, heading toward the chief's office. Kim remembered when all four of them had been summoned here, early one morning not long ago, nursing hangovers as they tried to explain how they'd ended up in a knock-down, drag-out brawl at the townies' local bar. Kim could remember it like it was yesterday—but at the same time, the image of the four of them moving down this corridor together seemed like it came from impossibly long ago and far away.

"Kim," Will said, stopping in his tracks and turning back toward him, his fist already raised to knock on Malloy's door. "Anything we need to get straight? Before we go in there?"

Kim narrowed his eyes. "I don't think so."

And what do you mean by that, Mr. Taylor?

Will nodded tersely, rapping loudly on the door.

"Come," Agent Malloy's harsh voice barked out from inside the office. Hearing it, Kim could feel his gut tightening with apprehension.

Here goes, he thought as Will turned the knob on the high-security metal lock plate and they strode into the chief's office.

Will's first impression was how tired Malloy looked. He was seated behind his smooth, empty desk, the bright sunlight gleaming on the edges of his high-backed leather chair, his hands folded neatly on the leather desk blotter in front of him. Will could see the redness in his eyes, the rawness of his drawn face.

It's cold in here, Will noticed. He'd noticed the same thing the last time he was here. For some reason, the chief seemed to thrive in a dry, frigid office air-conditioned to within an inch of his life. He and Kim stepped to the front of the desk and stood side by side at parade rest, waiting for Malloy to say something.

He let them wait. The leather chair squeaked as Malloy leaned back, flicking his dark eyes back and forth between the two young trainees. As usual, it was utterly impossible to guess what he was thinking.

"You can sit if you'd like," Malloy began. He *sounded* tired, too, Will realized. The chief's computer was running, but the afternoon sun gleamed on its screen, rendering it unreadable from this side of the desk. He and Kim remained standing. "Taylor," Malloy went on. He was rubbing his eyes with fatigue. "First things first. Progress report on the lollipop case."

"The lollipop case—yes, sir," Will began, clearing his throat. It was a bad beginning, but he couldn't help it. The problem was that he had almost nothing to report. All he was thinking about were Gaia's piercing eyes and her soft, shimmering hair. "I can't report any progress beyond the written statement I submitted at 1430 hours yesterday. We're still waiting for lab results, as I reported in writing. Beyond that, I'm afraid the case has hit a dead end, sir."

Malloy nodded. He didn't look mad—but you could never tell. It was like trying to predict which number a roulette wheel would land on.

"Kim Lau," Malloy went on, turning to face Kim. He hooked a thumb at his computer monitor—Will still couldn't see what was on it. "Agent Bishop and I have been looking over your course data, and in particular your performance in the Hogan's Alley exercise. You really did quite well—I didn't have a chance to focus on your individual performance before."

"Thank you, sir," Kim said. To Will's ears, he sounded surprised.

"I'm sure your friend Taylor has followed the rules and hasn't told you anything about the murder investigation he's working," Malloy observed dryly. "But assuming you can speculate about the case, do you think your particular insights might be of help in this matter?"

"Yes, sir. *Absolutely*, sir," Kim said fervently. Will wanted to make a shushing gesture—Kim was so excited, he seemed like he was about to grin from ear to ear. Will knew how badly Kim wanted to put his formidable skills to use on a real case. Not just for personal advancement—they all wanted that—but as an intellectual exercise, to find out if his methods and techniques would work outside of the classroom, out in the real world.

Malloy abruptly reached into a desk drawer and produced a small object that he slung across the table at Kim. As Kim picked it up, Will saw that it was an active duty badge—exactly the kind Will had been given days before. Kim took an avid look at the laminated card and then slipped it into his pocket. Glancing sideways, Will saw that Kim couldn't quite contain the triumphant smile that played across the corners of his mouth.

"You're hereby promoted to full active duty," Malloy told Kim. "I want you and your partner Agent Taylor here to do whatever you can to catch the serial killer before he strikes again."

"Yes, sir," Kim repeated happily.

So now we're partnered up, Will thought. He wasn't sure how he felt about that. He hated to admit it, but the idea made him nervous. What if Kim performed so well on the case that he actually caught the killer on his own? Will had worked too hard just to let Kim come in and figure out the whole thing by himself.

"Now, Taylor," Agent Malloy went on in his gravelly voice, leaning forward on the desk and staring keenly at Will. "Here's how we're going to work this. Right now, you're going to open your mouth and tell me everything you know about Gaia Moore's whereabouts and actions."

Will was already shaking his head. "I'm sorry, sir. I don't know, sir."

"Think before you speak," Malloy went on, tapping his fingers on the desk. His voice was low and dangerous. "You have no idea how important this is—how much pressure I and this whole division of the bureau are under because of that damn girl. Twelve hours ago she left this facility, and as far as I know, you were the last person she saw. It's inconceivable for me that you don't have some inkling of where she went."

"I *don't*, sir," Will insisted, staring straight back into the chief's eyes. It wasn't hard to keep up the staring contest because what he was saying was the truth. He had no idea where Gaia was. They were supposed to meet for dinner, but she'd never shown up. "I'm sorry, but it's true. She refused to tell me anything about her plans."

Because she saw this coming, he realized. *And she didn't trust me to keep my mouth shut.*

Malloy didn't blink as he returned Will's stare. Then finally he leaned back in his chair, nodding sadly. "All right," he told them both. "Back to work on this case. And Will, if I find out you've withheld evidence about Agent Moore, I swear I'll make you wish you never even heard of the FBI."

"I understand, sir," Will said tightly.

"And if either of you receive any kind of contact from Moore, I want you reporting it straight to me. Is that clear?"

They both told him that it was.

"Dismissed. Catch that killer," Malloy said briskly. He had already turned his attention back to his computer screen.

Will and Kim glanced at each other and then turned in unison to leave. Will could read Kim's face easily. He was absolutely thrilled to be working the lollipop case. Will wished he felt the same way.

Damn it, Gaia, Will thought helplessly as they walked through the freezing office air away from Malloy's desk. *Where are you?*

the bloodstained luggage
she'd never seen

BARE AND FEATURELESS AND EMPTY

Gaia wasn't exactly sure where she was—the outlying townships
and suburbs that surrounded this part of Baltimore all seemed to
fade together into interlinking networks of residential streets,
highways that led through crowded commercial areas with parking lots, gas stations, and small, lurid shopping malls. She had
been very tired of driving already before this strange journey
with the man who called himself Winston Marsh, who was pointing at the intersections and telling her where to go. Marsh kept
glancing behind them, as if he *knew* they were being followed
and was making only a halfhearted attempt to prevent it.

This is where he wanted to talk? Gaia thought. *I wonder why?*

They were in a small town park, in one of the nameless
checkerboard townships that surrounded Baltimore's industrial
outskirts. Gaia's car was parked in the street, barely in view of
the stone-and-wood park bench they sat on. The overcast sky
had darkened as this strange afternoon wore on, and now a mild
wind was whispering through the dark treetops that surrounded
them. There was nothing else in the park except a few other scattered benches, some of which had lost their wooden slats and

were just strange-looking, L-shaped cement foundations. A tall white bandstand stood in the center of the park, surrounded by thinning grass. The bandstand's festive white paint was peeling. Its six-sided floor was bare and featureless and empty.

They were alone except for three other people. An elderly man in a dark raincoat leaned on a cane, a hundred yards away. The man sat peacefully, tossing bread crumbs from a paper bag down onto the cracked asphalt, where a sea of dirty-looking pigeons waded around, cooing audibly. A mother sat at another spot in the other direction, past the bandstand, reading a magazine while her toddler played in a sandbox a few feet away. They were far enough away that their faces were just white blurs.

Gaia and Marsh sat side by side on a worn-out park bench, surrounded by clumps of weeds and a discarded Mountain Dew can that had faded nearly white. It was colder now, and Marsh had turned the collar of his suit jacket up against the wind.

"I retired from the FBI a couple of years ago," Marsh began in his rich, raspy voice. "And since then I've been working as a detective. I do fairly routine stuff just to keep my hand in—skip traces, woman checking if her husband's cheating on her, occasionally a missing person case."

I don't need your life's story, Gaia thought impatiently. She was picturing Catherine tied up in the back of a car, pounding her fists against the metal trunk lid as she was moved to another secret location for whatever mysterious reason. By now she'd be pale, hungry, and exhausted. Too tired to fight back. Gaia couldn't tolerate the vision. She bit down hard and tried to shake it off.

"That's how this started. A week ago a man named Sanders came to see me." Marsh gazed at the dismal park surroundings as he spoke. "Early fifties, graying, soft-spoken—a professional or academic type, I thought immediately: a nice guy but frightened. Out of his mind with fear, actually. He told me he's got a twenty-year-old daughter, raised her alone, the girl went off to join the FBI. Now she's disappeared—vanished into thin air—and he can't get anywhere with the bureau."

"What do you mean?" Gaia frowned. "Won't they tell him—"

"Oh, they're not going to say a word," Marsh said confidently, "because the girl is dead, at least according to the current FBI thinking. That part's quite clear: when Sanders told me what he was going through—all his frantic phone calls to Quantico, when they wouldn't answer his questions—I immediately thought, 'Dead trainee.' This is how they would handle it if they were reasonably sure she was dead."

The duffel bag, Gaia thought suddenly. The image flashed into her mind again of the bloodstained luggage she'd never seen. She remembered Malloy's insistence that she forget about looking any deeper into it—that the FBI was ready to drop the whole matter for good.

"There are procedures for informing family members of deaths in the line of duty," Marsh explained. "I remember from my time in the bureau. It's something I know much more about than I'd like to—I've had to do it way too many times. But the point is, the FBI has to allow a reasonable amount of time before declaring a missing agent 'presumed deceased,' even if they've privately closed the case. And you have to understand that the bureau wouldn't take that step lightly. They must be nearly certain of whatever evidence they've got. Pretty much a guarantee that you're not going to find anything new—you'd better get ready for bad news."

Closed the case, Gaia thought angrily. *They're just going to sit and wait and do nothing until it's time to say she's dead.* "You didn't tell that to Catherine's father," Gaia said. "Did you?"

"Of course not. I told him I'd look into it."

"Why?"

Gaia was watching the old man feeding the pigeons as she listened.

"See, I've got this little problem. I think the girl's alive," Marsh said calmly. "I'm not sure why; there's really no evidence that shows it, and the trail just gets colder by the minute. But there's something wrong with the story. Bright girl, shy but well adjusted, looks pretty in the graduation photo I saw. Decided she wanted to join the FBI; the father was against it. Afraid of exactly this sort of thing. He didn't want his daughter placing herself in harm's way—he just had this terrible feeling that one day he'd get the phone call, the one every parent dreads. But during her *training?*" Marsh squinted critically. "The day after she called him on the phone to make vacation plans, and suddenly they can't find any trace of her? That's extremely unusual, don't you think?"

"Yes," Gaia said forcefully. *That's what I've been saying all along—that's why I'm here.* "So what happened? Where is she? What was she doing in that basement?"

"My guess is that she's been abducted," Marsh said. "The facts don't lead us there, though. The duffel bag doesn't tie in until you acknowledge that she could have been *going somewhere*, traveling on her own, when it happened. I talked to the Virginia police. Someone named Parker—local sheriff who knows the girl in question—apparently worked with her. He asked around on his own if anyone saw her going anywhere; he's sent me notes on some eyewitness sightings."

"Sightings in *Quantico*?" The wind had picked up, blowing Gaia's hair around her head—she impatiently reached up to brush it away. "*When?* Who saw her? Where was she going?"

"Don't get excited; it's hardly positive identification. She *might* have stopped for gas on her way out of Quantico, heading north. I've got it all written down." Gaia imagined this private detective on the phone to Gus Parker, a man with whom she and Catherine had worked side by side. "If you come with me, I'll show you the evidence I've gathered."

"Come with you? Where?"

"Just a place nearby," Marsh said easily. "Someplace safe— where you can wash your face and drink a cup of coffee and we can have a calm, rational conversation about the whereabouts of Catherine Sanders."

"We've got to go back to that *house*," Gaia argued. "Rossiter's house. She was *there*."

"And that's one place she'll never be taken again," Marsh snapped. "Full of cops waiting to arrest *us*. Come on—you're not thinking clearly. You need to calm down."

"Don't tell me to calm—"

"We're being watched," Marsh interrupted in the same easy tone. It took Gaia a moment to register what he'd said.

"The blond man?" Gaia said quietly. She was pretending not to look at the strange, motionless figure in the perfect suit and raincoat sitting on a bench at the far edge of the park. She spoke softly with her eyes fixed on the tips of her shoes. "He's watching us?"

"No, he's just a businessman on his lunch break," Marsh said sarcastically. "Silly me. Never mind."

Gaia realized that the woman with the toddler and the old man with the bread crumbs were gone. Gaia hadn't seen their departure, but it had obviously happened. They were alone in the park with the strange man in sunglasses. The wind was gusting, blowing the dark trees that flanked the field.

"Okay, but who *is* he?" Without looking over, Gaia tried to put together a mental image of the blond man in sunglasses. It was impossible; he was too typical looking and too far away. "Have you seen him before?"

"Never," Marsh said assuredly. "No idea who he is."

One more thing to worry about, Gaia thought. She could feel her shoulders sinking with fatigue and a growing hopelessness that she angrily shrugged off.

"Okay, look: I just want to make one thing clear to you. I've got to find Catherine." Gaia gazed intently into Marsh's eyes. "Do you understand? I've *got* to. You may be the best detective in the world, but it's still just a puzzle for you to solve. For me it's a little more personal."

"I understand."

I hope you do, Gaia thought. *Because I really wouldn't like to find out you're wasting my time. I wouldn't like that at all.*

"We'd better leave," Marsh said quietly. Glancing quickly over, Gaia saw that the man in the sunglasses had stood up. "When I tell you, we'll stand up and head for the car."

Judging the distances, Gaia realized they could get there pretty fast—before the man across the park reached them—but they'd have to start moving soon.

"Now," Marsh said suddenly, clapping Gaia on the shoulder. "Let's move."

In unison, they rose to their feet and headed for the car, and behind them the man in the sunglasses kept watching. Gaia didn't look to see if he was following.

Kim

People tend to make the same mistake about profilers that they do about psychiatrists. They assume that just because we diagnose other people's neuroses and psychoses, we must have no neuroses and psychoses of our own. As if our study of the human mind should somehow qualify us as Zen masters or something. Well, of course, that couldn't be further from the truth. I've got just as many neuroses as the next guy. The only difference is, I do my best to be aware of them and own up to them as often as possible. Today, for instance, I've been all over the map. Elated for an hour, then guilty for the next, and then elated again.

Malloy has given me the opportunity of a lifetime here. An actual murder case—not hypothetical, not theoretical, not a practice run, not a game. The real deal. The moment I've been training for since my first criminology class in junior high. This is everything I've ever wanted.

But then comes the guilt. I think about Catherine. My mind flashes through all the horrific crime scene pictures I've seen over the last few years. I know the common fate of a missing girl in this country. I know the statistics, and I know what the bodies look like once they're found. I know it all too well. We have to see these kinds of images. We have to see them over and over again until we become immune—or at least until we claim we're immune. But when I think about sweet and brilliant Catherine as just another one of those bodies . . .

I can't say for sure what's happened to her. I can at least take some solace in that. But the fact remains, her disappearance is the only reason I got this case. Whatever Malloy says, the lollipop investigation belongs to Gaia and Catherine, and it always will. But once I truly accept that fact, then the guilt begins to fade away again. And an even stronger resolve takes its place.

I owe this case to them. I owe it to Gaia, and *especially* to Catherine, to put every ounce of my training and discipline into this thing. I owe it to them to eat, live, and breathe this case until it's solved. I don't just owe it to them; I owe it to the victims this bastard has already taken and the victims I'm not going to let him take.

So it's time to put my emotions aside and start focusing on the facts and only the facts. Organization is key. This is the pertinent information I've gathered thus far from the case file:

1. *Suspect is a male, approximately six feet, muscular build, no facial identification.*
2. *There have been three murders to date—all of them single mothers: Ann Knight, Laurel Halliday, and Terri Barker.*
3. *Each of them left behind a young son, and in every case the assailant gave the child a flavored lollipop at the murder scene.*
4. *Each victim had her throat slit by a left-handed assailant.*
5. *The murder weapon has been identified as a Yukon Bay double hunting knife, model sc-42.*
6. *Some wool fibers have been recovered—possibly from a fisherman's sweater, though that can't be confirmed.*
7. *One of the children (Sam Knight) identified the assailant as "smelling wet"—also inconclusive.*
8. *Suspect Ned Riley, a fisherman, was brought in for questioning but was cleared of all suspicion.*

Those are all the primary facts in the file, as far as I can tell. Some of it could be interpreted as useful, I suppose. But just as Malloy suggested, the truth is that this case is getting colder every day.

That is to say, it *was* getting colder. Until today.

Perhaps now would be a good time to mention it: I started my investigation this morning . . . and I've got a lead. A serious lead. A break-in-the-case kind of lead.

Like I said before: I'm not just stepping in to keep things status quo until Gaia returns. I'm stepping in to solve this thing. Before another woman gets murdered.

"We're changing our strategy."

Kim had dispensed with the knocks, hellos, and any other superfluous pleasantries and simply barged into Will's dorm room unannounced. Anything else would have wasted precious time.

Will barely had a chance to react before Kim was leaning hard on his desk and slamming his forensic psych book shut for him.

"Changing our strategy?" Will uttered, shifting back in his chair. "Since when?"

"Since now," Kim replied.

"I didn't even know we had a strategy. We haven't even talked since this morning."

"I know," Kim said. "Because I was busy finding us a new lead."

This announcement produced just the effect Kim had expected. Will's jaw dropped slightly open, and his body froze in position.

"A new lead . . ." Will repeated. It wasn't quite a question yet—it seemed more like a placeholder while he tried to process the information.

A smile began to creep up at the corners of Kim's mouth as he nodded slowly, waiting for Will to catch up. "A new *lead*," he confirmed. He grabbed hold of the other chair and dragged it right next to Will's so they were sitting knee to knee. "Just listen," he began. Kim couldn't contain his enthusiasm, and he began to speak in fifth gear—something he thought he'd trained himself to stop doing somewhere around the fifth grade, but this apparently would have to be an exception.

"I wanted to catch up on the file ASAP," he explained. "So I went down to Henderson Elementary to do my own follow-up on the Terri Barker murder—"

"Wait," Will interrupted. "Why didn't you bring me with you?"

"You had fingerprinting till two—besides, you'd already been through all this; I was just trying to get up to speed. Anyway, it was all just par for the course, you know—just confirming the basics—unwed mother, nurse's aid, everyone adored her, all the facts were checking out, and I was packing up to head out when the school nurse—Nurse Perez—says to me, 'God, if she'd just taught that class that night.' Well, of course, I looked like you look right now—I just froze and stared at her. 'What class?' I said. We didn't have anything in the file about her teaching a class. And then the nurse *tells* me, it was only once every couple of months, but Terri Barker would teach a CPR class to the lifeguards in training. Two hours, usually on a Saturday evening."

Will still looked unpleasantly puzzled. "Yeah, so . . . ?" His shoulders rose with a half shrug. "So she taught a CPR class. Was one of the students a fisherman or something?"

"*No.*" Kim groaned with frustration. "You've got to let me finish. The *point* is, on the night she was murdered, she *didn't* teach the class. She asked Nurse Perez to fill in for her."

Will still looked somewhat nonplused. "Okay . . . ?"

Kim squinted at Will. "Okay? That's all you have to say? Okay?"

"What am I missing here?"

Kim poked his finger at the side of Will's head. "Where *are* you today, man? Wake up. Terri Barker *bagged* on her class the night she was murdered. She asked Nurse Perez to fill in for her.

She *canceled*. People always cancel for a *reason*. Why do you think she canceled?"

"I have no idea."

Kim leaned closer to Will and lowered his voice for dramatic effect. "Because she had a *date* that night. A *blind date*." He let this gigantic piece of new information linger in the ensuing silence.

Will's expression finally began to shift. Slowly but surely his pursed lips passed through the puzzled impatient stage and opened into a cautious smile. "A blind date? How the hell did we miss a blind date?"

"Because she didn't *tell* anyone it was *that* night," Kim explained, relieved to see Will finally getting on board with this blockbuster. "Apparently she'd only mentioned to one of the kids at school that she *might* be going on a blind date that weekend. But she didn't actually tell anyone the night she went. So I did a little asking around, and I checked with her favorite restaurant, and they *confirmed*. She was at the restaurant that night with some guy no one had ever seen before."

"Jeee-*zuss*." Will unleashed a full dose of his Southern drawl.

"We've got to find this guy," Kim declared. "Forget trying to go through the knife for now; forget the lollipops, too. New strategy. Find Mr. Blind Date. We find him and this thing is over. Do you concur or what? What do you think?"

Will looked at Kim and shook his head slowly. "Jeee-zuss," he repeated, shooting out of his chair and grabbing his coat and keys. "I think, what the hell are we still doing here?"

Gaia

[*Recorder on*] Agent Gaia Moore recording, field log, additional. No case number, like I said before.

I don't want to be here. I don't want to be sitting at this plastic table, in this moldy room, looking at cigarette burns on the walls. I don't think anyone in a right frame of mind would want to be stuck in a room at the Clavarak Motel.

[*Pause*] I'm pissed. I'm pissed at myself for stopping, even if it's only for a cold shower and another slug of gas station coffee and a chance to breathe. I want to be back out there. I want to be on the road, tracking her down. I want to go back to that dungeon of a basement and find James Rossiter and beat the truth out of him. I want to just keep pounding and pounding until he tells me what he did with Catherine—where she is now, who's got her if someone else does, *why* they took her. If this is just about some backwoods pervert who found himself a pretty girl, then I swear to God . . .

But that kind of thinking won't get me anywhere. Jesus, if I haven't learned that, then all this training really has been for nothing. That was how Gaia, the lost girl, dealt with a problem: pounding despicable men's faces in and getting absolutely nowhere. The fact is, it doesn't *matter* how much I care about Catherine. It doesn't *matter* how desperate I am to find her. That's what you would say, Agent Bishop, and I know you're right. I'm not just some pissed-off girl looking for her friend. I am a federal agent conducting an investigation. And if I lose sight of that, then I know I'll lose her.

I've heard you say it so many times, Agent Bishop, but I'm finally starting to understand it: "An investigation is never about wants. It's about needs. We want to punish the bad guys. We want to save all the victims—we want to save the world. But what we *need* are facts. And a focused mind to collect them."

I needed to take this breather and I needed this shower. I can't help Catherine if I'm a goddamn zombie. [*Pause*] And I think I need Marsh. As much as I'd love to trust no one but myself in this investigation, the simple fact is that I'd be shooting myself in the foot trying to do it alone. The one thing I do know about Marsh is that we both want the same thing. We want to find Catherine and bring her home. He's been on her trail longer than I have, and I need to pick his brain until I know everything he knows.

And I could pound Rossiter's face until every bone in his skull was shattered—that doesn't mean I'd get any closer to the truth. Besides . . . after our unfortunate run-in in that basement, I'm sure he's made himself scarce. No, I don't need to pound James Rossiter. I need to investigate him. I'm sitting here in the middle of freaking nowhere and I need help. And I'm not going waste any more precious time feeling too proud or embarrassed to say it. [*Pause*] I need Will.

Phone calls are out of the question. Even a cell phone call could be traced. So how, then? How the hell can I talk to him? [*Recorder off*]

NO CHEMISTRY

It was Kim's first time in the Quantico sheriff's office interrogation room. Will, obviously, knew his way around—he had waved casually at the local cops and the town's two plainclothes detectives on the way in and showed Kim where to get coffee and where he could hang his jacket. Will hadn't been running the lollipop killer investigation very long, but he'd already developed an easy rapport with Sheriff Gus Parker's Quantico police. Kim tried not to smile as he watched Will deploy some of his patented Southern charm, smiling easily at the female secretaries before leading Kim into this interrogation room.

Showtime, Kim thought excitedly. Now that he was actually *doing* it—participating in an investigation—he was absurdly pleased. He wanted to call his mother and gush, starting with the cliché of "Guess where *I* am?" and finishing with a breathless description of the windowless interrogation room: its metal tables and foam-tiled walls, just like in the movies. He wasn't dressed in his nicest suit—that was only for really special occasions—but in one of his nicer ones, cut in such a way that the shoulder holster didn't interfere with the suit's lines. He was planning on letting Will take the lead in the interrogation, but he was ready to jump in at a moment's notice.

"Bill, it's Agent Taylor," Will was saying into the intercom phone. "Would you send Mr. Dix in?"

Kim followed Will's example, pulling out one of the metal folding chairs, undoing his jacket's top button, sitting with his hands folded on the table. Will glanced over at him, smiling reassuringly, before turning a bland implacable gaze on the door.

He must have practiced that look, Kim thought. He was impressed—Will seemed to imitating Special Agent Malloy's ice-cold facial expression.

The door opened, and Jason Dix entered the room.

Kim's first impression was that the man overwhelmingly wanted to be somewhere else. It was clear from his posture, the way he held the doorknob, his embarrassed look, the perspiration stains on his shirt, and the obvious fact that he'd wetted and finger-combed his thinning brown hair just before coming in. Which meant a visit to the sheriff's station men's room, which meant a nervous bladder, which meant—

Okay, give it a rest, Sherlock Holmes, Kim reminded himself. Here he was, already willing to convict Mr. Dix as the killer before he'd even had a chance to sit down. He had to relax—relax and keep his eyes open.

"Jason Dix?" Will was asking.

"Yes."

The man was small and round-shouldered, with a pleasant, plain face and puffy eyes. He wore a blue dress shirt and full-cut, off-the-rack pleated khaki pants.

Worried about his waistline, Kim thought.

"Thank you for coming in, sir. I'm Special Agent Taylor; this is Special Agent Lau—Federal Bureau of Investigation." Will gestured toward the opposite metal chair. "Have a seat."

"Um—thank you," Dix said. The metal chair scraped as he pulled it out.

Will took his time opening a file folder, gazing down at the pages inside before turning his eyes back to Jason Dix. It was a good technique—give the man time to stew.

"Do you know why you're here, Mr. Dix?"

Excellent first question, Kim thought. Will was cutting right to the heart of the matter—that this was a *murder* investigation—but at the same time he was making Dix do all the work: broaching the subject, finding the right words, figuring out how much detail they wanted to hear.

"Well—yeah," Dix said quietly. "It's because Terri got—got killed."

"You knew Ms. Barker?"

"Yes. No. I mean—I mean, I'd just met her."

"But you are aware that she was murdered?"

"Yeah. I saw it in the paper."

"And when you saw it in the paper," Kim asked, speaking for the first time, "did you happen to notice the time and date of the murder?"

"Um—I mean—I'm not sure. I think so."

He's sweating, Kim noticed.

"You 'think' you noticed," Will said. "Sir, the murder was reported on page twelve of the Quantico *Gazette* the day after it occurred—August 20. The news item makes clear that Ms. Barker was killed the previous night."

"That's—" Dix was squinting, puzzled. "Yes."

"How did you meet her?" Kim asked, leaning forward against the metal table.

Dix looked at Kim straight on for the first time. He had pale blue eyes that reflected the room's fluorescent overhead lights. An unusual color, Kim noticed.

"It was a blind date," Dix said quietly. He coughed to clear his throat.

"When?"

"The night before. I mean—the night before the newspaper article."

Will raised his eyebrows. It was perfect—he looked for all the world like this was the first time he'd ever heard anything about a blind date. "You went on a date with Terri Barker the night she was murdered?"

"Well, yes—"

"So when you saw the newspaper article," Kim cut in, "what was your reaction?"

Dix turned his blue eyes back to Kim. He was definitely perspiring—there was no question about it. His hands were leaving visible prints on the metal table.

"I was—I was shocked. I was surprised. It was very strange. I didn't know how to react."

"Did you consider contacting the police?" Will asked the question as if he had no idea whether Dix had done so or not.

"You mean, like helping them solve the crime? Yeah."

"But you didn't do it," Will said. "Why not?"

Dix rubbed his fingers over his upper lip. "Honestly? I thought about it. But I chickened out. I just—I thought it would look weird, I guess."

"What do you do, Mr. Dix?" Will seemed to be changing tactics.

"I work at the shoe store," Dix said. "Digby Shoes? Down on Marlin Street. I've been there about four years."

"Do you like working there?" Kim put in. He wasn't wild about the line of questioning, but he followed Will's lead.

"Sure, I guess."

"Who arranged the date?" Kim went on. He wasn't sure where he was going with the questioning, but he knew from his classroom experience that it was important to move around the subject matter in unpredictable patterns.

"It wasn't—it's an online service," Dix said, blushing a bit. "This local Web site? It's called SecondChanceVA.com—I saw the ad and decided to try them out."

"This was your first time using that service?" Will asked in a bored tone.

A Web site, Kim was thinking. *Wait a minute—that could be a huge lead.*

"Yeah—I'd never had the guts before," Dix said, coughing. "Anyway, I filled out their form and a few days later I got an e-mail back and I was set up with—with Terri. We made plans to meet that night."

"To meet where?" Kim asked.

"La Croix," Dix said. "Expensive place. I wanted to go to Montano's Steak House, but she kind of insisted. La Croix is like her favorite place—everyone knew her there. *Was* her favorite place."

"Did you have a nice dinner?"

"Sure. It was fine," Dix said. "No big deal. We talked about her job, my job, what kind of music we liked—you know. Usual first date stuff."

"Did you like her?" Will asked.

"Honestly, not so much. There wasn't much of a spark there. By the time we got to dessert, I was thinking I probably wouldn't call her again."

"And what time did you leave the restaurant?" Kim asked.

He already knew the answer—8:07 p.m., plus or minus two minutes, according to the MasterCard receipt and the La Croix coat check attendant's story.

"I think around eight?" Dix said, squinting. "I'm not sure."

"And then?" Will asked. Kim realized that he wasn't imagining it—Will was genuinely disinterested, as if he'd already given up on Jason Dix and his story.

"I drove her back to her car," Dix said. "I remember I was wondering if we were going to get another drink somewhere else, you know, after the date, but it was pretty clear that neither of us was interested. It was pleasant enough between us, just, you know, no chemistry. Anyway, she said she'd left her car downtown, and could I drop her off. I said sure."

"And where'd you go after you dropped her off?" Will asked, turning a page of his notes, not looking at Dix.

"I'd made plans to meet some of the guys from the shoe store, over at Wagner Lanes. A bowling alley near the Civic Center. I got there pretty fast because I knew it was Free Fixins Night—they have this free salad bar. So I got there around eight forty-five and met up with Louey and Pete and we bowled awhile. I think we stayed there until closing time—just after midnight."

Will and Kim looked at each other. The ME had placed Terri Barker's time of death at somewhere between ten and ten fifteen.

"You never left the bowling alley?" Will asked, in that same maddening bored tone.

"No. I mean, just to go to the bathroom. But once I'm bowling, I'm bowling."

"All right," Will said briskly, flipping the file closed. He leaned back in his chair. "Thanks for coming in, Mr. Dix. We'll contact you if we have any further questions."

What—?

It took Kim a moment to react since he was so startled.

"Just a second," he said, leaning forward. "Jason, you said you dropped her off downtown. Do you remember *where?*"

Dix looked at the ceiling, concentrating. "I'm not sure. A pretty crowded area. Somewhere near Loren Avenue, I think."

"Did you actually *see* her get into her car?" Kim went on.

"No, she walked away. We kissed good night, you know, just friendly, and then she said she had an errand to run or something and she left."

"All right, the important thing is that we know where *you* were," Will said briskly. "Thanks again, sir—we appreciate your taking the time to talk to us."

"Hang on," Kim said impatiently. He knew he was doing exactly what he told himself he wouldn't do—outflanking Will's lead and taking over the focus of the interrogation as well as contradicting Will's obvious desire to conclude the interview—but he had no choice. "You say you're 'not sure' where you dropped her off. Do you think you might recognize the spot? It we drove you downtown, would it jog your memory?"

Dix was nodding. "It might. I remember that I took a left on—"

"We may indeed have to put you through that, Mr. Dix," Will interrupted, looking at his watch. "At a later date. Like I said, we'll call and schedule any follow-up interrogation if we need to. Once again, sir, thanks for coming in. We sure do appreciate it."

"Um—that's fine," Dix said, standing up. He looked at Kim

hesitantly and then turned and walked out of the interrogation room.

"Well," Will said, frowning down at the file on the table in front of him. "We'll have to check out his bowling story, but if it's legit, I'd say that rules him out."

Kim was not, by nature, an angry person—he liked to think of himself as fairly levelheaded. But right at this moment he could feel the heat flooding into his face as his blood pressure went up. "We don't know the names of his bowling friends," he began tightly. "We didn't even ask—"

"Louey and Pete," Will said, standing up. "He told us already."

"But we don't have their last names," Kim said, "and furthermore—"

"He said shoe store friends," Will interrupted casually. "It shouldn't be too hard to figure it out, Kim. You'll get used to how this works. Come on—I'm starving."

And Will moved to leave the room, not even seeming to notice as Kim lagged behind, staring at him in mounting frustration.

the maddening, intoxicating ways that a girl could get under your skin

THE LAST ONE TO SEE HER ALIVE

Will's uncle Casper had sent him a fairly tacky poster that said SOUTH CAROLINA, with a richly colored photograph of the rolling grasslands near the blue ridge range of Table Rock Mountain. Will had gotten a frame and put the poster up on his dorm room wall. He knew it wasn't exactly high art, but it had a soothing effect. Late at night, when he was sitting in here thinking, invariably his thoughts turned to home, and when they did, he liked to look up at the poster. It made him feel better.

That afternoon, as the last reddened remnants of the sunset had faded away, Will was sitting in his desk chair, still sweaty from the gym, staring at the poster. He found that he could get lost in it—he looked at it when he was on the phone, when he was taking a break from studying, and even when he'd just gotten dressed and was about to go out and face the world. It was like a window into his home, into his past—and corny or not, he couldn't stop doing it. Now he was tracing the lines of the mountain range with his eyes, trying not to think about Gaia—it was just getting to be ridiculous, how often he was letting her face into his mind's eye—when there was a loud rapping on the dorm room's door.

"Come in," Will called out.

The door swung open and Kim Lau was there. He was still dressed in the suit and tie he'd worn that afternoon at the sheriff's station. He looked frustrated.

"Hey, partner," Will said, concerned. "Ready to go hit the vending mach—"

"What was that?" Kim asked tensely.

Will was genuinely puzzled. "What do you mean?"

"This afternoon," Kim said, stepping forward and staring down at him. "That interrogation. What were you doing in there?"

"Kim," Will began, rubbing the bridge of his nose. "Look, I understand that it's your first day doing this, but you'll realize how you develop shortcuts to—"

"This isn't about shortcuts," Kim interrupted. His jaw was clenched tightly, and Will began to realize just how annoyed he was. "You totally shut the witness down—you weren't interested in his story at all."

"That's ridiculous," Will said. "It was a textbook interrogation. Anyway, he's not the guy, Kim. Maybe you didn't realize that, but it's true. He's got an airtight alibi that's very easy to confirm. And he wouldn't have gone into detail about—"

Kim was shaking his head impatiently. "Of course he's not the guy. That was obvious from the moment he sat down. But where did he take her? What happened when he brought her downtown to a crowded street somewhere in Quantico? When did

78

they get there, and who saw them? And in what direction did she walk?"

Will frowned. "Okay, good questions," he admitted. "Maybe we can get him back for—"

"'Good questions'?" Kim repeated. "He was the *last* one to see her alive, Will. The *last person to see her* before she walked away into a crowd and showed up dead the next morning. So I want *every single bit* of information in his head. How can you *possibly* disagree?"

Will looked at Kim, standing over him in his impeccable suit with his patented penetrating stare.

"Look, I'm sorry," Will said, sighing and rubbing his eyes. He gestured toward his other chair, inviting Kim to sit—always the Southern gentleman. "You're right. I'm distracted. I've got stuff on my mind."

"You're thinking about Gaia," Kim said. He pulled back and collapsed into the chair. "Gaia and Cathy. I know—I miss them, too."

But it's probably not the same, Will thought sadly. Sure, Kim was gay, but he understood in abstract terms what kind of bond had formed between Will and Gaia. Maybe Kim had never—and *would* never—daydream about a girl and about all the maddening, intoxicating ways that a girl could get under your skin. Maybe Kim couldn't be that kind of buddy, the kind you talked to about girls.

But Kim understood. That much was clear. There wasn't much about people's feelings and emotions that Kim *didn't* understand.

"I'm sorry, partner," Will said quietly. "You're right—I wasn't on my game. Good thing I've got you aboard now, huh? Next time you can be primary in the interrogation."

Kim shook his head. "Never mind that. What's the next step in the investigation?"

Will found his eyes drifting back to the mountains in the South Carolina poster. "Do you have any bright ideas?"

"Yeah," Kim said intently. "We've got to go look at that dating Web site. SecondChanceVA.com. I think that's the next move."

Will gestured at his own desktop computer monitor, which was open to his e-mail program. "Be my guest," he said politely. "Maybe the Web site's got—"

"I did that already," Kim interrupted. "My point is we need their records. The company's offices are right here in Quantico. We might need a court order, but maybe Terri Barker went on *other* blind dates, too."

"Okay, genius," Will said, smiling broadly at Kim. "Makes sense to me. That's our next stop."

"Fine," Kim said. He was squinting at Will, as if he'd seen something in Will's face that he didn't recognize or understand. "Tomorrow, then?"

"Tomorrow."

After Kim left, Will leaned on the desk, frustrated. He was dimly aware that he still hadn't showered—his hair felt sticky and dirty, and the sweat from his workout was still drying on his face. His watch said it was closing on six-thirty. Time to unwind with some music and then hit the dining hall . . . and then early to bed. Because tomorrow would be—

Will caught a flurry of movement out of the corner of his

eye. He wasn't sure what he'd seen until he turned his head and looked at the bright surface of his computer monitor. The "you've got mail" indicator on the screen was flickering, its miniature numbers changing as ten or twenty e-mails arrived in rapid succession. He glanced idly at the messages' subject lines.

222Will Your Guy Allow You to Smoke??
Sent 180:29:01
222Will Your Guy Allow You to Smoke??
Sent 18:29:01
222Will Your Guy Allow You to Smoke??
Sent 18:29:01
222Will Your Guy Allow You to Smoke??
Sent 18:29:02
222Will Your Guy Allow You to Smoke??
Sent 18:29:02
2526Will Your Guy Allow You to Drink??
Sent 18:29:02
2526Will Your Guy Allow You to Drink??
Sent 18:29:02
2526Will Your Guy Allow You to Drink??
Sent 18:29:02
2526Will Your Guy Allow You to Drink??
Sent 18:29:03
2526Will Your Guy Allow You to Drink??
Sent 18:29:03
2526Will Your Guy Allow You to Drink??
Sent 18:29:03

2526Will Your Guy Allow You to Drink??

Sent 18:29:03

2526Will Your Guy Allow You to Drink??

Sent 18:29:03

1212Will Your Guy Allow You to CHAT??

Sent 18:29:04

1212Will Your Guy Allow You to CHAT??

Sent 18:29:04

1212Will Your Guy Allow You to CHAT??

Sent 18:29:04

1212Will Your Guy Allow You to CHAT??

Sent 18:29:04

1212Will Your Guy Allow You to CHAT??

Sent 18:29:04

1212Will Your Guy Allow You to CHAT??

Sent 18:29:05

1212Will Your Guy Allow You to CHAT??

Sent 18:29:05

1212Will Your Guy Allow You to CHAT??

Sent 18:29:05

Will frowned in annoyance. Junk e-mail (or spam) was a
growing problem for everyone—not just in the FBI, but anywhere people used computers to communicate. Will's computer
was connected to the Quantico base's master network, and the
security filter was supposed to prevent e-mail like this from coming in. Yawning, he reached for the mouse and moved to delete
the new messages—

—and then he stopped.

"Will Your Guy A"—*twenty-one times in a row.*

Will looked up and down the row of e-mails, absently realizing that his pulse was quickening.

No—it couldn't be.

Except Gaia Moore knew as much about the Quantico base security system as *he* did. She knew how intently she was being looked for. And she knew that all base and dorm e-mail could be eavesdropped on for security purposes.

Without giving in to the sudden wave of excitement he was feeling, Will selected one of the e-mails and opened it up. It was a lurid-looking commercial solicitation:

LIVE SINGLES CHAT LIVE SINGLES CHAT LIVE SINGLES CHAT
Hey, singles! Want to connect? Visit our JAVA-BASED Web site for
SECURE, PRIVATE CHATS with singles of your choice! Talk to the
whole room or go one-on-one! Just $0.99/minute!
IT'S FUN ! IT'S SPICY! CLICK HERE TO START!
http://www.livesingleschat.com
Minors, please ask your parents before connecting.
Some restrictions apply.

Will clicked on the link, reaching to fish out his wallet with his other hand. A Web browser came up, connecting to a Web site with the same lurid purple-and-pink color scheme as the e-mail. *LIVE SINGLES CHAT,* a headline insisted. A smaller window in the center of the page showed scrolling text of a conversation already in progress.

FOXYGIRL5: of boys

BADBOY: hi everyone

FOXYGIRL5: What about you?

PETER56667: anyone here from Vancouver

GIBSONTOWNGIRL: hi badboy! And welcome

PAULGLASER: foxygirl what do you look like?

BADBOY: thanx gib

PETER56667: I'm from Vancouver

FOXYGIRL5: that's for me to know ::grin::

Will had already started filling out the form on the bottom of the page, typing in his credit card number. When he refreshed the screen after the approval e-mail arrived, he saw that he could now enter the conversation.

SOUTHERNWILL: hi everyone

GIBSONTOWNGIRL: badboy where are you from?

BADBOY: I'm in Mason City IL. How about you towngirl?

SOUTHERNWILL: Any California girls here? Or from the Northeast?

GIBSONTOWNGIRL: Florida originally

SOUTHERNWILL: City girls? I like blondes

NEWYORKERCHICK: Hi SouthernWill! Glad you could make it!

Will moved closer to the screen, nearly forgetting to breathe. Somewhere nearby, in another dorm room, someone was listening to Coldplay. Will could barely hear it. In his mind the only sound was the feverish tapping of his fingers on the keyboard.

SOUTHERNWILL: Thanx NewYorkerChick! Are you blond? I like blondes.

PETER56667: Nobody from Vancouver?

NEWYORKERCHICK: Sure am. ((blush)) My friend Cathy's got dark hair. I'll bet you're cute and blond too!!!

BADBOY: Anyone seen War of the Worlds

SOUTHERNWILL: Maybe I am, NewYorkerChick. You into lollipops?

FOXYGIRL5: I did badboy it rulz

NEWYORKERCHICK: I bet that's more your thing now

I don't believe it, Will thought. He was grinning from ear to ear. *I just don't believe it.*

NEWYORKERCHICK: Hey SouthernWill, want to go private?

SOUTHERNWILL: Sure would ma'am—but how?

NEWYORKERCHICK: You remember Cathy's favorite city?

Will blinked. Favorite *city? What the hell does that mean?*

But something about it sounded familiar. Staring at the blinking cursor on the screen, he suddenly began to remember something—a trick that Catherine Sanders had shown them weeks ago.

"Hackers chat all the time," Catherine had explained, taking huge bites of microwaved pizza and talking with her mouth full as she pointed at her computer screen. It was a rainy Sunday afternoon, and Will and Kim were sitting around Catherine and Gaia's dorm room, pretending to study for their upcoming Surveillance and Criminology exam. "If you're in the business of breaking into secure systems, you've got to be able to communicate with your brothers and sisters about what's going on—trade passwords, help each other find back doors, and all that good stuff."

"Isn't that how those guys always get caught?" Kim had asked, reaching for the last slice of pizza—Gaia playfully slapped his hand, taking it for her own.

"Not anymore," Catherine told them, typing too fast for any of them to follow what she was doing. "Cybercrime's gone way up, thanks to the hidden communities we've—I mean, *they've*—all built." Thunder had clapped outside the dorm very theatrically right then, and Catherine had taken advantage of the timing, raising her hands dramatically over the keyboard. "Watch and learn, my minions," she said fiendishly. "I'm going to show you how to get to Hacker City."

And then she did, Will recalled. *But the question is, can I remember the way?*

On the screen the singles chat kept rolling.

NEWYORKERCHICK: Still there cutie?
SOUTHERNWILL: Yes ma'am—Im a little rusty that's all
NEWYORKERCHICK: Text mode, ping KL's birthday + 6

Right—right—
Will nodded to himself. With Gaia's reminder, it began coming back to him.

As fast as he could without making mistakes, Will opened another window and went into text mode, so that his screen suddenly looked like an old-fashioned 1970s computer with blocky, plain white text on a plain black background. Tapping his fingers on his desk in frustration, he tried to remember Kim Lau's birthday and finally got it—March 5.

Zero three zero five, plus six, is zero three one one. That's a four-digit ping—

Will's fingers clicked on his keyboard as he typed PING 0311 and hit return.

Nothing happened.

April, he remembered suddenly. *Not March.*

Typing PING 0411 made his entire screen go black. Will watched avidly, wiping sweat from his forehead, as the screen filled with plain white text.

```
         - - - - - - - - - - - - - - - - - - - - - - - -

         - WELCOME TO HACKER CITY -
         - - - - - - - - - - - - - - - - - - - - - - - -

    busting boundaries and corralling code since 1990
         - - - - - - - - - - - - - - - - - - - - - - - -

         double-16-bit-encryption activated
         - - - - - - - - - - - - - - - - - - - - - - - -

              please select a function
    NEWS SERIALS CRACKS HACKS DIRECTORY STORAGE CHAT
                     MAILBOX
         - - - - - - - - - - - - - - - - - - - - - - - -
```

Will got up from his chair, his head spinning, and checked that the dorm room door was locked. Then he sat back down and started typing again.

GAIA13: Hello? Will?

WILL22: Gaia? Is that you?

GAIA13: Will!!! It worked. Thank God.

WILL22: Gaia, I can't believe it's really you.

GAIA13: That goes both ways.

WILL22: Are you all right? Are you okay?

GAIA13: I'm fine. Just a couple of bruises.

WILL22: You're sure?

GAIA13: yes

WILL22: Good . . . Then where the HELL are you? Why did you run out of the restaurant?

GAIA13: I'm so sorry about that.

WILL22: Get your ass BACK here.

GAIA13: PLEASE don't start now, Will. I apologize from the bottom of my heart. It's a long story that keeps getting longer. I think I've picked up Catherine's trail.

WILL22: How? Where? What do you know?

GAIA13: Not enough. I need a favor.

WILL22: What kind . . . ?

GAIA13: I need you to go into the crime database and find some stuff out for me.

WILL22: What kind of stuff?

GAIA13: Anything you can about a man named James Rossiter. Address is 1309 Cherry Lane, Baltimore, MD.

Caucasian American male, 6' 1", black hair, brown eyes. That's all I've got. I need ANYTHING else you can find.

WILL22: Wait . . .

GAIA13: Then personnel files: I need you to find out if there was ever a bureau special agent named Winston Marsh. In his fifties now, allegedly retired a few years ago.

WILL22: Can't you explain what this is about?

GAIA13: Not now. Just do it, Will. I don't have time to explain or argue. I need to stay on this trail.

WILL22: I repeat if you've found a trail, then COME BACK TO QUANTICO and GET HELP. If you're not safe, then GET BACK HERE!!

GAIA13: Damn it, Will, don't be like this! I don't have time to explain—I told you.

WILL22: Not good enough. If you were me, you'd say the same thing. I'm not going to get into trouble just because you say so!

GAIA13: You're not going to get into trouble!! You can get the stuff from your dorm computer by logging onto the Quantico local network files. I'll wait.

WILL22: *sigh* OK, Gaia. Stand by . . . I'll get back to you in like two minutes.

GAIA13: Thanks, Will XOXOXOX

Why am I doing this? Will asked himself as he leaned forward at his desk and logged onto the FBI's Trainee Information Network. *I don't want to be doing this.*

It had taken less than ten minutes for Will's utter joy at hearing from Gaia to change into familiar, maddening frustration.

89

She needed him to do something, and he was doing it. He could object or refuse, but they both knew he was going to do what she'd asked and it was as simple as that.

Will resented being so predictable.

Where is she? Why didn't she say where she was?

Because she didn't really trust Catherine's "Hacker City"?

Or because she doesn't really trust me?

Even if Will decided to run to Malloy's office right this moment and say he'd text-chatted with Gaia, he couldn't give away where she was since she had been careful not to tell him.

On the screen he could see the familiar interface used for pulling data from the FBI criminology database. It was common practice for trainees to use the extensive FBI crime files in their schoolwork—Will thought of it as one of the fringe benefits of life at Quantico. If you were interested in criminology and crime fighting—if you were an FBI trainee, in other words—it made for endlessly fascinating reading.

First, the easy part—Will did a quick FBI personnel search, looking for Winston Marsh. The results came back almost immediately.

FEDERAL BUREAU OF INVESTIGATION PERSONNEL FILES
WINSTON ELIAS MARSH
ID #45199-EDO-5
AGENT IN GOOD STANDING 1979–2002
CONGRESSIONAL MEDAL OF VALOR 04.13.81
SECURITY OPERATIONS, BOSTON OFFICE, 1985–1993
DISTINGUISHED ORDER OF SERVICE, 08.12.93
COUNTERTERRORISM TASK FORCE, 1994–2001

Impressive record, Will had to admit. It was the kind of record Will would have been proud of if it had been his. There was a black-and-white digital photograph showing a fairly handsome, clean-shaven man with wide, high cheekbones, a pleasantly lined face, blue eyes, and close-cropped, graying hair. Reading from the text on the screen, Will began taking notes on a legal pad. Paging through year after year of arrests, task forces, and assistance programs, Will saw a respectable, above-average career history. The system had no information about Marsh's retirement or his current whereabouts or activities—but, Will supposed, that wasn't uncommon. A lifetime of secrecy was a hard habit to break.

Copying down the details, Will went into the general crime database—the system that had all the FBI's criminology records, indexed and cross-referenced—and typed the name James Rossiter and the Baltimore address Gaia had given him.

This time there was a delay. Will tapped his fingers on the desk, watching the progress bar that indicated that the data were being retrieved. After a moment the screen gave him an unexpected message:

The requested data is NOT AVAILABLE at this station.
All terrorism and counterterrorism inquiries relating to keyword SOCORRO are restricted from access through this station. To retrieve the requested search data [ROSSITER, JAMES], you must access the central FBI database at records bldg. Clearance level 4 required.
— Thank You —
Quantico Library Secure Criminology and Investigative Records System Administration

Will frowned. He had seen this happen before—certain FBI information wasn't available to trainees, who didn't have the security clearance that would allow them access to sensitive, terror-related data. But it wasn't what he'd expected.

Counterterrorism?

Gaia was "on Catherine's trail"—and she had somehow run across a man the FBI computer wouldn't tell him about because he was so dangerous.

Socorro? What does that mean?

Will was wishing he'd asked Gaia more questions when he'd had the chance. Not that Gaia seemed likely to provide any meaningful answers—but he didn't know *anything* about where she was and what she was doing. Not to mention how she'd ended up crossing paths with suspects on the FBI's terror-watch lists.

She might not know *he's a terrorist,* Will realized unpleasantly. *She might not know anything about him at all except his name.*

Will's eyes were caught by the word *Socorro* on the screen. His fingers quickly tapping the keys, he performed a network-wide search.

FBI Database Retrieval System—321 Users Currently Logged On
SEARCH QUERY RESULTS
Search term:
S O C O R R O
Results: 8 unclassified, 543,432,001 classified
MOST REQUESTED ITEM: ATTF-20439 08.22.05 **click to read**

Half a billion classified documents—and eight they'll let me see. Will wasn't sure if the "most requested item" was anything

92

relevant (or even if it was unclassified), but he clicked the link anyway.

He was in luck. Apparently the system was willing to let him see this famous "most requested item"—a document created today, he noticed.

A moment later, as the familiar FBI seal filled the top of the screen, he realized he was looking at a standard "briefing letter"— the kind of low-security document that got routinely distributed through the bureau.

Leaning forward, Will read on.

FEDERAL BUREAU OF INVESTIGATION
ALERT STATUS—FOR IMMEDIATE GLOBAL RELEASE—ALERT STATUS

This FBI memorandum is hereby marked for mandatory distribution to all field offices and law enforcement communications networks throughout the continental United States and liaisons to CD-040 ("friendly power") international law enforcement agencies in accordance with the International Terrorism Act of 2001.

MISUSE OR UNAUTHORIZED DISTRIBUTION OF THIS MEMORANDUM IS A FEDERAL CRIME, PUNISHABLE BY UP TO FIVE YEARS IMPRISONMENT IN A STATE PENITENTIARY OR A FINE OF UP TO U.S. $5000 OR BOTH.

ALL-POINTS BULLETIN ALL-POINTS BULLETIN ALL-POINTS BULLETIN

[Washington, D.C., ATTF-20439]

The Federal Bureau of Investigation has learned that the international terrorist organization code-named "**SOCORRO**" has completed preparations for a **MAJOR TERRORIST ACTION**.

The details of the present **SOCORRO** operation are unknown. It may be assumed that **SOCORRO**'s plans are part of their larger political agenda, but this agenda is difficult to interpret and understand, and for this reason, the tactics and goals of **SOCORRO**'s plans remain a mystery.

THE BUREAU HAS LEARNED THAT SOCORRO IS PLANNING TO RECRUIT AN FBI AGENT AND "BRAINWASH" OR "REPROGRAM" THIS AGENT TO ASSIST IN THE EXECUTION OF THIS TERRORIST ACTION.

IMPORTANT: Reliable corroborating intelligence (available only to FBI personnel with A-21 security clearance and above) has shown that

94

SOCORRO's terrorist action is timed to occur on a single day, code-named "**EL DIA**"—08.24.05—and will definitely involve the aforementioned "reprogrammed" FBI agent.

URGENT: AS OF 08.24 THE BUREAU HAS LEARNED THAT SOCORRO HAS ALREADY MADE CONTACT WITH THE FBI AGENT WHOM THEY INTEND TO "BRAINWASH" OR "REPROGRAM." For this reason, all stations are advised to observe all FBI personnel having SOCORRO ties and to employ the highest-possible scrutiny in doing so.

SOCORRO (originating in Latin America) is considered among the most dangerous organizations of its kind in the world, with an established track record of successfully recruiting and "turning" law enforcement officials as well as civilians to their cause or forcing them to act in **SOCORRO**'s interests. **SOCORRO** has been responsible for many crimes to date, resulting in civilian deaths and the disruption of all free societies and their way of life. **SOCORRO has demonstrated a clear disregard for civilian life and for this reason must be investigated and pursued with extreme care.**

Given the extremely short notice of this worldwide terror alert, law enforcement personnel are urged to regard ANY AND ALL potential terrorist activity in their jurisdictions as URGENT AND IMPORTANT. All suspected links or information concerning **SOCORRO** or its satellites or cells should be reported to the bureau with all possible speed.

END OF BULLETIN—[Washington, D.C., 08.21.05]

ALERT STATUS—FOR IMMEDIATE GLOBAL RELEASE—ALERT STATUS

Will felt a cold wave passing over him, as if the temperature in the dorms had dropped a few degrees while he read the memo.

Terrorism, he thought bleakly as he got ready to re-enter the "Hacker City" chat room. *Gaia, I hope you know what you're getting into here. I really hope you do.*

On the screen Will had navigated back to the plain, text-based interface for "Hacker City." *Gaia?* he typed. *Hello?*

Even with the entry-level antiterrorism training Will had received, he knew enough to be scared. "Terrorist actions" were notoriously difficult to prepare for. In the movies terrorists made speeches, grandstanding on television and advertising their cause. In the movies terrorists did things like take over stadiums and office buildings, demanding money or political asylum and making clear what they wanted and what their deadlines and timetables were. Then it was up to some steel-jawed hero to come in and save the day.

But real-life terrorists were a very different story. In real life you never saw them coming. Until it was too late. They blew things up, shot people, crashed planes, all without warning or logic, and then they let the world do the hard work of figuring out what they wanted and why they'd done it. Bruce Willis couldn't save you from *real* terrorists. They lingered at the outer edges of society, drawing absolutely no attention to themselves until it was time for them to strike.

Gaia, he thought helplessly, *you're in over your head. You can't do this by yourself.*

You have to come home. Come back here and get help.

On the screen the cursor blinked on and off serenely, as if it had all the time in the world. Will had typed Gaia's name four more times, he saw—but he hadn't gotten any response at all.

Gaia? Are you there?

RAISED LIKE BLADES

Someone was watching her.

Gaia wasn't sure how she knew, but in moments like this—when she was suddenly, overwhelmingly convinced that she wasn't alone—she tended to trust her instincts.

She was standing on a threadbare brown carpet in front of a motel ice machine. Her right hand was wrapped around a plastic scoop, shoveling miniature ice cubes into a blue plastic bucket. To the right of the ice machine was a big plate glass window that revealed a nearly deserted parking lot beneath a fading afternoon sky and an enormous, revolving neon sign whose letters spelled out CLAVARAK MOTEL and, below that, CABLE, TV, POOL, AIR-CONDITIONING, and VACANCY. The sign had not yet been turned on. Along the edge of parking lot Gaia could see the brown doors of the motel's rooms, including her own closed door and the door to Marsh's room right next to it. The Altima was parked in front of the rooms, its chrome gleaming in the sun.

She and Marsh had driven quite a ways after leaving the park where they'd had their conversation. Marsh kept pointing Gaia in different directions, ordering her to reverse herself, making sudden lane changes and U-turns as she drove. He seemed determined to evade any conceivable pursuit. Gaia had to admit that his technique—his "tradecraft"—was excellent, right out of the Quantico training manuals.

Marsh had already checked in here when he'd arrived in Baltimore—his gray Audi sedan was parked in the shade to one side. Marsh had gone into his room to check his phone messages while Gaia checked into the motel, moved her suitcase into her room, set up her laptop, and contacted Will. He had promised to get back to her in a few minutes with the information she'd requested—just enough time for her to come out here and get some ice.

And get ambushed.

Gaia had no idea who was behind her—tall, short, male, female—but she could feel a presence. Moving suddenly, she dropped the ice bucket and slid toward the floor, pivoting out of the way of any possible blow as she rolled into a reversed fighting stance, crouched in place with her hands raised like blades.

"Don't try it," said the tall, blond man standing there. His large, dark sunglasses reflected Gaia's own face back at her. "Best advice you'll get all day."

It was the man from the park—the man who had been watching them earlier. He was reasonably young—in his thirties—and was dressed in a conservative dark blue suit and a gray tie. Up close, he looked healthy and well built.

"Don't be too sure," Gaia told him.

"I know; you've got unusually good fighting skills for a trainee," the man told her. His voice was quiet and ice-cold. "But I'm a ten-year field-combat veteran. Thom Kinney, FBI, Baltimore branch. You think you can take me"—Kinney's shoulders moved as he balanced himself—"you go ahead and try."

"What do you want?" Gaia asked. She was coming out of the crouch, slowly rising to her full height, never taking her eyes off Kinney's. "Why are you following me?"

"*Everyone's* following you," Kinney said, taking a step closer. "The whole bureau's running in circles obeying a directive to locate you and bring you back to Virginia. Me, I'm the lucky one—I happened to pick up your trail first. I'm surprised you're not surrounded by agents. You didn't ditch your *car*—you didn't even change your plates. It's like you *want* to get caught."

"You've found me," Gaia corrected. "It doesn't mean you've *caught* me."

"Moore, if you don't let me or another agent 'catch' you, you're going to be risking a lot more than a reprimand or a court marshal." Kinney seemed very angry beneath his cold demeanor. "We know what you're up to you— you *traitor*."

What?

Gaia was so surprised, she was momentarily speechless.

"I'm not a *traitor*," she finally blurted. This was ridiculous— she was standing in the vestibule of a cheap Baltimore hotel arguing with a man who wasn't giving her the slightest explanation of what he wanted—or what he thought she had done. "I broke some bureau rules, admittedly. I understand how seriously—"

"Don't talk to me about rules. I read the *memo*," Kinney said intently. "I know *exactly* what you're up to. You ought to be ashamed of yourself. You took an *oath*—an *oath* to uphold and defend the American Constitution."

"The Constitution?" Gaia was as puzzled as she was angry. "What memo? What are you *talking* about? Look, I don't want to have an ethical debate with—"

Gaia and the man both flinched at a sudden, loud crashing noise. Winston Marsh was right outside the aluminum-framed door, pushing it open.

"Hi," Marsh said brightly, looking at Kinney. "What's going on here?"

"Sir, I'm a federal agent," Kinney said, taking a menacing step toward Marsh. "I'm going to have to ask you to turn around and walk right out of here."

"Federal agent, huh?" Marsh was nodding. "Can I see your credentials?"

"Sir—"

"If a citizen asks to see your credentials," Marsh went on calmly, "you're supposed to comply. You actually have no choice but to comply." He was holding out his hand.

"Sir, please," Kinney went on. Gaia saw that his hand was moving, inching slowly toward his lapel. "This is government business—I'm going to have to ask you to step outside."

Drawing his gun, Gaia thought. *Getting ready.*

"Unless you're making an arrest," Marsh went on. "Are you making an arrest?"

"Sir," Kinney said loudly. He had turned completely away from Gaia and was clearly drawing his gun. "I won't tell you again. Please turn right around and walk out that door, or I'll have no choice but to—"

Gaia shifted her weight, stepped forward, and in one clean move brought the rigid inside edge of her right hand down on Agent Kinney's neck.

Kinney's eyes rolled back in his head. His body tensed, flailed, and then fell like a dropped mail sack. Before he hit the ground,

Marsh moved to catch the unconscious man by his armpits, pulling him toward the wall beside the ice machine. Incredibly, nobody was around. The wide concrete motel parking lot and the surrounding landscape—a two-lane blacktop, a 7-Eleven, and a gas station—were completely empty of passersby.

"That wasn't very smart," Marsh told Gaia, grunting as he pulled Kinney's large frame into the shadows by the wall. "He'll be out for, what, twenty minutes?"

"Long enough to get away," Gaia said, rubbing the side of her hand. She had acted very fast, without consciously thinking it through beyond on some level that any FBI agent she encountered was going to try to take her into custody and prevent her from finding Catherine. Now, looking down at the unconscious blond agent, Gaia wished that she'd come up with a better plan. "Come on—"

Marsh shook his head, pointing at the ceiling.

Gaia understood. *The other agent,* she realized. *Kinney's partner—he's got to be on the roof.*

"When I say so," Marsh said, stepping closer, "I want you to follow me and do exactly what I say."

"But—"

"Please don't give me a hard time about this," Marsh said impatiently. "I was a field agent before you were born."

Fair enough, Gaia thought. "What's your plan?"

RECOGNIZING FEAR

With a sudden, loud squeal of brakes a blue Ford sedan gunned its engine. The car lurched forward out of its parking space beneath the revolving Clavarak Motel sign. Brakes squealed as the Ford accelerated purposefully toward the highway. Behind the wheel was a man in a dark raincoat with a hat pulled low over his eyes. Beside him a young woman with long blond hair hunched down against the passenger seat, as if trying to disappear from view.

As the blue Ford sped away, the Clavarak Motel's office door crashed open and two men in suits and sunglasses hurried out, heading for their own Chevrolet sedan. One of the men—the blond one—was limping and groggy, holding on to his partner's shoulder for support.

The men in suits got into their sedan and gunned the engine. Just as the blue Ford disappeared completely from view, the government-issue sedan emerged from the motel parking lot and began to pick up speed.

Gaia leaned against the edge of the window, bending back the curtain and peering out at the darkening parking lot. Marsh stood beside her with his jacket off and his tie loosened, watching the results of his handiwork.

"How much did you pay that guy?" Gaia asked.

"Fifty bucks." Marsh shrugged. "But he gets to keep my car."

"When will they pick him up?"

"Oh, they'll follow at a distance all night," Marsh said confidently, moving to one of the motel's vinyl-covered chairs. "Remember, they think they're tracking Gaia Moore and 'unidentified male suspect' or whatever that kid's field report will call me."

Pretty clever, Gaia had to admit to herself. Sneaking them through the weeds behind the building, Marsh knocked on just three motel room windows before he had the good fortune to come across a man and his blond teenage daughter, who were willing to make some money and get a free car in the bargain. The man looked nothing like Marsh, but the hat and raincoat had fixed that. And now Agent Kinney and his partner were getting farther away by the minute.

"That guy is gunning for a promotion," Marsh said critically. "He jumped you too soon and you got away. Not to mention actually *warning* you that the whole bureau's after you. Agent Kinney didn't exactly help the FBI with that maneuver."

"Wait—'jumped me too *soon*'?" Gaia frowned at Marsh. "You won't give me any credit for the takedown?"

"You're still embarrassed about Rossiter," Marsh said, smiling slightly. "Get over it. Happens to everyone."

Gaia looked at Marsh, caught in the fading light from the curtained window of her cheap motel room, and in that moment she felt like she could see what must have been hundreds and hundreds of cases. How many fistfights, arrests; how many times was Marsh primary through a door? How many injuries had he sustained, bullets had he taken?

He's certainly got the moves, Gaia told herself. She seemed to be able to *see* twenty-odd years of field experience in the flawless way he carried himself. It made her feel like a clumsy, lumbering novice in comparison.

But that's not fair, she told herself. *You've only just started. This is your first time in the field. Soon you'll be as good as him.*

If she got that far.

"What is this, some kind of secure chat?" Marsh said behind her.

Gaia turned around. Marsh stood at the tiny laminated desk where she had set up her laptop. Its screen glowed like a miniature billboard, showing green lines of text.

"A hidden IRC channel for *hackers*?" Marsh whistled, impressed. He'd gathered the nature of the site in seconds. "Not bad. Your generation's got a whole new bunch of tricks."

"Don't read that!" Gaia yelled out sharply. "That's none of your b—"

"Medal of Valor," Marsh said. "I didn't know they'd put that there."

Gaia had stalked over and grabbed the laptop's screen/lid, ready to slam it shut—when she stopped. On the screen were several lines of bold green text:

WILL22: Gaia? Are you there?
WILL22: Gaia?
WILL22: OK, I'm going to assume you're still connected.
Here's the 411 on that ex-agent:
FEDERAL BUREAU OF INVESTIGATION PERSONNEL FILES
WINSTON ELIAS MARSH
ID #45199-EDO-5
AGENT IN GOOD STANDING 1979–2002
CONGRESSIONAL MEDAL OF VALOR, 04.13.81
SECURITY OPERATIONS, BOSTON OFFICE, 1985–1993
DISTINGUISHED ORDER OF SERVICE, 08.12.93
COUNTERTERRORISM TASK FORCE, 1994–2001

"Checking my story," Marsh said, nodding in appreciation. The glow of the laptop screen shone up in their faces as they stood there. Marsh didn't seem remotely offended or annoyed. "Very good."

"You were on the counterterrorism task force?" Gaia asked, impressed. She had heard about that elite Boston program and how notoriously difficult it was to get oneself assigned to it. Marsh had managed, apparently. "And now you're doing—what did you say—'skip traces'? Spying on cheating husbands?"

"And finding your friend," Marsh said tightly. He turned to move toward one of the orange vinyl-covered chairs. "Don't forget that little detail."

"But basically I'm right, aren't I? One of a hundred people in the whole country who could actually achieve something in counterterrorism and you're working for bail bondsmen in Philadelphia."

"Today," Marsh said quietly, "I'm finding your friend. Shall we get back to it, or do you want to make more clever remarks about me?"

He's right—that was unfair, Gaia reprimanded herself. *Why are you picking on him? He's trying to help.*

Was it just that she felt competitive—overshadowed by a more experienced and more skilled FBI agent? Why did Marsh's midlife career change bother her? *He was done with it, that's all,* she told himself. *He was tired of saving the world. Someday it'll happen to me.*

Gaia suddenly broke off that train of thought, staring at the laptop screen. She had missed something.

Below the reprinted lines from Marsh's FBI service record, Will had typed something else:

WILL22: Gaia (if you're still there): Ran the name James Rossiter. All data RESTRICTED. Rossiter is connected to a terrorist organization called "Socorro." This is no joke, Gaia . . . you are dealing with some very dangerous people here.

PLEASE be careful and PLEASE ask yourself if you are 100 percent sure of what you're doing.

WILL 22: Gaia, are you there? I searched just now for the word Socorro. Nothing's available except a single FBI briefing memo—a worldwide terror alert. Here it is:

FEDERAL BUREAU OF INVESTIGATION
ALERT STATUS—FOR IMMEDIATE GLOBAL RELEASE—ALERT STATUS
This FBI memorandum is hereby marked for mandatory distribution to all field offices and law enforcement communications networks throughout the continental United States. . . .

There was more. Gaia and Marsh stood side by side, reading the memo in unison. They didn't move, except when Gaia had to reach forward and scroll the screen down to read the rest. *Major terrorist action . . . brainwash . . . reprogram . . . disruption of all free societies and their way of life . . .* The words and phrases echoed in Gaia's head like gunshots.

"Very interesting," Marsh said. He was frowning at the screen, concentrating.

He's seen these before, Gaia remembered. Marsh had spent seven years on the elite counterterrorism task force—documents like this one must have passed through his hands dozens of times. *He can explain what it means.*

"This is from yesterday," Gaia said, pointing at the date on the screen. She was struggling to make sense of what she was looking at. "'Completed preparations for a major terrorist action . . .'"

"Yes. This is basically really bad news," Marsh said grimly. He was staring past Gaia, the laptop screen reflected in his eyes.

Gaia could see an intensity on his face that hadn't been there before. She assumed it was fear—although recognizing fear was difficult for her. "Your friend's right—you are dealing with some dangerous people."

"I've never heard of 'Socorro' in my life."

"An FBI agent hasn't heard of a particular terror organization." Marsh smiled humorlessly. "What a shock. The bureau's *extremely* careful about the security 'pyramid.' A lot more than you know. Very strict rules govern who has access to what information."

"But—" Gaia was thinking furiously as she stared at the briefing memo.

It's Catherine, she realized helplessly. *Of course—that's what's going on.*

"Catherine's the recruit," Gaia said. She went over and collapsed weakly into one of the room's ugly orange vinyl chairs. "Socorro's captured Catherine and they're going to try to deploy her against the FBI."

"Now you've got it." Marsh sighed heavily.

His nerves are going, Gaia realized, seeing Marsh's drawn, pale face in the dim lamplight. *One too many shocks and he'll be finished—ready for genuine retirement.*

The idea was horrifying, but it made all kinds of sense. If Socorro was in the business of turning FBI agents to their will, as the memo claimed, why not a young recruit? Why not Catherine? Abduct her, keep her prisoner in a basement while you force her to do whatever dirty work you need done on a computer . . .

The motel room was dim and quiet. She could hear the interstate traffic rumbling past outside.

"And they want to use her for something they're doing *two*

days from now," Gaia remembered. "For 'El Dia'—what the hell does that mean?"

"It's worse than you think," Marsh said. He was walking toward her, holding out something—Gaia suddenly realized it was a hotel glass full of iced drinking water. She hadn't seen him fill it.

"Thanks," Gaia said, reaching to take the glass. Gaia took a sip of ice water and then, before she realized what she was doing, drank it all down.

"More?" Marsh said, holding out his hand politely.

"Maybe later." Gaia wiped her mouth, handing the glass back. "Why is it worse?"

"Okay, I'm going to tell you a secret," Marsh said, sitting on the edge of the bed. Gaia saw the cheap mattress and box spring sag under his weight. "Something that nobody at your security clearance level knows. There's an FBI procedure called a 'gray operation.' Gray ops aren't outlined in any regulation book or mentioned in any briefing or directive. Officially there is no such thing as a gray op, and the FBI has never and will never acknowledge otherwise. They never will because gray ops are . . . well, they're pretty bad."

"What do you mean?"

"A gray op," Marsh said, "is when the bureau has no choice but to make an agent disappear."

What?

"You're saying," Gaia repeated slowly, "that the FBI is responsible for murdering agents. I heard you clearly, right? That *is* what you're saying? You're saying this happens all the time?"

"Yes," Marsh said quietly. "It's not a very attractive story, but it's true. I would estimate it's been done about thirty times in the last ten years, as the war on terror has heated up. When an agent or ex-agent gets too close to the enemy, is drawn into contact with terrorists somehow, the bureau has to weigh its risks very carefully. They have to consider the knowledge in the agent's head, the knowledge that could conceivably fall into an enemy's hands if the agent or ex-agent was somehow forced to reveal it. Sometimes they have no choice but to neutralize the agent."

Gaia was watching Marsh, feeling an emotional confusion wash over her. She was trying to picture an FBI that could work the way Marsh was explaining—a bureau that made the bureau she *thought* she was working for look like a fairy tale in comparison. A bureau that would kill to protect its secrets.

Is that true? Could that possibly be true?

Gaia didn't have time to pursue this unpleasant line of thought. "The FBI's going to kill Catherine," she said weakly. "I get it—that's what you're saying."

"And you too," Marsh said. "Make no mistake, Gaia—the sole purpose you're serving right now is to lead the FBI to Catherine, if she's still alive. Once you've done that for them, then you'll be terminated, too."

Terminated?

"There won't be an order," Marsh continued. "Word will come down from Washington, but officially nobody will hear a thing. And then one day you'll be dead, Sanders will be dead, and to keep things nice and clean, I'll be dead, too. With the three of us removed from the game board, the bureau's precious tactical secrets are safe from Socorro and all the rest, and their war on terror can go on."

Gaia leaned back in the ugly fake-leather chair, stretching her legs out and arching her back. Her fatigue was really overcoming her now. It was a tremendous relief to have someone on her side—she had to admit that to herself.

"It's very disillusioning," Marsh said gently. "I know. Generally agents are a little older when they find out. But this is a war, and sometimes you've got to play dirty to win. It's not nice, but it's true."

Gaia nodded. The cold feeling—the feeling that wasn't fear, but in many ways was just as bad—lingered in her body like a winter chill. She felt disoriented. Less than an hour ago she'd been driving into the edges of Baltimore with half a clue about a phone trace. Now she was in over her head, and it had happened very fast. Gaia's concern about her roommate was doubling and tripling in her mind.

"Listen, you look exhausted." Marsh stood up, glancing at his watch. "Time to get some rest. You need ammo? I've got steel-jacket .22 calibers for a Walther like yours if you want."

"Um—sure," Gaia said. Standing made her feel light-headed.

"Tomorrow we'll keep looking for Catherine," Marsh said, taking his room key out of his pocket. "Just pick up the trail wherever we can find it."

"That's right," Gaia confirmed.

"I don't know if you've got a toothbrush or anything like that," Marsh said awkwardly. He had gotten up from the chair and was moving toward the motel room door. "I can go buy you whatever, um, toiletries you need." Marsh paused as he stared at Gaia a moment longer. "You're going to be a good agent," he said quietly. "If you live that long."

"Thanks."

Marsh shook his head, his hand on the doorknob. "Just calling it as I see it. Come on—time to get some shut-eye. I don't have to tell you not to make any phone calls. You're on the run now, Gaia—better get used to it fast."

Night was falling. It was dark and cool outside, Gaia saw as Marsh pulled the door open. Outside, the air smelled like evening dew and gasoline. The 7-Eleven's emerald signs and windows were blindingly bright; Gaia could hear an Usher song playing on a car radio somewhere nearby. Cars droned past on the interstate, far in the distance.

Someday, Gaia thought weakly. *Jesus, where am I and what am I doing?*

She was too tired to think about it anymore.

"Morning comes early," Marsh said. "Sleep well, Gaia."

"You too," she answered.

Then the door closed and Gaia was all alone in an empty motel room, far from anyplace she'd ever called home.

A WHOLE DAY'S WORTH OF LUCK

Bright white light—sunlight—

Gaia was in her Quantico dorm, dreaming that she was float-
ing down a wide river. The water was calm and smooth, and the
boat she rode glided gently with the current toward the sun. The
sun was too bright, hurting her eyes, but the current was taking
her in the right direction: she had to follow the river.

In her dream Gaia knew she was on a long journey. The sunlight dazzled her, made it hard to see where she was going. She
knew that the current was strong and that her voyage would take
her through deep and rapid water, beyond the sunset, into
darker and darker territory. Somewhere far ahead the water led
into the night, and there, in the darkness at the river's end, she
would arrive—

Where?

To meet—

Who?

The dream was fading now as the light on her eyes got
brighter. The damn dorm windows faced east; she should have
asked Catherine if they could switch beds halfway through the
semester or something.

Morning sunlight. Too bright—roll over—sleep some more—

112

Gaia knew that was a losing battle. If the sun was up, that meant there was probably less than a half hour before the alarm clock, and then she and Catherine would be doing their usual routine, stumbling to the closets, not yet awake, their bare feet slapping the cold linoleum floor as they wordlessly dressed for morning calisthenics, side by side, not even trying to speak to each other. They had the routine down, joining the bathroom line in sequence, taking turns, pulling on FBI sweatshirts as the Virginia sunlight flooded their dorm room, the same light that was blasting in Gaia's eyes now.

Wait—

The light was wrong. Too pale, too weak. The bedsheets were rough, not her own well-worn, beloved blue cotton sheets from Stanford. The *sound* was all wrong: too quiet, with no birdsong and no wind, just the hum of traffic and honking horns nearby and a droning machine sound she couldn't identify. And there was a mild ache in her lower back, like the ghost of a fading bruise—

Oh.

It all came flooding back. The dank basement air, the hands on her throat, the sirens behind the car as she gripped the steering wheel, the gazebo with the peeling paint; the man on a bench in the distance, watching her as the pigeons circled in the white sky overhead. And finally this place. The Clavarak Motel, somewhere on the outskirts of Baltimore.

Gaia opened her eyes. A square of sunlight was blasting onto her bed, shining on the rough orange bedspread and the polyester sheets. Squinting, Gaia could see a heavily curtained window and through the window a cloudless blue sky.

113

Sitting up—noting with some satisfaction that the bruise on her back was mostly gone—Gaia looked around the hotel room.

Her clothes were strewn on the dark, worn-out carpeting where she'd dropped them. There was a water glass full of melted ice on the laminated side table next to her wristwatch, and the motel room key on its plastic paddle, and her Walther automatic.

Gaia stretched, yawning as she smoothed her hair back from her forehead. Through the white gauze curtain she could see the back of a parked white van, outlined sharply against the dazzling blue sky. A vacuum cleaner was running in a nearby room; its muffled drone resonated through the walls. That sound must have awakened her.

Straight ahead, Gaia could see her reflection in the dressing table mirror—disheveled, sleepy looking, with red marks on her face from the wrinkle of pillowcase that had pressed against her face, but basically healthy and rested. She *felt* rested—yesterday had been a long, long day, one of the longest she'd ever known.

Kicking back the covers, Gaia rose to her feet, picking up her watch and strapping it on. The watch read 11:06.

Gaia winced. She'd slept *way* later than she'd intended.

On the dressing table her laptop computer was still open and plugged in. Gaia remembered sitting right there, in the lamplit darkness, nearly twelve hours before, staring at the bright rectangle of the screen as she engaged in her text conversation with Will Taylor. And it had felt so *good* to be talking to him—as she leaned forward on that uncomfortable motel chair, peering at the screen, the miles between them seemed to vanish and she was back in Quantico, seeing his maddening, smirking pretty face—the face she legitimately wanted to punch so often and, so many other times, wanted to tenderly stroke with her fingertips as he dozed off with his head resting next to hers.

After showering, Gaia pulled on clean pants and a hastily folded shirt, sitting on the creaky bed to tie her shoes. She strapped on her shoulder holster and slipped her newly charged cell phone into her pocket.

The laptop battery was fully charged, Gaia observed as she packed her duffel bag. After her typed conversation with Will, she hadn't been too groggy to remember to plug her machines' chargers into the wall sockets. Thank God for small favors. With no phone and no computer, she might as well just give up. Gaia left the computer hooked up while she zipped up her duffel bag, finally opening the motel room door and letting the bright, warm day into the room.

The sun was dazzlingly bright. The air was crisp and clean, and the chrome of the cars in the motel's parking lot sparkled in the sun. The green-and-white 7-Eleven sign glittered against the clear blue sky, looking completely different from the ghostly green glow that had haunted the windows late into the night. Gaia took a deep breath of Baltimore air, stepping out onto the cement landing, pulling her drying hair back from her face as she turned toward Marsh's door—

—and something's wrong.

Gaia felt it instantly. Later, trying to remember what had tipped her off, she honestly couldn't decide what the telltale detail was. She stood just outside her room, beneath the Clavarak Motel sign, squinting in the bright sunshine and looking down the row of identical brown doors that lined the cement walkway.

Marsh's door was wide open.

Gaia squinted critically. *So what? He's left his door open—enjoying the morning air.*

But somehow that didn't seem right. The man who was nervous in a public park because he'd seen a man looking at them from fifty yards away—Gaia had trouble picturing him relaxing in his room with the door wide open.

That sound, Gaia thought. *The vacuum cleaner—*

Gaia stepped over to the wall and began edging slowly toward Marsh's door. With her right hand she unsnapped the strap on her shoulder holster. No question about it—the closer she got, the more certain she was that the vacuuming sound was coming from inside Marsh's room.

Big deal, Gaia thought. *He's getting breakfast, and the maid service is cleaning the room.*

But they cleaned your room when you checked *out*, didn't they? Not during the day. Somehow Gaia couldn't picture an establishment like the Clavarak Motel providing such a service unless they absolutely had to.

Moving closer to the door, sidling along the whitewashed brick motel wall, Gaia suddenly noticed the white van again. It was parked nose out in front of her own motel room; she had seen it through the window when she'd first awakened.

Now, as she moved along the wall, she could see the driver's side door mirror. As she watched, there was a flicker of movement from the driver's seat. She caught a glimpse of a man's chin and lips and a white shirt collar.

Someone's in the van. In the driver's seat, waiting.

Why?

Moving as quietly as she could, Gaia edged along the wall another few feet until she was just at the edge of Marsh's room's window. Leaning carefully over, hunching down, she peered through the corner of the glass.

She tensed, ready to pull back as fast as was necessary. She had to cup her hand around her eye to see. The curtains were drawn, but there was a small opening she could see through if she got her face at just the right angle. And she was in full view of the van's rearview mirror if the driver happened to look back here.

The room was cleaned out. The bed was stripped down to its bare mattress.

A woman in a blue-green uniform was pushing a vacuum cleaner back and forth on the same spot without looking.

A man in a black suit was standing next to the cleaning woman, talking to her. He wore mirrored sunglasses and was tall enough that he had to look almost straight down at the frightened-looking woman, who was listening as the man spoke to her at length. She kept vacuuming absently while listening to him. Gaia could see that her eyes were wide with fear.

As Gaia watched, the cleaning woman suddenly flicked her eyes toward the window.

Damn! Did she see me?

As fast as she could, Gaia whipped backward away from the window, flattening herself against the wall. *Lucky for that vacuum,* she thought. *It probably meant they couldn't hear me—*

Gaia backpedaled along the wall, her shoes squeaking on the cement as she got herself out of sight of the van's rearview mirrors. Then she stopped and allowed herself sixty seconds to think.

Men in black—FBI—were asking questions.

And Marsh was gone.

He's been taken out, Gaia realized slowly. *This is a gray op.*

And Gaia knew what that meant.

Next on the list: Gaia Moore.

Fifteen seconds later Gaia was back inside her own motel room, reaching to slap the laptop closed with one hand while she grabbed her shoulder bag with the other.

In twenty seconds that woman's going to tell them about the blond girl in the next room—and then the game's over.

Gaia figured she had maybe a minute and a half to get away.

Immediately she pulled the laptop's plug from the wall socket, banging her head on the desk edge because she was moving so fast, and took a final look around the room.

The box of cartridges—Marsh's parting gift—was on the bedside table. She didn't dare risk the time it would take to cross the room and get them.

The bathroom door was open; its light was still on. Gaia could see that the mirror was still fogged with steam from her shower. Her toothbrush, comb, and other toiletries were laid out along the edge of the sink, ready to be packed.

Too bad. Kiss them goodbye—stop thinking and move now.

As fast as she could do it without making any noise, Gaia ducked back outside into the bright sun. If anyone were to look this way—if the driver of the van leaned to the left and glanced in his mirror or if the tall man with the sunglasses chose that moment to stride out of Marsh's room—it was all over. She was standing in direct sunlight in front of a white wall. They couldn't possibly miss her.

The Altima was parked at the far end of the Clavarak Motel's small asphalt lot, in the other direction from Marsh's room. It was fifteen paces to the driver's door.

She got moving. Halfway across the lot Gaia fished out the car keys—and dropped them. They clattered to the hot asphalt, loudly rolling forward and nearly tumbling under the car. When she bent to retrieve them, the laptop nearly slipped from beneath her arm and smashed on the ground. Gaia barely caught it, pulling a muscle in her shoulder, and then grabbed the keys, ramming them into the Altima's front door.

The sun was hot. Climbing into the car, Gaia had already started to perspire. She threw her shoulder bag and the laptop onto the passenger seat, pulling the door closed gently, so it wouldn't slam.

Now what?

Gaia glanced backward. From here, she could see the van's occupant perfectly—he was a sharp silhouette in sunglasses, leaning his wrists casually on the steering wheel, just thirty feet away. If he turned his head, he would see her.

I can't start the engine, she thought helplessly. *He'll hear it and he'll look over at me.*

Just then Gaia heard a door slamming. The other agent had come out of Marsh's room—Gaia could see his feet moving beneath the van. The walking agent shouted something.

The agent in the van heard him—he twisted to his left, leaning out the window to better hear what his partner was saying.

Now or never, she thought furiously. *Hit it.*

Gaia turned the ignition, making sure not to flood the engine as the car started, bonging gently while the dashboard indicators flashed on. The wheels squeaked on the pavement as Gaia lurched the car forward toward the apron that led to the road. Behind her the van's driver was climbing down from the side door while his partner advanced on the room Gaia had just vacated.

Lucky, Gaia told herself tersely as she pulled forward toward the intersection and watched the hanging traffic light bob in place against the brilliant blue sky and turn a beautiful shade of emerald green. *Lucky, lucky, lucky . . .* As she hit the gas, gathering speed, she just barely caught a glimpse in the rearview mirror of the tall agent drawing his gun and entering Gaia's hotel room.

Lucky I woke up when I did, Gaia realized. *Lucky the light changed.*

That was a whole day's worth of luck—and her morning was only beginning.

permanent disappearance

A FAKE SMILE

At noon Gaia pulled the windshield's shades down, squinting in the blinding glare from the interstate highway. Squinting was her only option: her sunglasses were in her toiletries bag, back at the Clavarak Motel, fifty miles behind her.

Or they're in an evidence bag, she reminded herself, looking for a faster-moving lane. *You know exactly what they're doing to that room.*

Gaia did indeed. That white van was probably full of equipment. They could be using a spectroscope to examine the bed linens, looking for hidden strands of hair or cotton thread, turning the room upside down to learn every conceivable scrap of information about its inhabitant. They probably had contacted the phone company and the power utility (for the voltage readings on the room's electrical outlets) and had figured out that she'd used a computer to go online. Now the FBI could be converging on her communication with Will from two directions and were twice as likely to figure out the clever use they'd made of a singles chat room.

The countryside around the highway was wide and flat, with industrial parks and farmland and strings of exits for various towns passing by as she drove. Gaia was moving fast, pacing the light traffic, but she wasn't really sure where she was *going*—her only objective had been to get as far away from the Clavarak Motel as she could.

But now, staring at the converging lines of the highway and the flawless blue dome of sky above, Gaia began to seriously wonder what her next move was. The vast American landscape around her only emphasized the truth: when you were looking for one single person, it was an awfully big world.

Gaia glanced downward at the laptop resting on the passenger seat.

Will. I need to get back in contact with Will as soon as I can.

Gaia started scanning the roadside turnoffs. If she could find a place to connect to the Internet—anyplace at all—then maybe she could contact him again. She could leave a message for him in "Hacker City" and hope he picked it up fast.

Because we're expendable, she thought grimly. She still could barely accept it. *We've been in contact with Catherine, who's in contact with Socorro—so we're both gray ops waiting to happen.*

Now that she was paying attention to the road signs, Gaia realized she was headed north on Interstate 95. She had left Baltimore far behind—she was headed parallel to Chesapeake Bay, approaching the Mason-Dixon line. Soon, if she kept going, she would reach the Susquehanna River as it ran inland toward Harrisburg, far beyond. The land was less flat now as she moved inland; there were rolling hills and protruding rock faces in the countryside she passed.

REST STOP AHEAD 1 MI, a reflectorized blue road sign announced—FOOD FUEL. There were signs for the different businesses available there: Mobil Gas and Hardee's and Superwhiz, whatever that was, and below that Starbucks.

Aha.

Gaia had spent more time in Starbucks than she wanted to think about. In particular, her precollege memories of the Astor Place Starbucks would probably stay with her the rest of her life—the green decor, the rich smell of grinding espresso beans, the hiss of the steamer, and the constant babble of the FOHs from the Village School. Not to mention all the other New Yorkers, young and old, alone or in groups, with newspapers and iPods and knitting needles and paperbacks, part of the tapestry of New York life. Just the green logo gave Gaia a pang of New York homesickness. Who would have ever thought she'd be yearning for those times again? Even running from her demented uncle was less twisted and confusing than running from the FBI.

In less than a minute Gaia was in the exit off-ramp, behind a station wagon whose backseat was filled with four young kids, all grinning and waving at her. For some reason, she felt strongly compelled to force a fake smile for these children she didn't even know—as if her true feelings were some kind of contagious disease they might catch. But she could only muster a stiff line of clenched teeth, which only seemed to scare them away. They stopped waving and turned quickly from her.

Now Gaia was driving onto a gigantic parking lot filled with parked cars. The brilliant afternoon sunlight was shining off dozens of chrome bumpers, rooftop luggage racks, and radio antennas. A wide green lawn behind the lot was dotted with picnic tables, where families were eating lunch, playing Frisbee, and walking their dogs while small groups of children ran aimlessly around. Even from here, on the approach lane, Gaia could hear their peals of laughter.

Ahead of her was the rest stop's main building—an enormous round concrete structure the size of a supermarket, with gigantic metal signs advertising the businesses inside. The revolving Mobil sign was turning gently in the sun atop a hundred-foot steel pillar in the distance, near the gas pumps—Gaia glanced quickly down at her fuel indicator and realized she was all right for a while longer.

She stopped her car for a moment, staring at the gas pumps, where a white van was getting refueled. *Is that—*

No. The printing on the van said something about Pinkett Plumbing.

So what? Gaia told herself. *The bureau loves to disguise their vehicles. You're never going to see them coming if you pay attention to labels.*

Gaia forced herself to stop thinking that way. If she didn't, she'd start seeing the FBI around every corner.

Paranoia is healthy, Gaia told herself. But this didn't feel like paranoia at all. She couldn't get the haunting question out of her mind: What had they done to Marsh? Could they really just erase him like that? Did he have some perfectly average suburban family out there somewhere who would have to live with his "permanent disappearance" for the rest of their lives? Just as Catherine's father was being forced to do right now? Just as Gaia had basically been forced to do with her own father for five years? She couldn't dwell on it. She knew if she allowed herself to dwell on those thoughts, she'd begin to slow down, and the last thing she could do right now was slow down. Not while Catherine was still out there somewhere—which Gaia once again convinced herself she was.

The main thing now was to find a parking spot close to the building, which, of course, every arriving car was trying to do. She was in luck—a young, happy-looking couple in sunglasses, holding matching ice cream cones, grinned as they got into a Nissan sports car right in front of the main revolving doors, and Gaia managed to zoom forward and pull into their oil-stained parking spot right ahead of a sour-looking man in a green Jetta, who honked angrily at her while shouting something that was inaudible through two sheets of safety glass. Gaia was tempted to flash her badge just to shut the man up, but she knew that really wasn't a good idea.

Let's not do anything to draw attention, she told herself, standing in the warm breeze beside her car, pulling on her jacket as quickly as she could to cover the gun. *Let's just get in and get out without anyone even noticing I was here.*

NO SUCH THING AS PRIVACY

The inside of the building was cold and loud—the tile floor seemed to echo every footstep and baby's scream. After the events of the past day it was strange to be in a *crowd,* surrounded by a hundred or so random people moving around with their food and maps and purses and sunglasses. Gaia had her laptop tucked under her arm, and her badge and gun were quickly accessible, but she knew they were invisible to the untrained eye. Her watch told her it was getting on one in the afternoon, which made her inadvertently quicken her pace, striding forward along the brown tile floor and craning her neck, looking for the Starbucks sign.

Starbucks. Wireless Internet. A quick anonymous chance to make contact with Will . . .

It had been almost thirty hours since James Rossiter's basement. In her mind, she could smell the Neutrogena conditioner again and see the indentation on the cot's white pillow. *The closest I've gotten to Catherine since this started—and it wasn't that close.*

At Starbucks she took one look at the crowd by the counter and turned away. Craning her neck, Gaia saw what she needed to see—the Wi-Fi emblem on the counter.

Thank God, she thought, making her way to a table near the windows. The air here wasn't just full of the familiar coffee smell—it was invisibly flooded with Web sites and e-mail, too. *Not the most secure way to communicate,* she thought, *but it works, and it's fast—hopefully I can get what I need and be on the road before anyone has a chance to see me here.*

She flipped her laptop open, anxiously checking to see if she could pick anything up. The computer's Wi-Fi indicator immediately gave her five bars—a perfect connection. She immediately typed PING 0411 and watched as most of the laptop screen went black. Just as had happened the night before, there was a brief wait while the "Hacker City" backdoor encryption system began working, logging her onto the underground network— Gaia tapped her fingers on the green plastic Starbucks table, trying to be patient.

Suddenly she looked up, staring out the window, where a black sedan was cruising slowly along the blacktop in front of the building. The sedan had tinted windows—it was impossible to see inside.

Agents?

How could she tell? It could be anyone—the important thing was to finish what she was doing and get moving. Looking down at the laptop, she suddenly noticed something down in the corner of the screen.

A flashing e-mail icon.

What the hell—?

Gaia hadn't been thinking about her regular FBI e-mail account at all. Using it was out of the question since the bureau routinely kept tabs on personnel's e-mail and phone communications. It was the open secret of the FBI: there was no such thing as privacy. Most of the time it didn't matter—you went about your business and didn't think about it. But that was obviously why Gaia had gone to such elaborate trouble to contact Will.

Now her laptop had just gone ahead and checked her e-mail—and there was one message. She opened it:

To: gmoore@fbiquantico.gov
From: admin@cmps.gov
Date: August 23, 2005, 11:55 EST
Subject: [no subject]
Dear Gaia, please come help me. The people I'm with are

Gaia stared at the screen. The surrounding sounds—the crying babies, the Muzak, the hundreds of loud footsteps on the half acre of tile around her, the hiss of the Starbucks milk steamer—all seemed to fade away. Gaia was alone in the world with the message, this eleven-word e-mail that was sent less than two hours ago.

Catherine.

It was her. There was absolutely no question about it.

Catherine had found a way to try and contact her friend—and then suddenly had been interrupted.

She thought she could get away with it, Gaia realized. *She had a moment when they weren't watching her, and she did this.*

Gaia could picture Catherine imprisoned in another dank basement, a gun to her head, being forced to do . . . something . . . on a computer. And then, when nobody was looking, frantically beginning an e-mail to Gaia.

But they caught her.

Or did they? The e-mail had been sent, after all. Nobody had *stopped* her. What was more likely was that Catherine realized she was being watched again and had quickly hit the send button without even getting a chance to finish her sentence.

Which means, Gaia realized, *she thought she'd communicated something I could understand.*

The e-mail had another message—one she'd missed.

Outside the building Gaia saw that the black sedan had pulled up in front of the revolving doors. As she watched, two men in black suits and sunglasses got out, adjusting their jackets and slamming the car doors. They didn't seem to be in any hurry—they stood there in the sun, with the wind ruffling their close-cropped hair, gazing around impassively.

Uh-oh.

Looking back at the laptop screen, Gaia stared furiously at the message. She couldn't get anything from it. *Dear Gaia, please come help me. The people I'm with are—*Well, are *what?* There was nothing meaningful, nothing helpful—but Catherine had sent it. How could Gaia possibly figure out where she—

Oh.

The e-mail address.

Wherever Catherine was sending from, she knew the e-mail address would give it away. Gaia took another look: admin@cmps.gov.

So what am I supposed to get from that?

The two men in suits had entered the rest stop building. They weren't the same men Gaia had seen in the motel. They stood on the tiles just inside the door, side by side, scanning their eyes back and forth, taking their time.

Time to go, Gaia thought. But she had to figure out where Catherine was.

Maybe there's a Web site, she realized. *Maybe that's Catherine's point.*

There was a potted fern between Gaia and the door, and she hunched down in her chair, returning her attention to the laptop. Going to a Web browser, she typed in the address from the e-mail—http://www.cmps.gov—and hit return.

Come on, come on, Gaia thought frantically, watching the Web browser. Nothing was happening—the computer's little hourglass pointer was turning over and over, waiting for data.

Glancing over, she saw that the two men were leaning to confer with each other, and as she watched, one of them suddenly pointed toward the Starbucks. They started walking toward the coffee bar.

Finally on the screen a Web site started to come in. It had to be the world's slowest-loading site. The page turned an ugly shade of green, and then a murky image started to appear, showing an enormous, low-slung, hulking building, huge against a dark, cloudy sky. She couldn't see any detail. Text flooded onto the page, including a large, bold headline:

Welcome to the Home Page of the

COLLINGSWOOD MUNICIPAL PUMPING STATION

This meant nothing whatsoever to Gaia—but she had the page, and that was enough. Slapping the laptop closed, she immediately ducked near to the ground and began backing away from the revolving doors toward the back of Starbucks.

Gaia slid between two more potted ferns—ignoring the puzzled glances of a group of college students drinking Frappuccinos—and once she was out of the Starbucks area she began sprinting toward the glass double doors at the far end of the rest area building.

There was a big crowd of motorists in the way. Gaia's shoes squeaked on the tiles as she jumped and weaved, darting around people as she propelled herself toward the doors that led outside. Her laptop computer was clutched in a death grip in her left hand—its metal surface was hot from all the activity the computer had been doing. She couldn't look back—not while running—so she had no idea if the men in the suits had seen her.

Gaia actually thought she was going to make it all the way outside. She had bumped into at least four people and had knocked one man flat on his stomach—there was no way to avoid it—but so far nobody had shouted or tried to stop her. When she was ten feet from the glass doors, the shouting began.

"Stop!" a deep male voice yelled out from behind her. "FBI! Stop that woman!"

"Stop, ma'am! Federal agents!"

A woman screamed. Gaia could hear a collective gasp from the crowd as rather than stopping her, the people in her path seemed to pull back.

Skidding to a stop at the door, Gaia frantically pulled it open, diving through and out into the hot Maryland sun.

Will they shoot? Gaia wondered. She pushed between a middle-aged married couple in sunglasses, knocking a big road atlas out of the husband's hands as she passed. *They're not going to shoot me, are they?*

Gaia was sprinting across the blacktop toward the Altima, trying to fish the car keys out of her jeans pocket as she ran. Behind her she could hear the glass doors being slammed open again.

"Stop, Ms. Moore!" the deeper male voice cried out. "Don't get yourself in any more trouble!"

Word will come down from Washington, Marsh had told her the night before, *but officially nobody will hear a thing. And then one day you'll be dead, Sanders will be dead, and to keep things nice and clean, I'll be dead, too. With the three of us removed from the game board, the bureau's precious tactical secrets are safe from Socorro and all the rest, and their war on terror can go on.*

Gaia was twenty feet from her car. She had the keys out. Another woman screamed off to one side.

"Don't run away, Gaia!" the other voice pleaded. Echoes bounced through the parking lot. "You've still got a chance to give yourself up!"

They won't just open fire, Gaia thought. *Not with all these people around. They have to warn me first.*

Gaia had made it to the car—she was pulling the driver's door open as she finally risked a look behind her. The two agents were running toward her at top speed, their guns drawn. A crowd of motorists, frozen with fear, stood on the sidewalk in front of the building, staring wide-eyed. Another woman screamed. Gaia tossed her laptop into the car and heard it thump onto the passenger seat.

The first agent got there, dropping to a shooter's crouch and pointing the gun at her. He was so close that Gaia could see herself completely reflected in his Ray-Bans. With her left hand on the roof of the Altima and her right hand on the open door, she swung a two-legged double scissor kick that knocked the gun out of his hand and bashed her other foot against the man's jaw while the gun was still sailing through the air. The agent jerked backward, his back arching, blood spraying from his mouth. Gaia landed on both feet and drove her right arm against his neck. The agent toppled backward to the ground, unconscious.

"Stop right there!" the second agent yelled, pointing his own gun two-handed at her face. More people were yelling, ducking, screaming back at the building. *"Stop or I'll shoot!"*

There was really no choice but a straight standing attack—she had to charge the gun. Some part of her mind knew that even a federal agent given direct orders to kill her wouldn't shoot her in the face as she attacked—his training would make him hesitate for a split second—but it wasn't a conscious choice. Gaia launched herself into the air and dove directly onto the agent, knocking the gun down and pushing him backward onto the hot asphalt of the parking lot, landing on top of him. Getting her wind back while the agent tried to stand up, Gaia drove her interlocked fists into his head, once and then again until he was unconscious.

Stumbling backward, she rose shakily to her feet, looking around. The crowd stared back at her, not moving or speaking.

Don't pass out, Gaia told herself. *Come on—don't pass out.*

The sky was a vast blue dome overhead, and the sunlight dazzled her. Panting, Gaia leaned back on the door of the Altima, edging around the other agent, who appeared to be waking up. His gun was on the ground twenty feet away; Gaia wondered if she should do something about that and realized she didn't have time—she could already hear sirens approaching.

She dropped into the driver's seat, checking that her laptop—with the precious Web page that revealed Catherine's location—was safe. Reaching to pull the door closed, Gaia furiously willed herself not to faint as she started the engine. She had to back out carefully, avoiding the two agents in black suits lying on the ground. Once she was safely past them, she sped up the exit lane, merging back into the interstate traffic and quickly accelerating as the rest stop disappeared behind her.

I'm coming, Catherine, Gaia thought. *I'm on my way.*

second chance

SUDDENLY ALTERED BEHAVIOR

Watching the Quantico streets go by, Kim wondered if he was handling this new "partnership" correctly. Next to him in the driver's seat Will was also gazing out at the town, following the directions they had been given by phone. It was four-thirty in the afternoon, and the two of them had spent the whole day together on the lollipop case.

Kim wasn't sure if he should take this opportunity to have another conversation with Will. He knew what he would say: he wanted to apologize for being so aggressive the night before. *It was my first day as a "real" agent,* he would tell Will. *I'm sorry I got in your face. It's easy to criticize what someone else is doing—especially if you've never done it yourself.*

But Kim hadn't said a word.

There was a specific reason for this. From the moment he and Will had met up at the Quantico courthouse that morning, Kim instantly knew that something had happened. Will had *changed.* To Kim, the difference between Will's behavior the night before in the dorms and today as they busied themselves with the case was as vivid as black and white. Will was in a completely different mood.

He was whistling to himself at breakfast in the cafeteria. He laughed too much at some of the trainees' jokes at the table, but then at other times he seemed to be off in some kind of private reverie, not listening to the people around him at all. Kim caught him smiling for no reason at least once.

And—the most peculiar thing—each time the two of them got anywhere near a computer connected to the Internet, Will seemed to *linger*. It was so subtle that Kim barely noticed it, but three times Will had craned his neck, slowing down and dragging his feet when he saw someone using a Web browser. Kim almost expected him to say, *Hang on one second, Kim—I know we're investigating a serial killer, but I have this sudden urge to go shop for books on Amazon.*

Strange.

The funny thing was that Will's suddenly altered behavior was *recognizable*. It reminded him of the way that Will used to get around Gaia Moore. Kim once told Catherine Sanders that he knew Gaia and Will liked each other before either of them knew it—the spark that had passed between them was so blindingly obvious to Kim on those first few days as trainees that he found it endlessly amusing to watch them earnestly pretend they didn't like each other.

And now Will was back in that same state of mind. If Kim didn't know better, he would have guessed that Will and Gaia were in contact with each other—that they had talked on the phone or had some kind of conversation.

And of course, that was impossible. It was obvious that Will's phone, mail (both paper and electronic), and all other communication were being monitored. Kim assumed that his was, too. And they both had firm standing orders from Special Agent Malloy to report any attempts by Gaia to contact either of them.

So there was no way Will and Gaia were talking.

Yet Kim felt sure he was missing something. Will was working very, very hard all day on the case. It was almost like he wanted to get it all done early so that he could go do something else. It reminded him of a kid hurrying home after school to catch a favorite TV program.

But he couldn't imagine what else Will needed to do besides catch the lollipop killer. And he wasn't about to ask. But Kim had decided to keep his eyes open when around Will and see what he could figure out on his own.

"Here it is," Will said, pointing out the windshield at a drab, two-story office building. "Ready, partner?"

"Sure," Kim said, adjusting his badge and gun yet again. It was going to take him a while to get used to walking around among actual citizens while wearing a firearm. Will seemed to have taken to it like a natural, but for Kim it still felt a little bit like playing cowboys and Indians. He got his notebook and pen together as Will eased into a parking spot in front of their destination. "You go first—I'll follow."

"No, not today," Will said, looking over. "Listen, I'm sorry again about what happened yesterday. Why don't *you* be primary today? I'll follow your lead. Let's see how that goes."

Kim looked back at Will. He couldn't read his face at all. *But something's up,* he thought again. *He's not even thinking about me right now. His mind's a million miles away somewhere.*

As they slammed the car doors and dashed up the steps and into the building, various Quantico passersby looked at them curiously. Kim kept a blank facial expression, trying to look casual as Will checked the building's directory.

"Here it is," Will said, pointing. "SecondChanceVA.com—on the second floor."

Vaulting up the stairs, Will made an exaggerated show of holding the doors for Kim when they passed the pebbled-glass sign that read SECOND CHANCE and, below that, Virginia's Best Online Singles Service.

NOTHING TO HIDE

They entered the office. It was a small, carpeted waiting room with a few upholstered chairs and couches where five or ten young men and women sat reading magazines or filling out forms on clipboards and generally pretending that they didn't see one another. There was a window with a counter behind it, like in a drugstore, where two or three staff people stood around, dealing with paperwork.

These are the "singles," Will realized, looking at the chairs' occupants. He didn't know how much of SecondChance's business came from the Web site and how much from people walking in; it was one of the things that they needed to find out.

The singles in the room were mostly divorcees, Kim figured, based on the Web site's statistical projections. As Will and Kim came through the room in their suits and ties, the singles glanced up at them and quickly away. *Lonely people,* Kim thought. It was very obvious. He could tell from the naked openness of their faces, from the neediness in their eyes that they revealed and then immediately hid from view.

Will was leaning on the counter, smiling back at Kim as he

waited for him to catch up. *He's being a model of courtesy,* Kim realized—*he wants to make up for yesterday.*

"Excuse me," Kim said to the man behind the counter. He looked about forty and had neatly combed hair and a small mustache. He wore a sweater-vest and a wool tie. "My name's Kim Lau and this is Will Taylor—we're federal investigators." Kim showed his badge, smiling gently at the man. "Have you got a moment?"

"Yes, Mr. Lau. What can I do for you?" The man smiled back, clasping his hands behind him.

Nothing to hide, Kim noted.

"We're here to take a look at your records, if it's not too much trouble," Kim went on. "In particular"—he lowered his voice, looking behind himself before continuing—"the information that your customers provide when they sign up for your service. I understand that you collect data from your customers whether they show up in person or fill out the form on your Web site."

"Yes," the man said agreeably. "Yes, that's quite true, Mr. Kim. But unfortunately all of that information is private. You must understand that we keep our clients' personal details in the strictest confidence. A business like this can't survive if it can't make secrecy an absolute guarantee."

Will stepped forward, holding up a sheaf of papers. "Sir, this is a subpoena issued in superior court," he said, smiling pleasantly. "Please feel free to read it at your leisure, but I can spare you the trouble. It says that you're required by state law to hand over any and all records that we ask for concerning your clients."

"But I don't understand," the man said, alarmed. "Why? What's the reason for—"

"This is a homicide investigation, I'm afraid, sir," Kim told him. He had lowered his voice even more, but unfortunately it made no difference. Everyone in the room was pretending to do something else but clearly straining to hear what they were talking about.

This is going to be all over town, Kim thought dismally. *We should have interviewed him in private. Too late—my fault.*

"All right." The man sighed, looking dismally at the court order. "What do you need to see?"

"Have you got a list of your current customers?" Will asked. "Let's start there."

"I *know* you!" said a female voice.

Kim was surprised. He looked over and saw a young woman farther back behind the counter, standing with a stack of file folders. She was looking right at Will.

"I'm afraid not, ma'am," Will said, smiling brightly. "Can't say I've had the pleasure."

"Oh—I'm sorry," the woman said, flushing as she turned awkwardly away. "I guess not. You just looked so familiar."

She's flirting, Kim thought distractedly. *I guess if you don't know how to do it any better than that, you end up working in a place like this.*

"Here you go," the man with the mustache announced, hefting a large loose-leaf volume onto the counter. It was the size of a telephone book. "These are the female clients—we keep them as two separate lists."

Will opened the book and started flipping through it. Leaning over his shoulder, Kim could see printed-out lists of names, dozens and dozens of them, each with an identifying computer code. The list was alphabetical, so Will could quickly narrow his search, flipping pages looking for Terri Barker.

Once we get her ID number, Kim realized, *we can find out what other dates she went on. And maybe one of them is the killer.*

Now that they were actually investigating it, Kim suddenly felt like this was a very slim lead. But it was the only thing either of them had been able to think of.

"Here we go," Will said, stabbing at a name with his forefinger. Kim looked:

BARKER TERRI   F-48673869284

"Let's make a note of that number," Will said, clicking his pen and writing it down. The man with the mustache stood waiting, still looking uncomfortable.

Look at all these people, Kim thought, grabbing the bound volume before it slipped shut. He could see hundreds—maybe thousands—of single women, all somewhere in the state of Virginia and all dealing with this one office, trying to find true love. It was sad and hopeful at the same time, Kim thought, thumbing the book. People seemed willing to go through all kinds of—

Suddenly Kim dropped the thought completely. He flipped the book back a few pages, wondering if he'd actually seen what he thought he'd seen. And he was right. There it was:

HALLIDAY LAUREL   F-4550112343454

"Holy—" Kim grabbed Will's shoulder, shaking it, and pointed down at the book. "Will, look at this," he said breathlessly.

"Well, if that don't beat all—" Will took the book, flipping back toward the beginning. "Let's see if another one's here."

"K," Kim said. He realized he wasn't breathing, and he forced himself to take a deep gulp of air. "Look in the *K*'s . . ."

Will was nodding. He flipped the book forward, scanning the names, until he found what they were looking for:

KNIGHT ANN   F 1121308855999

Kim and Will looked at each other. Kim could see the surprise in Will's eyes.

They all *came here,* Kim thought dazedly. *All three of the victims.* The realization bowled him over. He was amazed at the sensation of having discovered a clue—a real clue—and having it pay off. In that instant he almost felt like he was drunk, but at the same time he felt absolutely alert and wide awake.

"Sir," Kim said, trying to keep his voice level as he turned back to the man with the mustache and the sweater vest, "we're going to have to ask you for your complete client database."

"If you can give it to us on a computer disk," Will added politely, "we'd sure appreciate it."

The man nodded gravely. "I suppose I can do that," he allowed, nodding at them and moving off toward the SecondChance.com back office.

"You haven't cracked it yet, son," Will told Kim, with that same twinkle in his eye, that misplaced euphoria, that Kim had been noticing all day. "Don't get a swelled head or anything."

"No," Kim agreed. "I haven't cracked it. But suddenly it looks crackable, doesn't it?"

"We'll see," Will said, watching as the man headed back toward them, holding out a computer disk. "We'll see."

Too slow, Gaia reprimanded herself as she drove. *Taking too long.*

It was one-thirty in the afternoon, and any hope of getting to Collingswood before two was fading from her mind. The problem was that she couldn't risk getting pulled over for speeding. She could flash a badge, sure—but after the events at the motel and the roadside rest area, she had no assurance that it would work. She'd avoided getting apprehended—just barely managed to avoid it—twice today. Gaia didn't have much faith in what might happen a third time.

Even crossing the state line into Pennsylvania, Gaia had been concerned. It was entirely possible that a priority all-points bulletin was out on her. As she drove through the toll booth, smiling at the man who took her ticket, Gaia was half expecting the man to slap an alarm button and for cop cars to converge on her, sirens blaring.

And if that happens, she had thought behind her smile, *then I'll have to ram the barrier and outflank them—and if it means a high-speed chase, then it means a high-speed chase.*

But Gaia had been tremendously relieved when the tollbooth operator had smiled back and waved her through. It was amazing that the FBI hadn't mobilized to keep her from leaving Maryland, but she wasn't about to look a gift horse in the mouth. And now, driving northeast as the afternoon sky deepened into a rich, cloudless blue, she was forcing herself to stay within the speed limit. Because she really didn't want this trip to end in a local jail cell. That wasn't part of her plan at all.

The land was changing again as Gaia followed the Delaware River, which was just a mile or so out of view behind the rolling hills that she could see out the Altima's passenger window. She had stopped just once, quickly, to fill the gas tank and to finally pry open the laptop and take a good look at the Web site that Catherine's email had pointed to:

Welcome to the Home Page of the
COLLINGSWOOD MUNICIPAL PUMPING STATION
Built in 1921, the Collingswood, PA, Municipal Pumping Station is a landmark example in the history of American hydroelectric power generation. This beautiful monument is one of the five oldest pumping stations in continuous operation in the continental United States. <u>Click here</u> for a full history of this American institution.

There was more. Gaia had taken a moment glancing over the rest of the Web page's text and the big, murky photograph that showed the building's low, impressive silhouette. But really the only part she cared about was the directions of how to get there. She had no idea what Catherine was doing in such a place or what it meant, but Gaia figured that the best way to find out was to just *go* there as fast as she could.

Because that's what Catherine wanted me to do, Gaia told herself firmly. *That's why she sent the unfinished e-mail—because she knew I'd figure that out.*

And Gaia wasn't about to let Catherine down.

Finally, at two-ten in the afternoon, as the sun was just beginning to move toward the western horizon, Gaia began seeing signs for Collingswood. She had copied the Web page's driving directions onto a sheet of paper, but it turned out not to be necessary: the pumping station was visible almost immediately, a silhouette against the hills, looming impressively over the town like a castle or a cathedral. The Web site wasn't exaggerating: the building was very impressive.

Leaving the interstate, Gaia drove through Collingswood's narrow, shaded streets, finding her way by sight—the pumping station was visible through most of the town. As she got closer, Gaia realized the building was much larger than it looked from a distance or from the picture on the Web site. It was a mammoth granite-and-concrete structure, low and wide, with enormous, old-fashioned curved windows cut deep into its front surface, almost like eyes in a face. As Gaia got nearer, she could hear the roar of the river getting louder and louder. She drove uphill, rising higher and higher over the town, seeing how the Delaware River's tributaries flowed through the town and over the dams and conduits that ran beneath the pumping station. Even from this distance Gaia could hear the throbbing and humming of the pumping station's machinery.

But why bring Catherine here? Gaia thought as she drove the Altima along the chain-link fence that flanked the pumping station's empty parking lot. *What possible reason could Socorro or anyone else—political activists or terrorists, whatever they are—have be in a place like this?*

Gaia slowed the car down as she approached the gate in the middle of the fence. There was a small stone guardhouse that looked like it was as old and well built as the pumping station itself. An elderly guard in a drab uniform sat inside beneath a yellow lightbulb, reading a newspaper.

Not particularly high security, Gaia thought, stopping the car just out of view and getting out. The air had grown cooler as she'd moved northeast, coming closer to the river. She got out her jacket and pulled it on, once again covering the shoulder holster. Locking the car, Gaia moved down into the shrubbery at the edge of the road, approaching the gate.

Crouching down and moving quietly, she sneaked past the guardhouse, glancing up at the white-haired guard as she passed. So far as Gaia could tell, he didn't have the slightest idea that someone had gotten right past him. He lazily turned a page in his newspaper, totally unconcerned.

Once past the guardhouse, Gaia picked up her pace, moving across the nearly empty parking lot toward the enormous, looming face of the pumping station. She could feel the vibration through her shoes as she walked, and the closer she got, the louder the rhythmic throbbing and pumping noises got. The station, with its huge, steel-framed half-circle windows, *did* look like a face, an angry face staring down at her as she approached.

The building had a set of ornate, carved double doors. There was nobody around, and the doors were padlocked shut. The words Collingswood Municipal Pumping Station were spelled in carved letters over the door. Below that, another carving was inscribed 1921. A brass plaque bolted to the wall read Official Registry of the American Landmark Commission, 1952.

Great—but how do I get in?

She was standing there, confused, for about a minute before she saw a small utility entrance to one side. It was so small and plain that she nearly missed it. Walking over, Gaia saw there was a small window set into the door. The window had been smashed, creating an opening large enough for someone to get their arm through.

There was broken glass on the ground near the door.

This is recent, Gaia realized. *Somebody broke in here not too long ago.*

Are they still here?

Reaching through the broken window frame, Gaia found the metal lever that opened the door. Swinging it open, she entered the Collingswood Pumping Station.

Inside, it was nearly pitch black—and the rhythmic pumping and throbbing noise was much louder and deeper, vibrating from her shoes through her entire body, so that she could feel it in her teeth. Gaia waited a moment to get used to the darkness, but she couldn't really. It was like walking into an ancient tomb—there was just a pale glow somewhere straight ahead, reflected from a distant window. The cool, dark air washed gently over her, carrying a faint smell of water and electricity.

A flashlight, Gaia told herself helplessly. *Next time bring a flashlight. Can't you get anything right?*

And something else was on her mind, from when she first saw the smashed glass on the ground: *Is someone else here?*

There was no way to tell. Holding her hands out in front of her, Gaia moved forward into the darkness.

ONE TINY STEP BEHIND HER FRIEND

Walking forward a few paces, Gaia realized it wasn't so bad. In front of her was a cool, damp stone wall and, feeling its edge as she turned around a corner, suddenly she came into an area that was bright enough for her to see. Gaia looked around, amazed.

The turbines were enormous steel cylinders the size of Greyhound buses, half buried in the vast stone floor upon which she was standing on the edge. The ceiling was far out of view overhead—the only light was weak daylight from the big windows on the building's front. She could hear the splashing of the river's water far in the distance as the teeth-vibrating hum of the turbines continued.

Her eyes adjusted a bit more as she saw a row of normal-size doors off to one side. Heading over there, Gaia realized that there were administrative offices behind the doors.

And then she saw something so surprising, so utterly unexpected that she had to blink to make sure she hadn't imagined it.

Hanging on the doorknob of the leftmost door was a bracelet. She could see it clearly from this far away even in the dim light: a silver band with a turquoise inlay.

Catherine's bracelet, Gaia realized, amazed again at her friend's ingenuity. She recognized it immediately; Gaia remembered that it had belonged to Catherine's mother and that Catherine wore it all the time. She remembered one or two times when Catherine had practically turned their dorm room upside down looking for it.

And here it was, hanging from a doorknob.

It's a signal to me, Gaia realized. Suddenly she felt choked up again. Catherine was trying to communicate with Gaia.

Gaia, please come help, she remembered.

I won't let you down, Cathy, Gaia thought, clearing her throat and blinking away the hotness that was gathering in her eyes. *I promise.*

Lettering on the door Catherine had marked read Municipal Works Technical Records Department. Gaia pocketed Catherine's bracelet and opened the door.

Behind it was a small room with one other door at the back. There was a low ceiling and no windows. Closing the door she'd come through, Gaia flicked on the overhead lights, looking around. The room was empty except for a large oak worktable, a water cooler, and a desk with an older-looking computer workstation and a large freestanding machine that Gaia didn't recognize. The computer had been left on, and, Gaia realized, the big machine was on, too—a yellow light on its face was glowing.

Catherine was here, Gaia realized. The humming and throbbing of the pumping station's machinery was still making Gaia's body vibrate as she went over and awakened the computer.

After a few baffled moments examining the machine's unfamiliar desktop, Gaia realized that this computer's main purpose was as a filing system. Clicking the mouse on various folders, she saw the categories for a tremendously detailed database network—hundreds and hundreds of technical documents, including building blueprints, sewer maps, subway station plans, streetlight power diagrams, water pipeline schematics.

So what do I do now? Gaia's heart was sinking as she looked through the folders. It was all very technical, and she had no idea where to start looking or even what she was looking for.

Finally, when she was about to give up on the computer in desperation and begin searching the rest of the room, Gaia saw something she hadn't noticed before—a small icon that was blinking in a corner of the computer's screen.

Clicking on the icon, Gaia saw a small window open on the screen, with a label that read PRINT QUEUE.

Below that, the window had a list of technical documents, with dates and times next to them. And, Gaia realized excitedly, the most recent document was printed that morning, at eleven fifty-five.

When Catherine sent the e-mail, Gaia remembered. She had gotten it at the Starbucks at one in the afternoon—but the date attached to the e-mail showed that it had been *sent* at eleven fifty-five. Right when that document were printing.

Exploring the computer's desktop some more, Gaia realized that the machine's e-mail program was running; its window had just been minimized down to the bottom of the screen. Looking at the list of sent mail, Gaia fixed her eye on the most recent item:

To: gmoore@fbi_quantico.gov
From: admin@cmps.gov
Date: August 23, 2005, 11:55 EST
Subject: [no subject]

Gaia rubbed her eyes, sighing with released tension. She'd found it: Catherine's e-mail had been sent right from here—from this exact computer. Once again Gaia was just one tiny step behind her friend. Catherine had sat right here, in this chair, at eleven fifty-five and sent that e-mail.

Leaning back in her chair, gazing around the room, Gaia attempted to visualize the scene. *Don't be afraid to use your imagination,* Agent Crane had lectured them all back at Quantico. *Sometimes it's the most powerful weapon you've got. If you can visualize events you never saw, then you can find details in them you'd never catch any other way.*

So what happened here?

Gaia looked over at the door—the one she'd come in through.

Catherine's captors had been over there, Gaia imagined. *Watching the door. They weren't pumping station employees—they broke in, too.*

The smashed window, Gaia remembered.

So they stood there while Catherine sat here, at eleven fifty-five, and she realized they weren't watching her, so she decided to send me an e-mail—

While she printed that document, she realized, nearly clapping with triumph as she figured it out. *That's why they brought her here—to steal that document.*

Clicking the mouse on the document's icon, Gaia selected the repeat print command.

There was a pause and then a click and a hum as the machine she hadn't recognized—the one with the yellow light on its face—started making chugging noises. After twenty seconds of this, a sheet of paper about four feet wide started to inch out of the machine.

It's a printer that makes big documents, like blueprints and engineering plans. That's how they store all their stuff—they just keep them in the computer and print the ones they need.

It took six minutes for the massive document, the size of half a bedsheet, to emerge from the big printer. It finally spilled to the ground, and Gaia picked it up, spreading it out on the oak table.

Gaia couldn't make heads or tails of it at first. It was a very complicated schematic or diagram of something. But it was all Greek to her—

Except, somehow, it wasn't. Squinting at the page, Gaia realized that there was something familiar about it; some pattern somewhere in the maze of lines and shapes that she'd seen before somewhere. And the computer had printed a single black *X* in the middle of the diagram. Moving her face close to the page, she suddenly noticed that the horizontal and vertical lines had small labels. *Federal . . . Mifflin . . . Bella Vista . . . Cantrell . . .*

Those names sounded familiar. They reminded her of something she'd seen very recently. Sometimes having a photographic memory was a hindrance rather than a help; there was so much information moving through her brain that she could have difficulty realizing *what* she was remembering. Moving in closer to the strange, rectangle-filled schematic, she saw another label that snapped it into focus.

Liberty Bell.

Now she had it. This was a map of the city of Philadelphia.

But why is that important?

Gaia didn't know. Furthermore, she didn't understand what all the lines and rectangles were—or what the black *X* meant.

Looking again, Gaia realized suddenly that like a buried-treasure spot on a pirate map, the *X* was marking a particular intersection in the city . . . Decatur and Main, the two crossing streets were labeled.

That was interesting. Of course, she still had to figure out what—

What was that?

A clanking noise somewhere in the distance.

The pumping machinery?

That elderly guard, making his rounds?

Either way, the message was the same: time to leave. Rolling up the enormous document, Gaia spared five seconds to go back and delete the e-mail Catherine had sent—just in case somebody came into this room later and discovered it—and then, flicking out the lights, holding the tube of paper that was covered with mysterious hieroglyphics she couldn't begin to understand, Gaia sneaked out of the Municipal Works Technical Records Department, closing the door behind her, and, retracing her steps by memory, began making her way back out of the ancient stone building. She couldn't stop fingering Catherine's bracelet in her pocket.

Gaia

[*Recorder on*] Okay, it's getting on three in the afternoon and I'm doing this again. At this point, as a fugitive from justice, on the run from the bureau, having directly disobeyed an FBI agent's order at gunpoint that I surrender myself, I guess it's fairly ridiculous for me to still be making agent's logs.

Except maybe it's part of who I *am* now. Maybe I shouldn't call all these new behaviors "FBI"—maybe they're just me. I'm going to keep making agent's logs because they help me think.

Not that it's doing any good right now.

When Marsh told me about gray ops, I didn't want to believe it. But then he disappeared. If he was wrong—if the bureau just wants to take me in and question me, if they're not trying to kill me—then why did Winston Marsh vanish?

It's a serious problem. Because anyone who would kill Marsh—who would surgically remove a private detective from the face of the earth just because he chanced his way into the edge of a federal investigation of terrorists—won't stop there.

If they get to me, they're going to find out about Will—and what he did for me. And then they'll have to "gray op" *him*, too.

I was so reassuring. I told him it wasn't any risk at all; I demanded that he just start doing research into what turned out to be a terrorist cell. And now he's in as much danger as I am. [*Pause*]

I think I've done it again. I've gone and gotten myself into that condition where there's a boy in my life and I can't control how I feel about him. I remember there was a time when I swore I'd never do that again.

But that was a long time ago. And I'm older now and maybe a *little bit* wiser. Maybe it's okay to be back in this condition. I have to admit that since this whole FBI thing began, this roller-coaster ride of love and death, Will's been the one consistently dependable thing in my life. I can't say that about Jennifer Bishop, who was, I guess, my first friend and ally in the bureau, or about Malloy . . . or even Catherine or Marsh, the latest would-be "spirit guide" to enter my life and then vanish.

I'm tired of making mistakes. I want to fix the ones I've made—and then I don't want to make any more.

Marsh—I hope you're alive. And I'll honor what you did for me—when I save Catherine, it will be thanks to your help. Without you I'd be nowhere.

But now I'm on my own again.

And I've got to warn Will. If they think he knows anything at all . . .

This really is like a twilight zone I've stumbled into. It's like that dream I had this morning when I was following the river deep into that dark country. I'm still driving, still recording, still looking for my friend. I could still use a little help. I still could use Will Taylor, right here next to me in the car—I guess that might be my one wish, but don't tell him I said so. And whether I'm a fugitive, a criminal, or an agent, I'm still on the case. I'm following this river all the way to the end.

Agent Moore signing off. [*Recorder off*]

WILL22: Gaia.

GAIA13: Will.

WILL22: Are you OK?

GAIA13: Yes. No. I'm not sure. I'm lying on a bed in a cheap motel in Collingswood, PA, near Philadelphia.

WILL22: What happened last night? I got worried.

GAIA13: Sorry about that. Rudely interrupted.

WILL: Did you get my info?

GAIA13: Yes, I did. Thnx for helping, Will.

WILL22: Don't mention it.

GAIA13: Catherine was here, in this town. She was here TODAY, Will.

WILL22: What?

GAIA13: She's been abducted by the terrorist organization in that memo, Will. Socorro. Rossiter took her to Baltimore and I fought him, but he got away and I never found her . . . she'd been moved.

WILL22: Damn.

GAIA13: Will, I could smell her shampoo on the pillow. It was REALLY HER tied up in that basement. I can't even think about it.

WILL22: We'll find her, Gaia. But we've got to bring the bureau in and tell them everything you've found out.

GAIA13: NO NO NO NO NO

WILL22: Gaia, don't be unreasonable. I know you think they don't care about finding Catherine, but I can't believe that's true.

GAIA13: Will, listen, you've got to PROMISE ME you won't say a word to anyone at Quantico about this. You have to PROMISE because it's life and death.

WILL22: What are you talking about?

GAIA13: You read Winston Marsh's record, right? You understand who he is? You would trust him if he told you about a secret undocumented FBI policy?

WILL22: ??

GAIA13: According to Marsh there are "gray operations," or gray ops, where they terminate—that's assassinate—agents who have come in personal contact with terrorists or terrorist organizations.

WILL22: And there's no record of it?

GAIA13: Exactly. At first I didn't believe it. But Will, Marsh VANISHED right after he told me that. And the FBI's been after me since yesterday.

WILL22: Gaia, listen. The memo I sent you says "El Dia"—the day they're doing whatever horrible thing they're doing—is tomorrow.

GAIA13: I know, and I've got to find out what it is because Catherine's going to be right in the middle of it.

WILL22: Do you have any clues at all?

GAIA13: Just this big chart that Socorro stole from the Department of Public Works, which I finally figured out is a map of Philadelphia. It's got a single intersection marked—Decatur and Main. But the map has a layer of lines over it that I don't understand at all.

WILL22: What do the lines look like?

GAIA13: Just like lines, running throughout the city and converging on particular spots.

WILL22: Could they be water pipes?

WILL22: Gaia?

GAIA13: Oh my God—yes. Yes, that's exactly what they are. Here, they lead to the reservoir and interlock with the sewers. Yes—this is a map of the Philadelphia water system.

WILL22: And Socorro has that map? Gaia, is Socorro going to poison the Philly water supply?

GAIA13: I have to go to that intersection . . . Decatur and Main . . . tomorrow.

WILL22: Gaia? Are you sure that's a good idea?

GAIA13: If you've got a better one, now's the time.

WILL22: I've got a MUCH better idea. TELL THE FBI that Catherine's in the hands of James Rossiter. They've got him on file, like I told you before. When they see his name, they'll jump.

GAIA13: Will, you're right. Rossiter. He's the key to figuring out what Socorro's doing and where Catherine is.

WILL22: Exactly.

GAIA13: This is important. Don't reveal ANYTHING to Malloy or Bishop or anyone else about any of this.

WILL22: Because I'm going to get "gray-opped"? Gaia, come on. You know how paranoid you sound.

GAIA13: DO NOT TALK TO THEM.Will, I am very serious about this. You've got to PROMISE ME you won't say a word. If you had heard Marsh's description of gray ops, you would take me seriously. And it was only a few hours later that the white van showed up. We can't trust anyone. We've got to do this alone.

WILL22: Gaia, don't go to Philly if you're not sure what you're doing.

GAIA13: Miss you. Really miss you.

WILL22: Miss you too.

GAIA13: Wish you were here.

WILL22: Me too. Gaia, please don't do anything risky or stupid.

GAIA13: God, I'm SO TIRED. So tired, Will. I feel like I've just been going and going and I had nothing but weird dreams last night and now my eyes feel like they're made of lead.

WILL22: Gaia?

WILL22: Gaia, are you there?

GAIA13: Tired. I'll

WILL22: Gaia?

WILL22: Gaia? Are you there?

WILL22: Gaia?

the lying was easier

OUT OF THIS NIGHTMARE

At three-thirty exactly, Will Taylor hurried across the Quantico base courtyard toward the administration building. He nervously checked his watch as he walked. This time of the afternoon most of the base's personnel were busy elsewhere, on the shooting ranges, in the laboratories, or in the classrooms. Trainees were working out or practicing their tradecraft in Hogan's Alley or doing research.

Any of which Will *could* have been doing that afternoon rather than sitting in his dark dorm room behind a locked door, secretly using an illegal Internet connection scheme to chat with a missing—and wanted—trainee. Had Will been doing something innocent, he would have been perfectly comfortable obeying Special Agent Malloy's telephone summons.

He spent an incredibly tense ten minutes pacing his dorm room, sweating as he watched the blinking cursor at the bottom of the Hacker City chat stream window, where he had typed Gaia's name five times in a row and gotten no response.

She's fallen asleep, Will thought frantically, drumming his fingers on the back of his desk chair as he stared at the frozen conversation on his screen and wondered what to do next. When the phone rang right then, Will jumped about a foot in the air—and the voice on the other end hadn't exactly calmed him down.

"Taylor? Malloy," the chief said quietly. "Meet me in the admin lobby at fifteen-thirty hours."

No explanation of what the meeting was about; no explanation of anything at all.

Why the lobby? Will thought randomly. *Why not his office as usual?*

Will had barely managed to croak out, "Yes, sir," before the connection was broken. Moving like a guilty teenager about to get caught with a cigarette, he turned on the room's lights and snapped off the computer.

Are they onto us? he worried frantically as he walked up to the glass doors of the administration building. The phone call had come right in the middle of his second "Hacker City" chat with Gaia.

Did that mean they'd somehow been detected?

Pulling open the broad glass door and walking into the cool, air-conditioned lobby of the administration building, Will concentrated on staying *calm*—he figured that if anything was going to make this difficult, it wouldn't be any problem he had in answering questions. Will was good at thinking on his feet. The problem would be if he got too excited, if he let his mounting fear show.

Will took a deep breath and stepped up to the security desk, flashing his entry badge. The guard waved him through, and Will nodded distractedly, looking around for Malloy.

It didn't take long to find him. "Taylor!" Malloy called out from the end of the lobby, past the row of steel-shod elevators. "Get over here."

Will hurried forward. Malloy was standing impatiently in

front of a black steel door that led to the basement stairwell. A sign on the door read BASEMENT and, below that, AUTHORIZED PERSONNEL ONLY.

"Yes, sir," Will said, walking up to the chief. He was unsure of the protocol—whether to salute or reach to shake hands—and stood motionless, not knowing what to do next. "You wanted to see me?"

"Come this way," Malloy muttered, reaching to swipe his own pass card at the steel door's sensor. There was a deep bass rumble and then a loud *chunk* as the door swung open. Malloy stiffly held the door for Will, who hurried past him and found himself at the top of a narrow, cement-walled staircase. "You need to see just how big a problem you're creating."

What does that mean? Will wondered. *And why down there?*

At the bottom of the stairs a wide glass doorway opened to a brightly lit, gleaming white corridor. A sign on the glass door read

NATIONAL SECURITY DATABASE NETWORK
W A R N I N G
THIS FACILITY IS AVAILABLE DURING RESTRICTED
HOURS ONLY
OPENS AT 1000—CLOSES AT 1700
EVERY DAY—NO EXCEPTIONS

Will had heard something about that rule. According to rumors, the base's most sensitive antiterrorism and anticrime computer networks and files were down here in this basement. The underground location meant that lead and rock shielding could protect the computer systems from even the most elaborate, cutting-edge seismic espionage schemes, where computers were probed from a distance using radio wave transmitters.

"I want you to see what we're up to down here," Malloy told

Will. He turned a corner into another corridor and passed through a doorway into a small room. There were elaborate computer terminals at opposite walls and several technicians working at server racks on either side of the terminals.

"Nothing on the credit card from Precinct 31, sir," an operative at one of the computer terminals called out. "Switching inquiry to Precinct 33."

"Thank you," a gray-bearded man with glasses and a clipboard said. Will recognized him: Dr. Wolfson, the director of the digital security and surveillance network.

"Local police in Rensulano County have received the description of the Altima," another operative said. "Sir, they speculate that the suspect could be anywhere in the Collingswood vicinity—we're cross-checking in order to narrow that down."

They're tracking her, Will realized dismally. *They're down in this basement using their antiterrorism crime-fighting data network to do it, and they're right on top of her. Have they always known where she was?*

"Taylor," Malloy said, "I want you to meet a visitor from our Baltimore branch—Special Agent Thom Kinney."

Malloy indicated a trim, well-built man in his mid-thirties. Will had never seen him before, but it was obvious that the man was a field agent—and probably a seasoned one, judging by his appearance. His blond hair was cut short. There was a large bandage taped to the side of his neck.

"So you're the one," Kinney said. He moved his jaw carefully, wincing in pain. "Gaia Moore's partner in crime."

"Excuse me?" Will squinted at Kinney. The older man stared right back. He was giving Will a *look*—a deliberately

162

confrontational gaze, as if he was thinking about fighting him. "I'm not a 'partner in crime' with anyone, sir."

"Shut up and listen," Malloy said furiously, stepping forward and pointing his finger at Will. "Agent Kinney encountered Gaia Moore yesterday afternoon in Baltimore, traveling with a man who, if we're sure of our information, is an extremely dangerous international criminal."

What?

Will forced his face not to move, but it was very difficult. He *knew* Winston Marsh—Gaia's traveling companion—was a decorated FBI agent or had been at one time. Why would Malloy be calling him an "international criminal"?

"Moore has been on the move for more than thirty-six hours," Malloy went on, "during which time she's used her credentials to engage in a completely fraudulent and unauthorized 'investigation,' not to mention conducting not one but *two* clandestine IRC chat conversations with somebody on this base. Dr. Wolfson here is absolutely sure of it."

"We've got the interrogation tapes of the gas station employees," one of the technicians announced. "They definitely saw her; the description matches the Starbucks surveillance video image. Downloading from the satellite feed in forty seconds. And we're getting closer to trapping that cell phone call—she apparently contacted someone in the computer department here at Quantico."

"I think it's you, Taylor," Malloy went on. "I think you're the one she's chatting with. I think you know where she is and what she's doing."

Will stared back at Malloy. It was torture to have to think so fast while maintaining a totally blank face, but he forced himself to do it.

I should agree right now, he thought. *Tell him where she is, and then they can come in and save the day. Helicopters, jets, National Guard—whatever it takes.* Gaia had successfully tied Catherine's disappearance to a Socorro operative, Will reminded himself. No matter how stubborn she was being, it was time for the bureau to take over—he had been insisting this to her all along.

"You have *no idea* how important this is," Kinney said stiffly, his jaw muscles flexing the edges of the bandage he wore. "It is absolutely imperative that we locate Moore as soon as possible, especially now that Marsh is out of the picture."

Out of the picture? Will found that phrase disturbing. *Is that what you say after a successful gray op? Is Gaia going to be "out of the picture" soon?*

"Well, Taylor?" Malloy said, stepping closer. His chiseled, weather-beaten face was very close to Will's. "What have you been chatting with her about? We are facing a ticking clock and an extremely serious threat to national security. I am *ordering you* to tell me where Gaia is and what she's doing."

She's in Collingswood, Will thought helplessly. *She's in a motel. She fell asleep about twenty minutes ago and when she wakes up, she's going to drive to Philadelphia and go to the corner of Decatur and Main, to a specific spot in the city water grid, and wait for Socorro to show up and do whatever they're going to do.*

The entire answer, as a series of clear, complete sentences, was on the tip of Will's tongue. With no effort at all, he could open his mouth and tell them everything.

Do it! a very sensible voice in Will's head was raging at him.

Tell them where she is! Get us all out of this nightmare! This is the cavalry. These are the good guys. Tell them all and let them help.

But as much as he wanted to, he couldn't quite make himself speak.

What if she's right? he thought suddenly. *What if they're launching a gray op from this room right now? What do I say to Gaia when she's dead? "Sorry, ma'am, but I didn't believe you, and anyway, I was worried about my own career?"*

"Sir, what's a 'gray operation'? Or 'gray op' for short?"

"Taylor!" Malloy snapped, so loudly that the technicians in the room turned around. "I want you to answer my question."

Will looked over at Kinney. He had just realized something.

"She did that, didn't she?" Will asked, pointing at Kinney's neck. "Gaia fought you. Looks like she won, too."

Kinney glared at Will. For a moment Will thought that the older man might actually take a swing at him before he visibly mastered his temper.

"There's no such thing as a 'gray operation,'" Kinney said.

And you, Will thought, looking at Kinney, *haven't said one word yet that I believe.*

"I haven't had any communication with Gaia, sir," Will said. His mind was made up—and the lying was easier now that he was sure of the position he was taking.

Kinney turned away disgustedly. "Oh, for—"

"All right," Malloy said, sighing heavily. "You may have just destroyed your FBI career for good. I want you to think about that very carefully over the next few hours, and if you decide to come to your senses, I want you to contact me. You've got to live with the decisions you make. Remember that, Taylor."

"Yes, sir," Will said, nodding gravely. "I will."

"Good. Now get the hell out of here," Malloy snapped, turning away.

HARBORED SUSPICIONS

Will was still breathing hard as he knocked on the double doors to the tech lab. He had run all the way across the Quantico base, from the admin building over here to the science building, in the hope that he would catch Lyle in his office. Lyle's desk phone had rung ten times with no answer, followed by Lyle's terse message ("It's Lyle; you know what to do"), then a beep. But Will figured he might be right there. Will and Gaia had spent a fair amount of time with the shy, reserved technician, and Will had seen him ignore his ringing phone many times.

Approaching the science building, his lungs burning for air, he felt a bit better as he looked up at the building's gleaming glass facade, looming against the bright Virginia sky, and saw the fluorescent lights glowing in Lyle's window—and could just make out the top of Lyle's head, barely visible behind a stack of books.

Thank God for small favors, he thought, racing up the stairs to the fifth floor.

"Go away," Lyle yelled out from within the lab as Will knocked again. "Access denied."

"Lyle, it's Will Taylor," Will called out.

"So?"

"So I need your help," Will said. And then, hating himself for doing it but doing it anyway, he added, "Gaia needs your help, too." He'd always harbored suspicions that Lyle had a little bit of a crush on Gaia, and he hated to exploit that knowledge, but he couldn't think of anything else to do.

And Gaia's on her way to Philadelphia, he thought for what must have been the fiftieth time. *And nobody knows what she's going to find. And nobody can stop her.*

"Uh-huh," Lyle called out. "Listen, I'm really busy—"

"Damn it, Lyle, will you let me in?" Will shouted. *"I'm not kidding! This is serious!"*

After an agonizingly long pause, the double doors clicked open. Lyle was standing there, his curly hair backlit by the fluorescent lights, his glasses reflecting Will's anxious face. He was wearing a brown, short-sleeve button-down shirt and holding a complex-looking computer board in one hand.

"What's so important? *Hey*—*!*"

Will had pushed past Lyle, bodily propelling himself into the tech lab.

"Look," Will began, still out of breath. Lyle was looking in alarm at Will's disheveled appearance. "I don't have time to explain, but I need your help. I need information that's on the admin building network—and you can get it for me."

Lyle frowned. "Don't you have a pass to that building?"

"*Yes*, but not to get into the secure terrorism network," Will explained impatiently, "and I don't have a password that will log me on because I'm not clearance level 4."

Lyle had moved to his cluttered desk and slowly sat back down. Will moved toward him, not wanting to appear physically threatening but realizing he was giving that impression nonetheless. "I'm clearance level 4," Lyle remarked conversationally. "But I can't—"

"Yes, you can," Will repeated urgently. "Come with me right now over to admin. Say you've got to, you know, repair the servers or something. Then we can go downstairs and get into the main terrorism datab—"

"No." Lyle vigorously shook his head. "Forget it. No more. I don't care if Gaia Moore wants that information. I don't care if Christina Aguilera and Britney Spears want it. *You can't have it.* I refuse to bend the rules."

Will narrowed his eyes. He was listening to Lyle, but at the same time he had just noticed something. Partially buried amid the disorganized piles of bric-a-brac on Lyle's desk, he could see two spare magnetic pass cards. They looked like featureless, off-white credit cards that happened to be a quarter inch thick.

He's got a few of them, Will realized. *He must go through them like Kleenex—constantly moving around the base and dealing with all those locked-up computers.*

"Okay," Will said, taking a step backward and exhaling loudly. "Okay, Lyle, I'm sorry. I truly am—I'm just in this crazy situation where Gaia's asking me to do something and I'm going crazy trying to comply." He faked a weak smile.

"Sorry, man," Lyle said reluctantly. "I just can't do it. I'd lose my job and worse."

"Sure," Will said, squinting critically. "Actually, that's the other thing I wanted to talk to you about."

"What?"

"If you go look at the base phone records," Will confided,

"just between you and me, you'll see logs from very early yester-day morning when you had your little conversation with Gaia."

The moment he saw Lyle's face, Will knew he'd guessed right.

"I didn't—"

"Yeah, but you did," Will went on mercilessly, "and more people know about it than you realize. In fact, I happen to know that Dr. Wolfson is trying to trace the call's origin. If I were you, I'd start making sure he doesn't succeed."

"Wolfson? Oh, hell," Lyle said anxiously, and turned to his computer, which was displaying a Jennifer Garner screen saver.

The moment his back was turned, Will started sliding his hand on Lyle's desk, reaching for one of the spare pass cards.

"I *knew* I should have just hung up," Lyle said, typing his password. He didn't seem to notice that behind him, Will was standing on his toes and staring avidly at Lyle's fingers as he logged on. "I don't know how I let her talk me into that."

Four characters, Will noticed. *A—I—A—*

He couldn't read the fourth one.

But one of the two spare pass cards was in his pants pockets.

"Thanks," Lyle sang out, peering at what looked like a secu-rity readout screen. "That was a close one."

"No problem," Will said. Now his only priority was to get out of the room before Lyle noticed that one of his spare cards was missing. "Sorry about coming down so hard. That lady's just dif-ficult to refuse."

Lyle smiled weakly. "I understand," he said. "No hard feelings."

None at all, Will thought as he turned to leave. *None at all, my friend.*

A RULE THAT TRAINEES ALMOST NEVER BROKE

With his back pressed against the basement wall, trying to sneak past a motion sensor, Will found himself thinking about his uncle Casper.

In his mind, Will was sitting with his uncle on Casper's back porch, the way they always did in the spring, looking out over the rolling fields behind the house, and Will was trying to convince Casper he wasn't stupid.

But you are *stupid,* Casper was saying. *You remember that movie? "Stupid is as stupid does"? That's you all over, Willy, because you're risking everything on a gamble. And where our people come from, a man doesn't do that.*

Standing flat against the wall of the Quantico administration building's basement, imagining this conversation, Will had to admit that Uncle Casper had a point.

It was five ten in the afternoon, and above him the Quantico administration building was humming with activity. But down here it was a different world. As the warning sign on the glass door made clear, the entire basement (and its millions of dollars' worth of seismic security protection) closed down at 1700 hours—5 p.m., or ten minutes ago.

And Will Taylor—star athlete, model student—FBI investigator, was breaking a rule that trainees almost never broke. The main deterrent was something far more effective than locks and combination codes. It was the consequences. There was a no-tolerance policy for trainees who violated security guidelines. If they were caught once, they were thrown out—and usually court-marshaled.

And that part's going to be especially fun, Will thought ruefully as he took another step to his left, with his eye fixed on the rotating ruby red LED in the ceiling that indicated the motion detector's cycle. Just another eighteen inches and he was home free. *I'm especially going to like sitting up there in front of a military court and explaining how I tried to sneak into the national security database network and actually had a fantasy that I could get away with it.*

Twenty minutes before, he had swiped his laminated active duty pass in the card reader, watched the red light turn green and the door open, and then strode up to the security desk and waved cheerfully at the uniformed marine guard.

"Afternoon, Burt—how goes it?" Will said as he signed in, writing his destination as Township Law Enforcement—4th Floor.

"Going to be a warm night," Burt pointed out.

"Yep. Have a good one, Burt," Will called out as he strode away toward the elevators, his shoes clicking on the stone floor.

This time of day, only a few FBI employees were scattered around the lobby. Nobody was paying attention to Will.

Here goes.

The elevator button bonged as he pressed it. While the elevator was on its way, Will reversed his direction and began walking as quietly as he could toward the black steel door that led to the basement stairwell.

While the elevator door was rolling open behind him, Will used the sound as cover while he swiped Lyle's stolen pass card. There was a frightening pause while nothing happened, and then on his second try the door flew open. Will slipped through it as fast as he could. The stairwell door was an official fire exit, Will saw—it had pneumatic latches on its inside with a red sign that said EMERGENCY EXIT ONLY—PRESS HERE—ALARM

WILL SOUND. Will caught the door before it could click shut and with the aid of a wooden pencil he'd brought for this purpose propped it open.

You can see the pencil from the outside, Will thought, looking at the edge of the door. *But that's just too bad. It's after five—I just have to hope nobody notices.*

Then Will had hurried down the stairwell and into the basement corridor, and here he was, playing the game of moving four inches to the wall every time he saw that the ceiling motion detector had cycled away from him.

Finally all this slow, careful work paid off, and now he was able to slip around the corner and into a secure computer annex down the hall from the main complex. It was a small room with two computer terminals against opposite walls.

Approaching the leftmost terminal and turning it on, Will was greeted with a forbidding looking log-in screen with a blue FBI seal and boldface type reading ADMINISTRATIVE SPECIAL CLEARANCE WORKSTATION and, below that, UNAUTHORIZED USE OF THIS FACILITY IS A FEDERAL CRIME.

Never mind, Will thought, typing *Lyle Perkins* into the screen's log-in panel. Then he stopped.

A–I–A—and a fourth letter, Will thought. *Artificial intelligence?* Without much hope, he typed AIAI.

INCORRECT PASSWORD, the system responded.

Will's shirt was already stained with sweat. He looked at the screen, trying to think like a hacker. They always used clever patterns, word reversals, personal secrets—

"Backward," Will said out loud, snapping his fingers. He

entered AIAG as the password. The computer responded immediately.

PASSWORD ACCEPTED
WELCOME, PERKINS, LYLE
YOU ARE LOGGED IN AT LEVEL 04 SECURITY ACCESS

Without preamble, Will logged into the terrorism database search function, typing in the word *Socorro*.

And now, finally, we'll get some answers.

It was torture to wait the additional thirty seconds that passed before the screen refreshed:

ERROR 512: TERM TOO GENERAL
System contains **349,909,210** entries for your selection
"SOCORRO"
Please narrow your search by selecting a cross-reference term
MOST FREQUENT CROSS-REFERENCE TERMS FOR
"SOCORRO":
Ramon Nino: 26,434 entries or **capsule bio**
Explosives and Explosive Detonations: 1,030 entries
James Rossiter aka Jimmy Rossiter: 26,434 entries
Poisoning Incidents: 9 entries

There was more, but Will fixated on the first entry: Nino.

CAPSULE BIO
Ramon Nino
Age 41. H 6'2". W 210. E Brown. H Brown. Birth San Miguel
Capistrano.

Ramon Nino is the undisputed leader of international terrorist organization 65-1, code-named "SOCORRO." Since 1982 Nino has been charged with forty-five separate illegal activities in Latin America and the United States, including twelve indictments for murder. None of these cases have ever gone to trial except one (see below). The list of atrocities committed by Nino is long and detailed, but Nino excels at hiding his true crimes—including **murder**, **arson**, **conspiracy**—from his followers, except for a trusted "inner circle" of advisers. In 2002 Nino was arrested and charged with conspiracy and reckless endangerment under the Homeland Security Act and was incarcerated in federal maximum security penitentiary #23459, where he will remain until his parole hearing on 08/24/05 at the Philadelphia County Courthouse, Philadelphia, PA. **Click for more information.**

August 24, Will thought.

Tomorrow.

El Dia.

Will could hear his pulse thumping in his ears. He clicked back a page and clicked on the link for Socorro cross-referenced with James Rossiter.

What was that?

For the second time Will was absolutely convinced he'd heard muffled footsteps outside the computer room. As if someone was approaching the room but was doing it very slowly and quietly so as not to get caught.

Meanwhile there was a pause while the computer retrieved the data, and then another summary page came up:

SEARCH QUERY RESULTS

"SOCORRO" CROSS-REFERENCE WITH **"James Rossiter aka Jimmy Rossiter"**

MOST FREQUENT SUBCATEGORIES

James Rossiter 03/02/02 SOCORRO Plastique Bombing Incident: 12 entries

James Rossiter 12/04/01 SOCORRO Dynamite in Auto Plant Incident: 6 entries

James Rossiter 05/10/04 SOCORRO Incendiary Gas Bomb in Office Tower: 4 entries

Will felt a sick feeling in the pit of his stomach as he read.

Bombs, he thought. *Rossiter's a bomber, a terrorist bomber. Tomorrow he'll be in Philadelphia setting a bomb.*

And Gaia's on her way to the spot it's going to explode.

In that moment Will was so completely consumed with the idea that he had to get Gaia out of danger that he didn't realize he wasn't alone in the room—until one second later, when a hand dropped onto his shoulder.

"Shhh," a voice whispered in his ear. "It's Kim."

some kind of big terrorist incident

THE PANIC BUTTON

"What the *hell* are you doing here?" Will whispered, genuinely baffled. He had jumped a foot in the air when Kim put his hand on Will's shoulder.

"This is for Gaia, isn't it?" Kim asked, glaring at Will. "You're stealing information for her."

"How the hell did—" Will started over. "How did you know where I was?"

"I followed you, obviously."

"But how did you get into the building? You haven't got—"

Kim wordlessly held up his own active duty pass. "I've got one of these now—remember? I waited outside the building, looking at the windows, and I never saw you arrive up on the fourth floor. You know you can see the window, right, and the ceiling lights coming on? Anyway, I looked around the lobby and I found your pencil."

"Very clever." Will sighed in defeat. "So you came here to stop me?"

"I think I came here to *help* you," Kim said earnestly. "But I really think it's time for you to tell me what you're doing, partner. For the past two days you've been—"

176

"Wait a minute," Will said, pointing at the computer screen. "What's that mean?"

A new alert message had appeared:

LOG-IN ACCESS ERROR
ACCOUNT IN USE
ACCESS DENIED

"That's weird," Kim said.

"Listen," Will began urgently. "Here's the story. Catherine was kidnapped by a terrorist group called Socorro. They're using her to help them with some kind of big terrorist incident that FBI intelligence indicates is going to happen tomorrow."

"What do you—what kind of 'incident'?"

"In Philadelphia. In the center of town. Gaia's on her way there to stop them and save Catherine. She doesn't know what they're going to do."

"But you do?"

"Yeah." Will was drenched in sweat and losing patience. Kim wondered how sharp his faculties were at the moment. He *seemed* to be in control of his thoughts, but it was possible his reflexes were slowed from stress. *"There's a bomb."*

"Oh, no—"

"There's a bomb, and there's no way to stop it."

Kim thought about it. It didn't take him very long.

"You need my help," Kim went on. "You need me to cover for you. You need me to take care of the lollipop case while you're gone."

On the screen the same message appeared again:

LOG-IN ACCESS ERROR
ACCOUNT IN USE
ACCESS DENIED

"Gone—?"

"You have to go to Philadelphia," Kim continued patiently. "Right now."

Another line appeared on the screen:

PASSWORD DENIED—POSSIBLE SECURITY COMPROMISE

Kim saw Will's eyes widen in sudden, frightened comprehension as he stared at the screen.

"It's Lyle," Will said, grabbing Kim's arm. "Damn it—I stole Lyle's access card and password, but now Lyle—the *real* Lyle—must be trying to log onto the system."

"That's bad," said Kim. "You realize what that means? We've got about two minutes before he hits the panic button, calls security, and reports a security alert."

"And they'll even be able to localize it," Will confirmed, looking at the door.

Kim held out his hand. "Give me the access card."

"What?"

"God, you're dumb," Kim said impatiently. "Weren't you listening to what I just said? You've got to get moving." Kim wiggled his hand. "Give me the card and go. If you hurry, I'll bet you can make it out of the basement before they get here. But you've got to *move now.*"

Will returned Kim's gaze, and then after a moment he nodded, handed over the card, and turned to hurry toward the door. Kim stayed where he was, listening to the sound of Will's footsteps as he made his way back along the wall toward the stairwell, and then, as Kim heard the distant stairwell door click shut, he sat down at the computers, took a deep breath, and waited for the sirens to ring out and the stampede of armed guards to arrive.

LOST TIME

More time lost, driving.

Gaia was hopelessly caught in traffic.

"God*damn* it!" she hollered uselessly. It must have been the twentieth time she'd blurted out those words. She still couldn't believe it. How could she have let herself fall asleep? How could she give in to the exhaustion *now*? She was furious with herself. And now she was losing time—pounding on her horn and jutting the car forward in futile spurts.

She'd done everything in her power to make up for lost time, but it was getting on the appallingly late hour of nine o'clock by the time she finally, *finally* saw the towers of downtown Philadelphia against the horizon ahead of her, protruding over the road like some kind of Emerald City.

The traffic was only growing worse as she drove. She had two maps spread out on the seat next to her. One was a folded gas station map of the city, showing the approaches that were available. Gaia had already taken a red pen and drawn in the quick route that she'd figured out before, the route that would get her to Decatur and Main, where the spot on Catherine's map was marked.

And the other map was the one Catherine had printed—the one that showed the lines radiating out from that same street corner, the lines that Will had convinced her were water pipes.

And then what?

Gaia wasn't sure. Maybe Catherine and her captors would be there—maybe, for the first time since this all began, she wouldn't be one step behind.

The office towers were growing larger on the horizon against the darkening night sky. Philadelphia Civic Center 20, a green highway sign told her. Impatiently drumming her fingers on the steering wheel, Gaia *willed* the traffic to move faster. Her technique was ineffective. She and the six lanes of cars around her were stuck at the same lurching ten-mile-an-hour pace and, judging by the near stationary mass of cars ahead, would be for some time.

TO SAVE GAIA

"Agent Lau," Agent Bishop said, her arms folded over her chest, "we don't know what you were doing on the basement computers, but we strongly suspect that it has to do with the crusade Taylor's been indulging in over the past twenty-four hours. Now, can't you just make this easier for yourself and for us? Why throw away your career—your *entire career*, Kim—for something that has nothing to do with you?"

Kim was in Malloy's office on the top floor of the administration building, standing in front of Malloy's desk at full attention. Along with Special Agent Bishop, they had been joined by a field agent Kim had never seen before—a blond man called Kinney. The armed guards who had found Kim in the basement computer room had grabbed him by the upper arms and brought him to face the chief. He had to believe that Will had gotten away and was en route to save Gaia, but he had no way of knowing and no way of asking.

"I want to know where Taylor has gone," Malloy insisted.

Kim took a deep breath, stared straight at the cloudless sky out the window, and then answered.

"As I told you already, I haven't seen Will Taylor since yesterday. I have no idea where he is or what he's up to. I illegally entered the administration building basement alone, without anyone's help or knowledge, for my own reasons, which I do not care to discuss."

"You're protecting your friends," Bishop said, "or trying to. But there's a lot you don't know."

"For two days," Agent Kinney said, "according to high-level chatter, Gaia Moore has unknowingly made personal contact with a major Socorro operative with a very high ranking. *Two days*, Lau—that's how long she's been in contact with Socorro."

"You're saying they're in contact with her and she *doesn't know it?*"

"She doesn't know what's going on," Bishop insisted urgently. "She's got it all wrong."

Kim stood staring straight past Special Agent Malloy's head at the window and the sky beyond.

He'll get to her in time. Will will make it to Philly and he'll find Gaia and they'll save Catherine. I believe it.

I have to.

CENTER OF A SPIDER'S WEB

The intersection—Decatur and Main—seemed to be right in front of a small federal courthouse.

It was closing on 10 p.m., and Gaia was *finally* getting somewhere. At least she was off the highway and away from the almost dreamlike series of lane changes, roadside stops, gas stations, and motels that had taken over her life for the past forty-eight hours. She was in the middle of a major city now.

She had driven three slow laps around the block, looking in vain for a parking place. It was a ridiculous problem to be having, but she couldn't think of a way around it. Finally she had decided to just forget it, to double-park and let her car get towed. She'd already given up so much on this journey, she was getting fatalistic about what little else she had to give.

And it's not my car anyway, she thought absently. *It's Catherine's.*

And right then she saw a spot. A couple in a Volvo were pulling out of a parking space right in front of the courthouse's stone front steps. Gaia swerved over, took the spot, shut off the engine, and then sat there, taking a deep breath.

Well, I'm here.

Looking around, Gaia didn't see anything unusual. The intersection was in a fairly lively neighborhood, surrounded by store-front shops and office buildings. The city felt different from New York and Stanford; Gaia had noticed this while driving in.

After climbing out of the car and locking it, Gaia walked onto the sidewalk, looking up at the small colonial building in front of her. Philadelphia County Courthouse, the carved letters spelled out. For the third time she looked up at the street signs, confirming that this was indeed Decatur and Main.

Casting her eyes down to the street, she noticed an iron man-hole cover.

Down there, she thought, *is the magic spot.* The point in the water network where pipes converged like the center of a spider's web.

There were many passersby on the sidewalk, mostly business-people. It was late, but Gaia could see that the courthouse was still open—probably because night court was in session. Its windows glowed yellow, and people were moving up and down the stone steps, carrying briefcases.

I should be hiding, Gaia thought wearily. *Out in the open like this, I'll get caught.* She remembered the agents in the motel that morning back in Maryland, the agents in the roadside rest area who had almost gotten her later in the day. And it wasn't just the FBI—there was Socorro and James Rossiter (whose hands around her neck were a vivid memory). Gaia was tired of hiding, tired of running and chasing. *At some point,* she told herself, standing on the sidewalk with her hands in her pockets, *they'll get me. There's no way around it.*

And amazingly, at the very moment she was thinking those words, a pair of hands landed heavily on her shoulders, gripping them tightly.

There were so many martial arts moves she could make from this position, so many ways to turn the tables on whoever was trying to grab her. She could have propelled her would-be assailant vertically over her head by grabbing his forearms the right way.

But somehow, oddly, the fatalistic mood she was in prevented all of that—which, as it turned out, was a very good thing. Instead of fighting, which in nearly any other circumstance she would have done without even thinking about it, Gaia just turned her head and looked behind her.

Will Taylor was standing there.

Gaia blinked. *Have I finally lost it?* she thought weakly. *Am I hallucinating?*

But it was really him. He stood there with his hands still resting lightly on her shoulders, the Philadelphia streetlights shining on his blond hair and the shoulders of his blue sweatshirt. The look on his face was indescribable—there wasn't the slightest trace of swagger or smirk about him. He looked at her face as if he was having the same reaction she was—as if he simply couldn't believe it was really her.

Without a word, Will pulled Gaia close and hugged her.

They held each other so tightly that Gaia almost worried she was making it hard for Will to breathe. Her face was pressed against his shoulder, and the *smell*, the familiar smell of Will Taylor, soaked into her nostrils like perfume. She could feel the stubble of his cheek and chin pressing into the side of her head and his wide hands flat across her back.

Finally they pulled apart. They stood facing each other, less than a foot away, with her face turned up toward his. Then, at nearly the same moment, they each took a step backward.

"Will," Gaia began awkwardly. "How did you—"

Will grabbed her wrist, pulling her toward the courthouse steps. "Later," he insisted. "We have to move now. Fast. There's a bomb."

A ZEN CALM

Will and Gaia came through the heavy iron-framed doors into the Philadelphia County Courthouse. They arrived in a large, well-lit lobby with marble walls. The lobby was full of business-people—attorneys and clients, Will figured—but most of them had their coats on and were carrying briefcases. It was just ten o'clock, according to the old-fashioned wall clock with the roman numerals.

Night court's ending, Will thought. *The place is closing down for the night.*

Which was good, he figured. If the building was empty, a bomb would be less dangerous—and potentially would harm fewer people.

Just us.

"How do you know there's a *bomb*?" Gaia was asking. "I don't understand."

"I'll explain later," Will said impatiently. "But it's *here*—in the courthouse."

"Why here?"

Will had to firmly shove aside all his excitement at seeing her again. "Because Ramon Nino's going to be in this building tomorrow," he explained. "It's his parole hearing. And James

185

Rossiter's going to blow the place up. Martyring Nino, I guess—for their cause."

"The snips of wire," Gaia said, seemingly to herself. "The colored wires on the Ping Pong table. Of course—he builds bombs."

"What?"

"Never mind," Gaia snapped impatiently. "We've got to evacuate the building."

"There's no time for that," Will said impatiently, scanning his eyes along the rows of marble-framed doors that faced the lobby. "We've got to find it—let's get moving."

"Where do we look first?"

Will cast his mind back to Agent Baxter's lectures in Quantico. *Your experienced bomber is going to use the rules of physics to help him plant explosives,* Baxter had told them. It had all sounded very intellectual and exciting back then—it was very different when you were actually standing in a building that had been primed to blow up.

"We need to use logic," Will said uncertainly. "Where would you put a bomb in this building in order to do maximum damage?"

Gaia was looking around at the walls. "Low," she said. "It's an old stone building, without any steel structure. You want the bomb *low to the ground* to guarantee a structural collapse."

"I agree," Will said hesitantly. He couldn't stop himself from darting his head around, looking at all the courtroom doors. He was trying to appear cool, like he wasn't frightened, but it was very difficult. His overwhelming instinct was to *get out of there,* to run out of the front door and keep running until the courthouse was miles behind him. Instead Gaia was talking about getting *closer* to the bomb.

She didn't seem frightened at all, Will noticed. It was strange—impressive, but strange.

"Let's not waste time with these courtrooms," Gaia argued. "They all have metal detectors and high security. No way to get explosives in there."

"Fine," Will said. They were both keeping their voices low to avoid alarming the people around them.

"Basement," Gaia said, reaching to grab Will's wrist. "Come on."

Moving against the tide of people who were leaving the building, Will and Gaia found their way to the back of the ornate marble lobby to a stairwell that led down. Their footsteps clattered loudly as they galloped down the stone steps, pushing through a swinging door with a pebbled-glass inlay.

The basement was warmer and quieter than the lobby above it. The walls were painted an industrial gray, and the floor was gray cement. The low ceiling was lined with rows of naked fluorescent bulbs.

"We have to go room to room," Will said. He was trying to keep his voice steady, but it was hard to do. He had never in his life felt his "flight mechanism" raging as strong as it was right now. He had to concentrate on forcing his legs not to run away. His body was trembling with the exertion it took just to stay motionless.

"Start there," Gaia said, pointing at a wood-framed door. She seemed to be having none of these problems. Striding over, she pulled open the door and flipped the light on inside. Following her, Will saw that they'd entered a small storage room—metal chairs were stacked against the wall. Looking around, he saw that the room was basically a featureless box—no closets or cabinets, no place to hide anything.

"This isn't it," Will said. He was struggling to remember more details from Agent Baxter's lectures, but he was so agitated that it was difficult to do. "Wouldn't a bomb be close to the *center* of a stone building? Not near its edge?"

"Right," Gaia said, pointing at another door with a pebbled-glass window on the other side of the hallway. It looked different from the other doors—Will wasn't sure why until he realized that, like the storage room they had just left, it had no lock. "Try here," Gaia said.

Will pulled open the door as Gaia flicked on the lights. This was a slightly larger utility room, with cabinets built into one wall. Will immediately began opening the cabinets and pulling out the contents—bottles of cleanser, boxes of lightbulbs that exploded on the cement floor as he dropped them, cellophane rolls of paper towels.

Gaia had started at the other end, pulling rubber gloves and plastic buckets out of the opposite cabinet. Will noticed the sudden quiet—he had to figure that the building had just about finished emptying out. The only sound was the hum of the basement's air circulation vents and the clatter of the supplies that they were tossing onto the floor.

"Found it!" Gaia yelled. She was on her hands and knees, facing the bottom of the cabinet—she pulled back, letting him get down beside her and look.

It was a bomb, all right. Not a model, not a practice mechanism. The real thing.

Will tried to clear his head and find a Zen calm like Gaia seemed able to do. He didn't even come close. Sweat was pouring down his face, and his heart was pounding so loud that he was sure Gaia could hear it.

There was an electronic timing mechanism with a fuse, a trigger, a large nine-volt dry-cell battery, and a mass of wires connecting it all. Will couldn't see the detonating mass, but a pair of black wires led from the back of the bomb to holes drilled in the cabinet's back wall.

Where do those wires go? Will thought fleetingly. Did the bomb have an additional power source somewhere?

He shrugged it off—there wasn't time. The bomb had a digital clock mechanism, and its motionless display read 01:02.

"We've got two minutes," Will said breathlessly.

"That's not *minutes,*" Gaia argued, crouching next to him. "Are you crazy?"

"The two? It has to be minutes," Will disagreed. "I mean, what else can it be, *seconds*? It's not *moving.*"

"*Obviously* it's not two seconds," Gaia said patiently, "or we'd already be dead."

"Well, if it's not minutes, then what is it?" Will demanded, wiping sweat from his face. "I don't understand what you—"

"*Hours,*" Gaia nearly shouted. "We've got two hours. Now will you pay attention to the wires?"

"So the one is what—days?"

"I don't know. Yes, days. Whatever. Will, damn it, will you just—"

With a beep the display changed to 01:03.

"What the hell?" Will said. "What does that mean? Now it's going *backward.*"

189

"Defuse it!" Gaia yelled. "Will, you're driving me crazy."

"Why should I do it?"

"Because you're better at it," Gaia said, shaking his shoulder furiously. "Now will you just—"

"You're admitting I'm better at defusing bombs?" Will asked, curious. "You're not just psyching me up, are you? Because—"

"Will!"

The talk was doing its job—it was siphoning off the fear. Will had been staring at the wires as if in a trance, remembering how he had been able to do this before. Reaching out with a calm, almost delicate motion, he plucked a white wire away from the bomb's network of contacts.

With a loud click the bomb's digital display went dead. The bomb was defused. Will breathed a tremendous sigh and collapsed against the floor. His entire body was coated in sweat. "That's over," he murmured weakly.

But he was wrong.

A distant, echoing thump sounded through the basement—as if the same automatic mechanism was activating simultaneously everywhere in the building.

"What the hell is that?" Gaia asked. But he could tell from her voice—she knew as well as he did.

The security system, Will thought dismally. *The building's automatic locks.*

He looked at his watch. Sure enough, it was ten exactly. The Philadelphia County Courthouse was closed for the night—and all its doors had automatically shut and their locks engaged, sealing them inside.

an overwhelming need to stop

BLOWN TO KINGDOM COME

Gaia and Will's escape efforts had officially grown futile. They'd searched the entire courthouse basement at least four times, from the stairwell doors to the maintenance doors to the storage doors—all industrially locked. Will had tried to give Gaia a leg up to reach the steel gratings on the ceiling that led to the air shafts. No luck. They'd even tried to wriggle their way through the barred windows that looked out on the pitch black alleyway. Useless. Gaia had come to terms after thirty minutes; it had just taken Will another hour to accept it. They were locked in this basement until morning—until security returned to unlock those doors. And although she hated to admit it, Gaia was actually grateful for the much needed breather.

They'd been running on pure adrenaline for too long. Will had told Gaia all about his James Rossiter discoveries, and she could only imagine what he'd gone through to make it to that courthouse in time to save her. Adrenaline had carried them both across miles of highway, and it had carried them through a class-one bomb scare, but Gaia knew at least one thing from all her years of street fighting: all that adrenaline came with a price. Yes, she and Will had made it through the crisis, but now the post-traumatic exhaustion was kicking in. She could see it in Will's eyes, too. An overwhelming need to stop. Just for a while. They didn't even have a choice.

They were standing just outside the utility closet where they'd defused the bomb. Almost simultaneously they fell back against the cold concrete basement wall and slid down to the floor. Will hung his arms over his knees and let his head drop forward. Gaia rested her face in her hands and took a few long breaths. She could feel Will's thigh pressing against hers. His body was actually helping keep her upright—that's how drained she had suddenly become. She might have even drifted off to sleep had Will not spoken at that moment.

"Man, my head hurts." He pressed his fingers to his temples and then scratched them wildly through his blond buzz cut.

"I can't even feel my head," Gaia replied. "Or my fingers or my toes. Everything feels detached."

Will shook his head regretfully, staring down at the ground. "I should have gotten here faster. If I'd gotten here faster, we could have taken out the bomb and still made it out of here before lockdown. And we'd be looking for Catherine right now instead of—"

"Shhh." Gaia flailed her hand tiredly at his face to shut him up. "Let's just not . . . Let's not freak about things we can't change right now. Let's just be quiet for a few minutes, okay?"

"Okay," Will agreed. "You're right. There isn't a damn thing we can do right now."

"That's right."

Gaia savored the moment of silence, but it didn't last very long. Will's voice began to echo off the dank gray walls of the basement again. "But if I'd just gotten here an hour earlier, then we could have—"

"Will." Gaia grabbed Will's muscular arm to silence him again. "Come on. We agreed. Let's not dwell, okay? We're alive. We've got to believe that she's still alive, too. But we won't be any good to her burnt out and exhausted. We need to rest."

Will nodded. "I know it. You're right."

"Okay," Gaia said. She squeezed her knees closer to her chest to form a personal cocoon. Her eyelids began to flutter and grow heavy. "You know what?" she breathed. "I think I'm going fall asleep for just a little while . . ."

This time Will grabbed hold of *her* arm. The jolt shook Gaia's eyes wide open again. "I don't think that's such a good idea," he said.

"Why not?"

"Why *not*? Maybe you've forgotten that we were almost blown to kingdom come less than two hours ago? Might be a good idea for you to stay alert down here, don't you think?"

Gaia tried to forge a reassuring smile with her tired lips. "Look," she said with a sigh. "Think about it for a second. We are completely locked in down here. That means that everyone else is locked *out*. This is probably the safest we're ever going to be. So I'm going to take advantage of that and get some rest. I highly recommend you do the same."

She tried to shut her eyes again, but now Will grasped her hand and nearly squeezed the life out of it. And for the first time she noticed . . . there was the slightest hint of a tremor in his strong fingers. She turned to face him, and she could see something strange in his eyes. Something she'd never really seen before. If she didn't know Will Taylor better, she would have sworn his expression was bordering on vulnerability. No, not exactly vulnerability, more like . . . need.

Will locked his eyes with hers. "Just don't go to sleep, all right?" The hint of his pale blond stubble was showing in the stark light of the overhead bulbs. He quickly let go of her hand and turned to face forward, but it was too late. She'd already seen that look in his eyes.

Gaia was at a momentary loss. This was not a Will Taylor she was accustomed to. Normally Will would rather die than admit that he needed something from Gaia, but the last few hours had pretty much done away with normalcy. Now that they'd stood over that ticking bomb together, they couldn't exactly go back to petty bickering and witty banter. At least not tonight.

"Okay," she agreed quietly. "I'll stay awake." She kept her tone as neutral as possible. She knew Will had just dropped his egomaniacal guard for a moment, and he was open to a direct hit. If she had sounded condescending or obnoxious about it, he would have shut down completely. And the truth was, now that she'd seen a glimpse of his more vulnerable side . . . she wanted to see more.

She stared at Will's Southern gentleman profile. His elegant features reminded her of old black-and-white photos from the twenties and thirties when men still looked like—for lack of a better term—men. She followed her gaze down his arms and focused again on his hands. Now she could see that his right hand was indeed shaking slightly. Will caught her staring, and he quickly closed his right hand in his left, keeping his eyes fixed straight ahead.

"Will?" she asked cautiously. "Are you okay?"

"What? Of course," he insisted. "What's that supposed to mean?"

"It's supposed to mean that your hand is shaking."

He clutched his hand more tightly. "No, it's not."

Gaia reached over with lightning speed and grabbed hold of his right hand before he could stop her. She pulled it over to her lap and couched it firmly between her hands. Now she could feel the undeniable twitches in his thick fingers. Will made a half-hearted attempt to pull it away, but then he gave in, knocking his head back against the cinder-block wall with frustration.

"It's been doing that ever since we defused the bomb," he admitted. "I mean, it's not like I couldn't handle it," he added, straightening his posture. "I took care of it—*we* took care of the bomb."

"I know."

"But the whole time . . . my heart was just pounding like . . ." He finally turned to face her. "I mean, Jesus, Gaia . . ." He swallowed hard. "That was the real thing in there. No game, no class, no stopwatch, nobody wins. You just live or die. That's it. I mean, hell, I've got confidence to burn, you know—but life or death's got nothing to do with confidence. My goddamn hand is shaking like a leaf. I swear to God, I know I'm ready for this job—I'm ready to be an agent, but . . . I guess I got spooked, all right? I got spooked, and I didn't even know it until just now—until it got so quiet and I really had a minute to think. And then I looked at you and I thought about what could have happened in there . . ."

Will stopped himself mid-sentence and fixed his eyes on hers. Something about the way he looked at her sent a flush of heat up her back. The heat grew in the silence between them, running like a warm current from her hands to his and his eyes to hers.

"I was scared," he said. It clearly wasn't easy for him to admit.

"Weren't you scared?" He searched her eyes for a connection.

Gaia's throat went bone dry. Her lips became glued to her teeth. But why? It was a simple enough question. Will obviously had no clue just how complicated the answer was, but that shouldn't have mattered. It had never mattered before. She was quite accustomed to deflecting that question with a quick and easy lie.

So lie, she told herself. *What the hell is the glitch? Kill the deaf-mute routine and lie.*

"Of—of course," Gaia said, clearing her throat. She let go of Will's hand and tucked her arms tightly around her chest. "Of course I was scared." She felt a wave of nausea rush through her stomach. Why was this so hard all of a sudden? Why was it making her physically ill?

Will looked unconvinced. "Were you really? Because I sure couldn't see it. And I am a perceptive son of a bitch, Ms. Moore. It was just . . . it was amazing." He shifted his body so he was facing Gaia head-on—leaning even closer to her than before. "I mean, forget all our competitive crap for now, okay? Forget all that stuff. I don't even *care* right now. I'm just going to sit here in awe and stew in the jealousy because I want to know how you do it. We were going to die in there, and you didn't even bat an eyelash—I didn't see one drop of sweat. You just went to it like it was a practice run—like it was just another plastic toy."

Gaia's back grew stiff with discomfort. Her head began to throb, and she still couldn't understand why. She just wanted Will to stop talking. "Let's forget it and move on," she muttered, avoiding his penetrating glance.

"Oh, come on." Will groaned. "*Now* you want to get modest with me? When I'm finally giving you all your props?"

"It's not that, I just—"

"I've never seen anyone be that brave. I mean it. And you can call me a Carolina sexist pig if you want, but I have *particularly* never seen a *woman* that brave. Come on. Tell me what the trick is. Is it some kind of Zen philosophy thing, or are you just the most tough-as-nails woman I've ever—?"

"Neither," Gaia snapped. "It's neither, it's none, it's *nothing,* okay? It's *nothing.*"

Her outburst echoed off the walls and faded into a long awkward silence. Her extreme response had obviously caught Will completely off guard. Hell, it caught *her* off guard. Will just sat there wide-eyed and frozen. Gaia pulled herself into such a tight fetal position, she looked like she was getting ready to crash-land.

Will seemed unsure what to even say next. "Hey, I'm—I'm sorry," he said. "I was just—"

"No." Gaia shut her eyes with frustration. "No, I'm sorry. I don't know what's wrong with me."

That was the most honest thing she'd said so far. What *was* wrong with her? She'd dodged this issue a hundred times before. Especially with all the baffled men in her life. They could never *quite* accept the notion of a woman this strong—this impervious to danger and peril. But of course, Gaia never truly explained it. She always had her rationales for lying or at least omitting the truth:

Telling him the truth will only put him in danger. Don't drag him into your tortured universe. What's the point of telling him anyway? He'll never believe you. He'll think you're a liar or crazy or both, and he'll go running for the hills.

All of a sudden Gaia was caught in a time warp. Her mind was flooded with those faces from the past—the short curls of Sam Moon's red-brown hair, Ed Fargo's eternally optimistic stubbly grin, Jake Montone's uncommonly green eyes. She'd lied to every one of those beautiful faces, and now, sitting so close to Will in the silence of this dark basement, one question was haunting her like hell . . .

What good had it ever done? All the evasive answers she'd given the men she cared about, all those strained and awkward silences when they searched her eyes for the truth. She had always told herself that she was lying to protect them, but now, looking back with twenty-twenty hindsight, it was impossible to ignore the facts. Keeping those men in the dark had never protected any of them at all. It had, in fact, done just the opposite. It had brought them all nothing but pain and tragedy. It was a mistake.

That's why she felt so ill right now. That's why she'd curled up like an infant. Because she was regressing and she knew it. Three years of lessons learned, yet here she was, about to lead Will Taylor right back down that same dark path? She couldn't do it. She couldn't bring deception into this thing with Will when they'd barely even gotten started. She couldn't do it to him, and she couldn't do it to herself. That tortured life of hers was long in the past, and Will was a grown man. He didn't need any protecting. And Gaia refused to make the same mistakes again. She refused to let her tragic ancient history repeat itself.

That was that. She had made up her mind. She was going to tell him her secret.

"I'm lying."

The moment she said it, she was overcome by a strange sense of calm. She had no plan here—no idea of what she would say or how she would say it, just the unmistakable sensation that she had taken a flying leap off a cliff and that it was the exact right thing to do.

"Lying about what?" Will asked.

"About being scared," she said. "You're right. I wasn't scared."

"I knew it," Will said. "But how do you steel yourself like that? What makes you so br—"

"It's not bravery," she stated flatly—almost shamefully. She had always wanted to feel the fear and then overcome it—like Will had done with that bomb. That was bravery. That was being heroic. But she had only felt it once or twice in her life. "Bravery's got nothing to do with it," she explained. Out of the corner of her eye she could see that Will looked stumped.

"What are you talking about?" he asked.

"I, uh . . ."

Where to begin? How was this supposed to come out without sounding like utter lunacy or a very bad joke? *The truth,* she reminded herself. *Just tell him the truth.* As long as she stuck to that plan, she knew she couldn't really screw it up. She reminded herself that the point wasn't really to make Will believe her. That was not something she had any control over. The only point was to *not* lie—to *not* drag Will down that same road that she'd taken Sam, and Ed, and, most important, Jake. Or maybe the real point was just to stay in this moment with Will. He'd created this unexpectedly naked moment here on this cold basement floor, and Gaia didn't want to leave it. What she wanted was to start putting some faith in the opposite sex again.

"Look," she said, "there's no way to say this, so I'm just going to say it, okay? I need to tell you something about me, and it's going to sound very strange, and you're probably not going to believe me, but I still need to tell you." He looked thoroughly confused already. "The thing is," she went on. "The thing about me is . . . I . . . I don't get scared."

"I know," Will said. "That's what I'm saying—"

"No," Gaia interrupted. "I mean, I *can't* get scared. It's like . . . it's like a genetic defect. I'm missing the chromosomes that trigger the fear response, so . . . I don't feel fear. I'm sort of . . . incapable of feeling—I mean, no, not sort of—I *am* incapable of feeling fear. Genetically incapable."

God, that was easy. She never would have believed it, but it was so easy to say it out loud. Or so she thought. A moment later, however, she became very short of breath. She felt strange needling tingles in her hands and feet, and she began to feel dizzy.

Okay, not so easy. Weird. Sickeningly weird. Literally. I feel sick. Say something, Will. Now's the time for you to say something.

She finally sneaked a glance at Will, and when she saw what looked like anger on his face, a wave of regret began to creep up from below.

Will narrowed his eyes at her. "Hey, I was trying to be *straight* with you," he complained. "I was being real with you, and you're turning it into a joke—you're screwing with me when I was trying to—"

"I am *not* screwing with you," she insisted. "And what I'm telling you is *not* a joke." All she could do was stare him down and stay honest. She'd made her decision. She'd committed to this confession—she *wanted* this confession, and she wanted to make it to Will. "You asked me if I was scared, and I decided to tell you the truth—the honest-to-God truth about me. It's not something I tell people about. It's not something people know. And if you don't believe me, there is nothing I can do about that. Not a thing. But I'm telling you the truth. You are the *only* person I am telling." Now she felt a sudden lump in her throat, and she didn't even know why. Apparently this kind of exposure stripped you of all emotional control, which was just one of the many reasons she had steered clear of this kind of exposure for most of her life.

Will stared at her long and hard in the silence, and she stared right back, despite the early signs of inexplicable tears that were beginning to blur her vision. She watched the anger drain away from his face as his eyes narrowed with bafflement. "Gaia, I don't . . . I don't understand what you're trying to do here. Why are you doing this?"

"I don't know," she said. Now she felt so naked it was almost painful. The tears in her eyes were just some kind of uncontrollable reflex. "I thought it was a good idea at the time, but now I'm not so sure. I told you that you wouldn't believe me, but I wanted to tell you anyway. It's not something I'm particularly proud of—this fearless 'gift' of mine—it doesn't really mean anything to me anymore, to be honest. It's just a fact of my life. It's the way I'm wired, like blue eyes or wavy hair. I was born this way, so it's beyond my control."

What am I saying now? I'm babbling.

Will just shook his head with confusion. He probably would have continued to accuse her of joking if he hadn't seen the tears in her eyes, but now he seemed to have no idea what to think. "I'm sorry, I just . . . I don't know what I'm supposed to say here. I mean, if you're going to keep on with this whole medical miracle story, then I've got to assume you're either joking, which you're obviously not, or that you're just . . . you know . . ."

She knew where this was going. "Crazy?"

"Well, not—"

"I'm not crazy, Will. If that's what you want to believe, you can, but I'm not crazy." Before she knew it, words were spilling out of her mouth. "If you want to know the truth, this little genetic malfunction has been the bane of my existence. It's made me a target for half my life. It demolished any chance I had of having a real family—I lost my mother, my father had to abandon me more times than I can count, it's made me a victim, and I *hate* being a victim. . . ."

This isn't going well. This is a mess. It wasn't at all what she'd envisioned when she'd made the decision to be honest. But then again, she hadn't really envisioned anything. Still, that sense of free falling was feeling less and less like freedom and more like plummeting to her doom.

"Look, I already told you," she said, swiping those pain-in-the-ass tears from her cheeks. "You don't have to believe me. I just needed to tell you. I had to. But you're making me regret it. Don't make me regret telling you this." She shifted to make some distance between them. She hated this feeling. She hated being this raw in front of him—in front of anyone, but especially him. Suddenly being this raw and this close was too much.

"Gaia . . ." Will wouldn't let her keep the gap between them. He slid across the wall and pressed his side up against hers again. "Don't cry, okay? Please don't cry. I'm sorry. I don't know what I'm supposed to say."

"You said that already."

"Well, what do you expect?" Will threw up his hands and puffed out a hopeless little laugh. "Okay. You're, uh . . . you're *clinically* fearless. You're a genetic anomaly."

"Yes. That's exactly right."

"Well, will you at least admit that it sounds a little insane?"

"Yes. It sounds a little insane. *Now get over it!*" She shoved her elbow into Will's side. Hard. It led to a much needed moment of silence.

Something changed in that silence. Gaia couldn't put her finger on it, but something changed. She finally realized that she'd done it. As torturous as it was, whether he ever believed her or not, she had made it all the way through her confession. She'd been completely honest about who she was . . . and the world hadn't come to an end.

And the next thing she knew, she felt his knuckles graze her cheek, wiping away the remaining tears. And then he clasped his fingers between hers and rested her hand on his knee. His hand had stopped shaking now.

Gaia was completely exhausted. She leaned back and dropped her head on Will's shoulder. She wasn't sure which was more tiring—defusing a bomb or confessing her secret.

"God," she breathed.

"What?" Will asked, leaning his head back against the wall.

"I feel completely different," she said. "I feel . . . lighter. I mean, I honestly feel lighter now that you know. I think secrets have an actual mass—a physical weight that literally weighs you down."

"I think you're right," Will agreed. "I do."

Gaia gazed up at Will's face. She couldn't quite tell what he was thinking at that moment. Then she settled back down on his shoulder. "I think extremely fat people must have a ton of secrets."

"I suppose it stands to reason."

"Will . . ." She peered up at his face again. She was close enough to smell the faint sweet remnants of sweat and Yardley soap on his neck.

"Yeah?"

"I honestly don't care either way," she said. "But I still want to know. Do you believe me?"

"You mean about your—?"

"Yes. Do you believe me?"

Will took a deep breath and let it out very slowly. He turned his face toward the ceiling and stared at the grating to an air shaft where they'd tried in vain to make their escape. "I didn't know you grew up without a dad," he said.

"He left when I was twelve. I didn't meet him again until I was seventeen."

"Where the hell was he hiding?"

"Long story," Gaia replied.

"Yeah, it always is." Will sighed. "You know . . . I lost my dad, too. He split before I was even born. Walked out on us while Mom was pregnant with me."

Gaia found her hand gripping Will's more tightly when she

heard this. For a moment she felt like she could see exactly what Will looked like as a child. He probably even had the buzz cut.

Of course, she thought. That explained all his macho alpha-male issues instantly. That's why he had so much to prove. He'd grown up without a father.

"Have you ever talked to him?" Gaia asked. "Have you ever met him?"

"Never," Will said. "To be totally honest . . . I don't think my mom much cared if I ever met him or not. I don't think she cared much about him in general. I think she's the reason he left. I mean, I wouldn't say that to her face. I probably wouldn't say it to anyone except my uncle Casper. But I said it to you." Will turned his face down to Gaia, grazing his stubbly cheek along hers until their eyes met.

"Why?" she asked.

"I don't know," he said. "I guess I wanted to test your theory. I wanted to see if I felt any lighter."

"And?"

"And . . ." Will's voice trailed off. He brought his fingers to her lips and traced along the curve of her mouth and then down her neck. Gaia felt another rush of heat rise up from the center of her chest, through the back of her neck, and into her cheeks. He ran his index finger along her collarbone, just beneath her shirt, and then pushed the wisps of her tangled hair back behind her ear. "I suppose I do feel much lighter," he said. "And yes. If you insist you're a genetic freak of nature . . . then I think I could believe you. I mean, I've yet to see anything about you that's even remotely normal."

Will tilted Gaia's chin up and their lips met—first for a soft kiss, but then for something much deeper. She wrapped her hands around the back of his neck and breathed him in, collapsing against him as they drifted down onto the basement floor. There was something new about this kiss. A new kind of urgency—a new kind of closeness. Like some thin layer of caution between them had been peeled away. Gaia had given all of herself over now. Not just the parts of herself she was willing to reveal, but the entire person, secrets and all. And she could feel it in the kiss. She could feel it in the way his strong hands spread out and gripped her entire back. He was holding all of her now.

There was no way of knowing what might have happened then and there on that basement floor. Will's fingertips had just found their way under her shirt to the small of her back when that ugly sound stopped them both cold.

First there was the high-pitched electrical snap that sent them both flying to their feet in less than a second. It sounded like a spark plug or a piston firing. Then there was the electronic whir. It started at a low-pitched rumble, but the ominous pitch was climbing awfully quickly. And it was coming from that utility closet.

There's no way, Gaia thought in that surreal little blip of a moment. *There's just no way. . . .*

Gaia and Will shared one painfully apprehensive glance, and then she leaped back into that cabinet. The numbers were the first thing she saw at its base. Flashing on the bomb's digital readout. It seemed so much like a clichéd bad dream, only it was actually happening.

The bomb—the very same bomb they had busted their asses to defuse—was somehow operational again. The goddamn thing had reactivated itself.

a big, ragged hole leading into more darkness

DISTANT EARTHQUAKE

You've got to be kidding, Will thought frantically. His mind, he realized, was not designed to cope with this. In the space of two hours he'd gone from mortal terror straight into one of the most tender, confessional conversations of his life—if not *the* most—and then into the sublime bliss of an embrace with Gaia—and then straight back into the adrenaline-soaked fear brought on by the sound of the bomb.

Gaia was already moving, propelling herself toward the cabinet where the supposedly dead mechanism had come back to life. She was already down on her hands and knees, her face up close to the digital display, peering at the bomb's components in the hopes of seeing something they'd missed.

And she's not afraid, Will noted. Some part of his mind was reeling from what Gaia had just told him. But that part of his mind wasn't in control right now. *Maybe Gaia is automatically rational and collected at a time like this,* he reminded himself, *but you have to force yourself. So, do it. Force yourself.*

"See anything?" he asked her, dropping onto the floor next to her. His lips were still tingling with Gaia's kiss, and he impatiently ignored the sensation and stared at the bomb. Its display was flashing. The numbers read 00:00.

What the hell does that mean? Will thought wildly. The bomb mechanism clicked and beeped again, and as he watched, the numbers changed to 00:10.

And this time there was no question what the 10 meant—it meant ten seconds. Because the clock was counting down.

"It's midnight!" Gaia said, looking at her watch. "It's El Dia!"

And this is where we both buy the farm, Will thought, watching the numbers dial down from 07 to 06 to 05, each change accompanied by a loud beep. In the face of certain death—in what he *knew* was his last moment on earth—he felt a strange, otherworldly calm. *At least I got to kiss her one last time,* he thought as he and Gaia reached for each other, pulling each other into a final tight hug. *And at least I can die with her in my arms. At this distance we'll be vaporized—we won't even be shadows on the wall.*

Will's eyes were clutched tightly closed, and Gaia's fragrant, silken hair was pressed against his face. He could feel the smooth muscles of her back beneath his hands. He was counting the beeps—just two to go. As last moments went, it honestly wasn't so bad.

Goodbye, Will thought on the final beep.

Nothing happened.

What the—?

That wasn't entirely true, Will thought. *Something* had happened. They had both felt a faint, deep tremor, like a distant earthquake. And Will's ears were popping; something had happened to the air pressure. But there had been no explosion.

Gaia was letting go of him and standing up. Will stumbled to his feet, glancing back at the bomb, whose mysterious display

208

had gone completely dead. Behind him Gaia was walking back out of the room.

"Will!"

He followed her.

There was something wrong with the air out here, Will realized, stepping back out into the courtroom basement's central area—the spot where they'd shared their secrets.

The smell, Will realized. *The air smells different.*

He could smell plaster dust—it was tickling his nose, threatening to make him sneeze—and behind that another smell. It was familiar, but he couldn't place it until he remembered a time at college when he'd joined a crowd watching firemen extinguish a burning dorm building. The aroma—burned air, charred paint, and blackened wood and stone—was the same as he was smelling now.

Will's eyes were itching and burning. Looking around, he could barely see tendrils of dust and smoke hanging in the air.

He and Gaia stared at each other, confused.

"The wires," Gaia said suddenly, snapping her fingers. "The wires from the bomb went through a hole in the wall, Will!"

"So?"

"So there *was* an explosion," Gaia said, grabbing his hand and pulling him down the corridor. *"Somewhere else."*

"What do you mean?" Will followed her, trying to keep from sneezing in the suddenly dusty air.

"You *heard* it, right?" Gaia said impatiently. "Exactly at midnight. A muffled explosion."

"Yeah, but—"

"Look."

Gaia was pointing at the floor. In the back corner of the basement, far away from the bright ceiling lights, Will saw a black metal plate sunk into the floor. It couldn't be larger than three feet square, covered in the familiar diamond pattern of the plates one saw on a city sidewalk and walked over without noticing.

Looking closer, Will saw that the plate was warped and bent—and that bands of dust were radiating from its edges along the floor.

"Down there," Gaia said, pointing. "Through that trapdoor."

"Yeah." Will realized that she was right. "There's got to be another basement—a sub-basement below this one."

"And that's where the bomb went off," Gaia finished, reaching down to pull the trapdoor's handle. She grunted with the effort it took. The door squeaked as it swung upward, releasing a cloud of dust and smoke. "Come on—we've got to see what happened."

Will came closer and peered down through the trapdoor. There was absolutely nothing to see except smoke and dust—Gaia had already sneezed once, and he was about to do the same thing. "But we don't know where that goes," Will argued weakly. There was no point—Gaia was already swinging her legs down into the hole. Will could see that she had found the iron rungs of a ladder leading into the darkness.

There's no point in arguing, Will thought. *I just have to follow her. But what's down there?*

As soon as Gaia's blond head had moved down far enough, nearly vanishing into the blackness below, Will swung his legs over and followed her. It was like disappearing down a well—if Will had been claustrophobic in the least, he would already be suffering.

"There's light down here," Gaia's voice echoed up from beneath him. He took her word for it, although he couldn't see anything. He was in a stone-walled tunnel leading straight down. The air was thicker with smoke, dust, and the smell of ash. His and Gaia's feet clanged on the metal rungs, echoing crazily in the darkness.

And then, after a moment, he could see.

Gaia had dropped to the floor below him. After a moment he did the same thing, and they stood side by side, looking around.

They were in a small chamber, the size of a one-car garage. The stone ceiling was very low. The air was filled with dust. The floor was flat cement, covered in dust, crumbling cement, and rough blocks of stone. The only light came from a weak overhead bulb that was protected by a steel cage. A yellow-and-black radiation symbol was on the wall.

Fallout shelter, Will realized. *This was the courthouse's fallout shelter. Probably nobody even knows it's here anymore.*

Ahead of them nearly one entire wall had been destroyed. It was now a big, ragged hole leading into more darkness. A cool, wet wind blew at them through the hole.

"The bomb," Gaia said, pointing upward to where Will could just make out the two wires that led from a hole in the ceiling. The wires extended a few feet and then stopped suddenly—their ends were burned and melted. "The explosives were down here, but the timer was up in that other room."

"Lucky for us."

"Right, but look," Gaia said, walking through the dust cloud, moving closer to the blasted hole in the wall. "They used, what do you call it, shaped charges—seismic charges. You remember from class? How you can use C-4 plastique to channel an explosion in the direction you want?"

"You're right," Will said. The explosives themselves had vaporized, but the pattern of the debris matched that in the pho-

211

tographs Agent Baxter had shown them of demolition-bombing sites. An expert had blown this hole leading—*where?*

Gaia and Will stepped closer to the hole, gingerly leaning on its ragged edges, which were still warm.

"Water," Gaia said. "There's water flowing down here."

And leaning his head out through the hole, Will realized she was right.

The hole went into a circular tunnel that stretched off into the far distance in each direction. There were weakly shining work lights at regular intervals. A wide, metal-grid catwalk with a railing led along the edge of the tunnel. And far below, in a stone channel deep along the tunnel's floor, water was flowing—a small underground river that moved through the tunnel.

The water pipes, Will realized. *That's what the map is about.* He remembered Gaia's description of the document she'd printed out, which apparently showed the Philadelphia water supply pipeline radiating out from the intersection of Decatur and Main.

On the opposite wall of the tunnel, on the stained, smooth concrete surface, someone had drawn an arrow in yellow chalk. Pointing down the tunnel to the left.

Gaia and Will looked at each other in the darkness. Will could only see the silhouette of her head through the dim, ghostly light from the work bulbs. Below them the rushing water roared past them, flowing like a bloodstream beneath the Philadelphia streets.

"Now what?" Will asked. His voice echoed crazily against the cement walls of the tunnel.

But he already knew what she was going to say.

A CHORUS OF WILLS

Gaia was crouched in the hole the bomb had blasted in the wall. Leaning out and peering straight down, she saw that there was a ten-foot drop at most—and at the bottom of that drop, she could see the steel grating of the catwalk that stretched off endlessly in both directions.

Simple to climb down, she realized, gauging the distance. *Not so simple to climb back up.*

The chalk arrow on the wall pointed left. It didn't look like something a Philadelphia engineer would have put there.

So who did? And why right there?

But the answers were obvious. In her mind, the Socorro plan was beginning to make sense. Someone had found the spot in the tunnel that butted up against the courthouse sub-basement—and had marked it.

As if somebody was supposed to come through the hole— once it had been blasted out—and follow the arrow.

Follow it where?

Gaia could only think of one way to find out.

"Gaia?" Will was asking. His voice echoed in the tunnel, repeating back over and over like a chorus of Wills. "I said, 'Now what?'"

"You *knew* there was a bomb," she remembered. She pulled herself out of the blasted wall opening, back into the comparatively quiet sub-basement room. "Because you did research on Rossiter, right?"

"He builds bombs," Will explained. "There's like three dozen incidents in the FBI database—Rossiter's blown up all kinds of things. Do you know him?"

"We've met," Gaia said, laughing humorlessly—a laugh Will had heard before. Gaia remembered the beard, the stinking breath, the weight on her back—where the bruise had almost completely faded—and the hands around her neck. "I'd love to meet him again."

"So what do we—?"

"Why do you keep asking that?" Gaia interrupted impatiently. "We follow the arrow. We go down the tunnel."

"And go where?" Will protested.

"We can't find that out," Gaia said doggedly, "without *going* there. It's *obvious*."

Will was already shaking his head. "There could be anything down there. Any number of people or guns. It's stupid to just go by ourselves—we've got to get help."

"What do you mean?" Gaia was in no mood for this conversation. Her legs and body were nearly twitching with the need to go through that hole into the cool, wet air and down that tunnel. "Get help from who?" She pointed up. "We *can't go back*, in case you forgot. The courthouse is completely locked. The tunnnel's the *only way*."

Will was still shaking his head. She saw that his face was suddenly illuminated by a piercing blue light—he had opened up his cell phone. "I'm not stupid, Gaia. I'm just saying let's get above-ground and call for backup. Call the FBI, call the Philadelphia police—damn it, no signal."

"Of *course* there's no signal," Gaia yelled. "Anyway, how are you going to call the bureau?"

"The *wall blew up*!" Will was yelling right back. "Don't you realize that the bomb changes everything? We're not *theorizing* anymore! You found the *real* terrorist plot—I think Malloy will listen to you now."

Gaia was listening, but she was also remembering Winston Marsh's words from the day before. *They want Sanders dead,* Marsh had told her. *You won't find an official order or anything on paper, but that's an absolute priority. She knows too much.*

And you too. Make no mistake, Gaia—the sole purpose you're serving right now is to lead the FBI to Catherine, if she's still alive. Once you've done that for them, then you'll be terminated, too.

"No," she told Will flatly. "No phone calls, no cops, no Malloy, no FBI." She moved closer to him, pointing over her shoulder at the jagged hole in the wall. "Catherine's down there. I'm sure of it. Tied up, bleeding, frightened. She took risks to contact me and asked me to save her." Gaia could hear her voice getting angrier, but she couldn't help it. She was tired of standing in this dust-filled underground room—she was aching to get moving. "Now I'm going to save her. You can come with me or not. But if you want to stop me, you're going to have to fight me."

"Gaia—" Will sighed theatrically. Gaia's eyes had adjusted to the darkness enough that she could begin to see his face. "Gaia, be reasonable. There's a procedure we're supposed to follow when—"

"*I don't want to hear it,*" Gaia shouted. "If *either* of us were following 'procedure,' we wouldn't be here. If you're scared, just *admit* it! Admit that this whole thing has you spooked and you want to run home to Daddy!"

"Gaia—" Will sounded hurt. "That's not fair."

He's right—it's not, Gaia thought sadly. *But I've got to do it—I've got to get his ego on the line so he'll come with me.*

"Then prove it," Gaia said, sitting down on the cold, jagged edge of the hole, swinging her feet over into the cool air of the tunnel. "Follow me."

"Gaia—"

"If you really are the man you act like," she told him, "you'll come with me."

"You know I can't," Will said miserably. "Someone's got to get backup—otherwise we're walking into a death trap."

"Fine," Gaia said. Tensing her body, she gripped the edge of the hole and dropped down. Her hands slid against the wet concrete and then her feet slammed into the steel catwalk. "See you later, Will."

"Gaia, wait!"

Gaia looked up. The sound of rushing water was louder now, echoing all around her like the roar inside a seashell. She could see Will's head silhouetted above her. The hole was ten feet up the smooth, wet curve of the tunnel's cement wall.

No way back up.

"Are you coming?" Gaia shouted. There was no answer. She couldn't see Will's face or hear anything over the loud roar of the water. She turned to the left—the direction in which the arrow pointed—and started down the tunnel.

216

A NATURAL CAUTION

This is the end of the journey, Gaia thought.

She wasn't sure how she knew, but she was certain of it. The road chosen in Quantico, when she drove off into the night—the road that led to Baltimore and Collingswood and finally to Philadelphia, the City of Brotherly Love—ended in this tunnel.

Gaia remembered the dream she'd had in which she was following a river. It was funny that she'd ended up here, deep underground, moving along this waterway. If Gaia had believed in premonitions, she would have been spooked.

After she had walked for five minutes the hole in the wall disappeared in the distance behind her. The tunnel seemed to continue forever, its work lights diminishing into the endless distance like highway reflectors. Her footsteps clanged and rattled against the steel catwalk, echoing and reverberating in an endless dull symphony of metallic percussion. The water shone like glass five feet below the catwalk, roaring past her at what seemed like high speed. From the temperature of the cool, damp air Gaia guessed that the current was cold and strong—and fairly deep, too. She didn't like to think what would happen to her if she fell in there. There was nothing to grab on to at the water's edges except smooth concrete; a person who fell into that raging river would probably we washed miles downstream after they'd drowned.

Gaia had no idea where she was in terms of Philadelphia geography. *That's what that map was for,* she thought, realizing that she'd left it behind in the courthouse's basement. *If I'd realized, I could have asked Will to toss it down to me.*

Will. Gaia frowned in the darkness as she thought about him.

It would be so much simpler if he were right here with her, following the underground river by her side. They could confer, make decisions—and she wouldn't be alone, as alone as she'd been since this whole surreal journey began.

But he's not like that, she told herself doggedly. *It's not in his nature. A boy like that cannot be made to throw away everything he believes in just because you tell him to.*

But Gaia knew she was being unfair.

Running her hand along the steel balustrade that flanked the catwalk—and bringing her hand away wet—Gaia realized that Will had actually done exactly that.

Didn't he steal all that information just because I asked him to? Didn't he sneak into that chat room with me even though it could have cost him everything? Maybe even his life?

Gaia's eyes narrowed in the darkness as she thought about it. *And didn't he run away from the base just to meet me here? Because he thought I was in danger?*

Will had come through for her—over and over. She forced herself to admit it. All he had done at the end was exercise a natural, sensible caution.

What if he's right? Gaia thought, looking ahead down the tunnel. *What if I can't handle whatever's down there?*

Should I go back?

But there was no way to go back. Her watch told her that she'd already been walking for nine minutes—she had no idea how far that meant she'd traveled. If she retraced her steps, she'd just be back at that hole with no way to climb up. She could shout for Will, but how could she be sure he would hear her? If he was back up the ladder, in the courthouse basement where they'd kissed, then he *definitely* wouldn't hear her. A *bomb had gone off* and they'd barely picked up the noise—there was no way the sound of a yelling girl would penetrate through all that stonework.

Up ahead, Gaia saw, the tunnel was ending.

Getting closer, peering through the dim light, she realized that it wasn't *ending*, exactly, but *forking*. The tunnel ran into another tunnel that moved off left and right. Gaia noticed that the catwalk formed a bridge up ahead, allowing her to go in either direction.

So what do I do?

Gaia wasn't interested in getting lost in the Philadelphia water system. Images flashed through her head of herself spending the rest of her life down here, wandering like a wretched shipwreck victim, her pale dead body eventually washing out to sea.

Getting closer to the junction, Gaia suddenly saw another chalk arrow on the opposite wall. Pointing right.

Someone's supposed to follow the path, she realized again. She was absolutely sure of it. *Through the new hole and down the pipes to—where?*

But there was no way to find out except to keep going.

Gaia thought about the journey she'd taken—about Rossiter, and Marsh, and the basements and motel rooms and rest areas, about the decayed city parks and pumping stations, all leading to this tunnel. Thinking through the steps she'd taken, she was convinced she hadn't made any mistakes—that every move had been logical.

I'm coming, Catherine, she thought again, following the arrow across the metal bridge and moving farther down the tunnel. *I'm nearly there now. I can feel it.*

Will

This is ridiculous.

I *know* I'm right. Every instinct, every bit of knowledge and experience *tells* me I'm right. But I feel wrong.

The argument I gave Gaia makes perfect sense. Catherine told me how Gaia won the game back when we first started—how she laid out the evidence for Agent Bishop, point by point, justifying each leap of logic, and, once she'd finished, it didn't matter anymore what rules she'd broken. In the end, what's important to the bureau is solving and preventing crimes, not upholding rules and regulations.

Right?

I mean, in Hogan's Alley, Gaia realized that the empty medicine cabinet pointed at the doctor as the perp—and she was right. Now she's traced a series of clues to a terrorist bomb—and she's right again. The FBI will care about that more than they'll care about that memo or all their misunderstandings. I'm sure of it.

But that was a game—it wasn't real. And like I just realized, when it's real, everything's different. It's one thing to be brave and smart and in command when you're just racking up points and trying to win. Hell, I've been doing that all my life. But when it's life or death for real—when you're staring at an *actual* bomb that will *actually* detonate, not a classroom model—suddenly everything's different.

And she saw me afraid.

That's the worst part. Pacing this damn courthouse basement, holding my cell phone, trying to decide who to call first, I keep looking at the room with the detonator and the spot on the floor where we sat and talked—and kissed. Okay, maybe somebody without fear doesn't have the right to give anyone grief about their moment of weakness. But that doesn't make it hurt any less.

She could be walking into a trap. She could be in incredible danger.

Could be? Of *course* she's in incredible danger. I can't get that image out of my head—the last view I had of her, a dark shadow moving away on that catwalk over that mysterious underground river. On her way into the heart of the mystery. And me, leaning over that jagged hole, watching her go. And doing nothing.

This is a waste of time. I'm letting a girl influence my thinking. Just like when I first got that message from her about the chat room—I effectively stopped thinking rationally and just did whatever she told me to do. Like a sap—like a man with no will of his own.

I shouldn't be pacing and debating with myself. I should flip this phone open and dial 911 and start talking. I could have the cops here in ten minutes, and then I could show them my badge and explain the situation and ask to be taken to the FBI's regional field office and then—assuming they believe my story and don't waste time with too many questions—the cops and the bureau will be down in that tunnel with as much artillery as is necessary. And with bomb experts and terrorism experts and full military backup—

—and I let a girl walk into danger.

I have to stop thinking about it and do something. I won't think about Gaia anymore. She made her own decision—I'm tired of covering for her anyway. It's time to do the right thing. I don't care what the consequences are; I've broken enough rules for one day. I'm calling for backup right now.

NOTHING BUT BLACKNESS ABOVE

Without her wristwatch Gaia knew she would have completely lost track of time. There was no frame of reference—just concrete, steel, and water running off in all directions. Gaia figured that it would be very easy to go insane down here if you somehow got lost and couldn't find your way out. In these tunnels there was no day and night, no north and south, no up and down. Just tunnels, connecting and reconnecting, with the same feeble, regularly placed bulbs and the same dull roar of water until you wanted to scream.

Since dropping through the hole in the wall and leaving Will behind, Gaia had made four turns, each marked with a chalk arrow. She was forcing herself to memorize the path she was taking, but the geography was very difficult since everything was the same—she kept losing track of how many junctures she'd passed through or turns she'd taken. Gaia knew that retracing your steps backward could be very difficult—anyone trying to follow trip directions in the other direction quickly found that out. And down here there seemed to be no way out but forward and back—only once had she seen a ladder going up, and peering through the hole she saw it led up through nothing but blackness above. *Probably leads to a manhole,* she thought, picturing herself trying to unseat a heavy iron disk from beneath, with traffic moving overhead as she did it. No, thanks. That was an easy way to get—

Gaia suddenly stopped walking.

The light had changed.

Squinting ahead, she was sure—the tunnel was getting brighter. There was another light source ahead, a bright one, around a curve in the tunnel's sloping wall.

Gaia moved forward hesitantly. Her eyes had gotten so used to the darkness that the yellow light ahead seemed blindingly bright, and she squinted painfully until her eyes adjusted.

There was a hole in the wall up ahead.

It was easy to see that it wasn't a part of the tunnel's original construction. But unlike the hole beneath the courthouse, which had been instantly created in the past hour by means of expertly placed explosives, *this* hole was much more regular. It looked like it had been neatly sawed out of the stone.

Bright light was shining out through the hole—and by concentrating, Gaia could hear murmuring voices.

On the opposite wall of the tunnel, illuminated by the brilliant yellow glare from the hole, a final chalk sign had been drawn. Not another arrow—a big *X*.

X marks the spot, Gaia thought dazedly. *I'm here.*

A metal ladder had been attached to the catwalk she was on, leading up to the hole in the wall.

Gaia unsnapped her holster and carefully drew out her Walther. She flicked the safety back. Her hands were slippery, and she dried them impatiently on her pants legs. It wouldn't be very smart to drop her gun in the water.

With the gun ready, Gaia took a deep breath and then walked to the ladder as quietly as she could. Gripping the gun tightly, she climbed up step by step, taking care to keep her head below the edge of the hole.

What am I going to see? What's in there?

Gaia had no idea.

She could hear voices, but the roar of the water was still maddeningly loud, and she couldn't make out how many people were speaking or what they were saying any more than she'd been able to hear Will an hour before, however many miles behind her they had said goodbye.

Without sound cues Gaia had no idea how to move through the hole. It was conceivable that she'd be shot dead the moment she stuck her face up into view. There might be some kind of acrobatic way to get through the hole, land without stumbling, and point her gun at any assailants who were there—but it would be very difficult, if not impossible. There was just no way to predict what the area in there was like. The floor could be right there or it could be ten feet down, with another ladder on the other side of the punctured wall. From her vantage point all she could see was a smooth, dimly lit cement ceiling.

Will was right, Gaia admitted to herself. *I can't do this by myself.*

But it was a little late to change her mind.

Slowly raising her head, Gaia looked through the hole.

IMPRESSIVELY FAST REACTION TIMES

She was looking into a brightly lit room with a low ceiling lined with industrial fluorescent lights. The room was wide and bare, about the size of a small warehouse. The walls were featureless white cinder block. The floor was clean, dry cement.

The room was full of supplies. Gaia could see stacks of crates and rows and rows of weapons—artillery, rifles, handguns, cases of grenades, bundles of dynamite. Several of the crates had warning labels that read DANGER: EXPLOSIVES and C-4.

Not a place where you want to be firing a handgun, she realized uneasily.

Five men were standing in a clump to one side. They all wore black T-shirts and baggy camouflage pants, and their hair had been shaved down to buzz cuts. All of them were well built and carried themselves like they had received physical training. Poised at the top of the ladder, Gaia kept her head low, peering over the cement edge of the hole in the wall, watching the men as they intently unpacked a crate, removing and assembling what looked like the mounting tripod for an large-bore artillery gun.

I can take them, Gaia thought, looking at the men. They didn't seem to have noticed her—but then, of course, they could be faking—just pretending not to see her so that they could capture her by surprise once she moved toward them. There was no way to tell.

The men were all armed, she saw, with what looked like Glock handguns in belt holsters, but the same restriction applied to them as to her—a stray bullet in that room could mean an explosion big enough to vaporize a city block.

So, no shooting—hand to hand. One against five.

The problem was that she couldn't see the whole room. It was too big, and there were too many crates and boxes in the way. Any number of other men could be hidden from view, ready to pounce.

So be it, Gaia told herself. *What are you going to do—wait for everyone to leave?*

As quietly as she could, Gaia reholstered her gun, carefully flipping the safety back on. With the holster snapped shut she took a moment to calculate her move, setting her hands in the right places on the top rung of the ladder, and then, when she was good and ready, surged upward and jumped through the hole.

She landed neatly on floor, her shoes squeaking slightly as they hit the cement. The five men turned toward her instantly and displayed impressively fast reaction times. They didn't stop and ask themselves why this blond girl had suddenly jumped into the room—they just dropped into fighting stances.

"Hai," Gaia hollered from her center, leaping toward them. She jumped forward, aiming a kick at the head of the man nearest to her. With incredible speed the man whipped his head back, and Gaia twirled in the air, fighting not to lose her balance before landing heavily on her other foot. The men to either side of the first man moved toward her—

And suddenly Gaia felt cold metal pressing against her head and heard the unmistakable sound of an automatic pistol being cocked.

"Stop right there," ordered a voice she instantly recognized. "Move one muscle and you're dead."

Someone else in the room, she thought furiously. *I knew it, I knew it—*

"Hands behind your back," the deep, resonant, almost theatrical voice continued. "I'm watching your feet, Gaia—if you look like you're even *thinking* about performing a scorpion kick, I'll hit you with a nerve-block punch and you'll be immobilized for hours."

The gun remained pressed against the back of her head as a hand reached around to pull her own Walther roughly out of its holster. The five men in front of her stared dully into her eyes, their arms poised in ready position. Gaia stared right back. She could feel the gun pressed to her head suddenly pull away.

"Okay, I'm out of your kill zone," the voice behind her said, having moved farther back. "But I've still got you covered—and I *will* shoot. Turn around slowly with both hands showing."

226

Gaia had placed the voice. She knew what she was going to see as she slowly turned around. But even expecting it, she still found the view a sickening surprise.

"Very good," Winston Marsh said, leveling his Beretta between her eyes. He was exactly far enough away that she couldn't reach him with a flying kick. He was dressed like the others, in a tight black T-shirt and camouflage pants. As she watched, she could hear the men behind her circling around back into view. "Hello, Gaia—and welcome. Do you know where you are?"

"I think so," Gaia said. "This is Socorro headquarters, isn't it?"

"Exactly." Marsh smiled, his eyes crinkling pleasantly. He looked exactly the same as he had in the Clavarak Motel room the last time she'd seen him, but the change of clothes—and the whole situation—made a tremendous difference. "You realize there's nothing to be gained by attacking, right? Even if you subdue everyone in this room, which is extremely unlikely, you'll never make it through those doors and out of here alive. Anyway, we've got a lot to talk about."

Gaia couldn't even muster words. She knew she should be shocked and bewildered. After all, he was standing there before her—alive and well. Smiling, even. The man who was supposed to have been gray-opped into oblivion by the FBI. The man who'd somehow reminded her of her father.

But there was no more room in Gaia's psyche for shock or bewilderment or horror. She'd exhausted every last bit of it in the first seventeen years of her life. No, this was a scenario with which she'd become far too depressingly familiar: betrayal.

Apparently she was no less gullible now than she had been at the age of six. That big fight with Rossiter obviously had been staged, and she'd been duped by the charade. It wasn't her father she'd sensed in Winston Marsh. It was her uncle.

It was too pathetic even to admit to herself. But it seemed, no matter how much training she'd gotten at Quantico, there were still some things she would simply never learn.

"You're upset," Marsh said. He hadn't made the slightest move toward lowering the gun. "I don't blame you—it's reasonable. I want you to understand, I took no joy in deceiving you. But if you'd known about my involvement in Socorro, there's simply no way we could have brought you here. And we need you here, Gaia. You have no idea how badly we need you here with us. You'll begin to understand." Marsh turned to the others. "Gentlemen, would you leave us alone, please?"

The five men didn't ask any questions—they just turned and moved toward one of the metal doors at the far side of the room. Gaia kept her eyes fixed on Marsh while in her mind assessing the physical situation. She couldn't charge the gun, as she had that morning with the FBI agents. They were afraid to shoot her; she had no way of knowing if Marsh harbored the same qualms. And if she was dead, then nobody could save Catherine.

Gaia briefly considered trying to jump back *out,* through the hole. It would mean a spectacular leap, mostly from memory, since a glance backward would give her away. She'd have to chance not getting shot as she jumped and then clearing the cement edges and somehow managing to miss the catwalk and land in the water, dodging the bullets from above while fighting the current—

No. An Olympic diver couldn't do it. Not even without the bullets. Not a chance in hell.

"Forget about jumping backward," Marsh said in his maddeningly calm voice. "Good, I can see you've already given up on *that* madness. Obviously I didn't tell you the full story about Socorro, but I'm sure you can see the ways in which my hands were tied. It's so easy to misinterpret what we do or what a visionary like Ramon is capable of."

Visionary? Gaia thought. *What's he talking about?*

"And the bureau," Marsh went on. "The fabled FBI. By now you've checked my background; you know I was telling you the truth. Do you realize that their entire purpose is to keep things from changing? To maintain the imperialist status quo no matter what the cost? If people around the world heard our message in an unbiased way, if they could really listen to Ramon Nino and hear what he's trying to tell them, the freedom he's offering to them, they would rise up together and follow him. Which is why your FBI is working so hard to make sure that never happens. I may have bent the truth slightly, but make no mistake: the FBI *is* interested in locking people up and in silencing them, not in liberating them."

"I don't want to listen to this anymore," Gaia said quietly. "I want you to put the gun down so I can beat the crap out of you."

Marsh smiled. "You're really impressive, Gaia," he told her fondly. "So sure of yourself; so iron willed. She was absolutely right about you—and I'm so glad I listened to her."

She—?

"Who's 'she'?" Gaia said impatiently. "And believe me, Marsh, I've heard just about enough of your mysterious—"

Gaia stopped talking because the metal door had swung open again and a third person had entered the room. Gaia's gaze was finally torn away from Marsh and from the gun barrel pointed at her face.

There was Catherine Sanders.

She was dressed like the others, in a black T-shirt and camouflage pants. The military getup didn't make her look any less pretty, Gaia noticed, although the brush cut she'd recently gotten radically altered the look of her jet black hair. She still wore the same round glasses—they glinted and flashed in the fluorescent lights as she stepped forward into the room.

Cath— Gaia tried to speak, but her throat was utterly dry. She coughed and tried again. "Catherine—?"

"Gaia," Catherine said warmly. "God, it's good to finally see you."

And she looks like she means it, Gaia thought. She was so stunned that she had to willfully force herself not to collapse to the floor. *She's not being held captive.*

She's one of them. She's always been one of them.

"*Catherine?*" Gaia said again. She seemed to be practically speechless.

But there were more surprises to come.

"Would you leave us alone, Dad?" Catherine said to Marsh. "My ex-roommate and I have a lot to talk about."

"Sure, kid," Marsh said, backing toward Catherine, covering Gaia with the gun as he moved. Gaia watched in utter disbelief as Marsh put his arm around Catherine's shoulders, kissing her on the forehead as he handed over the gun. Catherine hugged Marsh back before fixing the gun on Gaia. There had been a moment when they were both distracted, and in that moment Gaia might have attacked—but she was simply too stunned.

"I'll see you soon, Gaia," Marsh said over his shoulder as he moved toward the door. "We've got a lot of planning to do."

Planning? What did that mean?

The door slammed shut, and Catherine and Gaia were alone in the room.

the truth with a gun
pointed at your head

A TERRORIST TRAITOR

The long silence was sickening. Gaia could only stand there and stare at Catherine's face—her glasses, her cream-colored skin, the intelligence in her eyes. This was absolutely her friend and roommate, the woman she'd literally thrown everything away in order to save—yet at exactly the same time she was a complete stranger now, someone Gaia didn't know at all. Someone who was pointing a gun in her face.

A word began to buzz through Gaia's head, repeating itself endlessly like one of those unbearable car alarms on a New York City street. It had become her least favorite word in the English language—one she'd sworn to avoid for the remainder of her adult life, even if it meant living in relative seclusion.

Betrayed. That was the word. *Betrayed again.* It kept growing louder in her mind like a permanent echo. The painful sensation of burning acid erupted in her chest and began climbing up her throat. . . .

How many times had she been betrayed like this? *Never mind,* she told herself. *Never mind all the "woe is me" crap.*

Never mind the laundry list of trusted friends and family who'd stabbed her in the back over the years. Never mind how sad it was to consider all the loyalty she'd wasted on her "part-ner" Catherine. This moment wasn't about her sadness or her confusion. It was about rage, pure and simple.

"Do you have any idea . . . ?" Gaia shook her head slowly. Her fingers curled into fists, the nails digging into her palms. "Do you have any idea what I went through to find you?"

"Look, Gaia, please," Catherine said cautiously. "Just try to stay cool, all right? I know this is a lot to process, but we can—"

"*Process?*" Gaia spat. "A lot to *process?*"

"Gaia, everything's going to be—"

"No, I don't think you *heard* me," Gaia barked. She took a step closer, closing the distance between her and Catherine's gun. "I asked you a question. I asked you if you had *any idea* what I went through for you. Wait, what am I saying? Not for *you*. What I went through for my *partner*, Catherine—my partner and my *friend*, Catherine Sanders. I don't know who the hell *you* are."

"Yes, you do," Catherine insisted. "I'm still your friend, Gaia. Your *best* friend *and* your partner. I need you now more than ever. We all do."

"Oh, you *all* do," Gaia scoffed. "As in you and—and your *father* out there and the rest of your terrorist organization?"

"No." Catherine shook her head vehemently. "No, we are *not* a terrorist organization. That's just what the bureau wants you to believe. We are not terrorists, Gaia, we're *activists*. All we're try-ing to do is send a message to this country and free people from modern-day slavery—corporate slavery. And we can't free them without our leader. We can't free them until we free Nino. I know you can see that. I know you—I know if you look in your heart, you'll see the truth."

"The *truth*?" Gaia narrowed her eyes with disgust. "You're talking to me about the truth? I guess that's what terrorists do, isn't it? They tell you about the 'truth' with a gun pointed at your head."

"I am *not* a terrorist!" Catherine shouted. "You think I want to point a gun at you? I don't. Of course I don't."

"Then put the goddamn gun down!" Gaia shot back. She lurched slightly forward, forcing Catherine to thrust the gun out more securely—tightening her grip on the handle with both hands.

"I will," Catherine promised. "I will put the gun down, I swear. I just need to be sure I can trust you."

"Trust?" Gaia bellowed. "Now you want to talk about trust? I trusted *you*. I promised myself I'd never make that mistake again, but I *did*. Like a true idiot, I put my faith in you, and this is what I have to show for it!"

"Gaia, you just don't understand, that's all," Catherine insisted. "You're just not seeing the big picture yet. You *can* trust me. I *am* your friend. I've always been your friend. You're the reason I came to Quantico, for God's sake. Socorro put me there to meet you—to find out if it was true about the 'fearless' girl from New York. Once I knew you were just as talented and smart as all the reports said, I knew I had to recruit you for this mission. I knew you'd be able to see the importance of what we're doing here."

Gaia had stopped listening when she heard the key word:

Recruit.

Jesus. Of course . . .

She'd been so busy feeling furious and betrayed she hadn't even bothered to put the pieces together. But now she finally understood. The memo . . . the warning about Socorro recruiting an FBI trainee for D-day . . . Catherine wasn't the recruit—*Gaia* was. She always had been, since her very first day at Quantico.

But still, it was Catherine who was missing the big picture here. Because Gaia wasn't about to be recruited for any kind of Socorro D-day. All she was thinking about was how to get that gun from Catherine's hands and get her ass under arrest and back to Quantico.

"Gaia, you've got to help us break Nino out of that courthouse," Catherine declared. "This is the day. His parole hearing. You need to help us create chaos in that courthouse and then lead him back here through those water tunnels. . . ."

The longer Catherine babbled about her ludicrous agenda, the more Gaia noticed that she didn't have quite the same discipline with the handgun as her father did. She wasn't pointing the gun at Gaia quite as relentlessly—in fact, she seemed not to be paying much attention to the gun at all. Gaia inched a step closer, feeling the adrenaline start to rush through her veins at full speed.

"With Ramon free and with Dad and *you* joining us, Gaia, we'll be unstoppable," Catherine continued. "Can't you see that?"

"No," Gaia snapped. "No, I don't see that happening."

"Don't say that, Gaia," Catherine warned. "Please say you'll do this. I told him I could get you to do this voluntarily, but if I can't, they *will* use force, and I don't want see that happen. I *need* you to see it now, okay? You're *perfect* for us. You're brilliant, a devastating fighter, a born leader—and you're just like me—you hate rules and authority. You've got to follow the beat of a different drummer. Believe me, when you hear what Nino has to say, it will all make sense to you—rebellion's in your blood, Gaia. And that's why you'll be a great freedom fighter—a natural Socorro soldier."

The door was opening, and through its aperture Gaia could hear a crowd of people moving to enter the room. Catherine heard it, too—her attention was pulled marginally away from Gaia, and her father's Beretta slipped farther downward.

This was Gaia's moment and she knew it. Not just the moment to escape this nightmare—but the moment to exact some revenge for everything Catherine had put her through.

In the blink of an eye Gaia leaped forward and dove into the air, aiming a swift downward kick at Catherine's gun hand. Catherine was fast, raising the gun and firing, but not fast enough—the bullet blasted downward, ricocheting loudly off the concrete floor and smacking into the concrete wall back out in the tunnel. The gun clattered to the cement floor and slid far away to one side. Gaia landed, spun, and aimed another kick, but Catherine had suddenly stabbed out her own fist for a block, knocking Gaia off balance.

Catherine was a *much* better fighter than Gaia had ever realized. She had obviously been hiding her strength and her skill since the day they'd met—the day that, Gaia remembered, Catherine had fallen off the obstacle course. She was extremely strong, and her moves were as precise and devastating as one would expect from a young terrorist who'd been receiving combat training from her father her entire life.

Catherine slammed a karate chop into Gaia's shoulder, and the searing pain distracted her while Catherine spun around and aimed a kick at Gaia's solar plexus. Gaia lost her breath completely, slamming to the floor, seeing red. Ignoring the pain in her bruised abdomen, she reached out from her position on the floor and grabbed Catherine's foot, twisting it to bring her down. Behind Catherine, Gaia could see that Marsh and several Socorro henchmen had re-entered the room—James Rossiter was among them. Once Catherine hit the floor, the five henchmen from before came forward and Gaia, her lungs burning, gasping for breath, barely had time to get to her feet before the men closed in and she was fighting all *six* of them.

And right then Gaia finally let all of her anger take over completely. Her entire hellish journey flashed through her head in an instant—the midnight drive, the horror of Catherine's hairs on Rossiter's basement cot, the agents chasing her down, the day spent on the run with Marsh, poor Will potentially throwing away his entire career for her and for this mad chase . . . and all of it for nothing. For a terrorist traitor who obviously had a screw loose.

Gaia let go of the last vestiges of her restraint and went into a near transcendent state of combat. She unleashed a series of moves so quick that even she wasn't altogether conscious of her combinations. Offense melded together with defense as she tore into Catherine and the five men. The moves were like a complex chess game at high speed, and she was seconds from prevailing, beating them all, when suddenly—

Click.

Gaia wasn't sure how she *knew*—how she recognized the sound instantly and what it meant and how it sent a chill through her body so complete that she stopped moving, her leg poised to kick one of the henchmen in the side of the head, and turned toward the quiet, deadly sound she'd heard.

James Rossiter stood with a gun held to the head of a figure kneeling on the floor.

It was Will.

He was poised there, halfway out from the crate he'd been hiding behind, and Rossiter was right behind him, his hand clamped on Will's shoulder, holding a .45 Magnum pistol against Will's head.

"Stop," Rossiter ordered Gaia.

Will—!

Will locked his eyes with Gaia's, telegraphing all his frustration, regret, and remorse in one ironic crooked smile. "Turns out I followed you anyway," he said. "I couldn't leave a lady in distress. Guess it didn't work out so well."

"It didn't," Rossiter agreed, the lights glinting off his yellowing teeth as he stared at her. Gaia could see the gun's cylinder moving as Rossiter began to squeeze the trigger. "Get your hands behind your back, Gaia. I got no problem blowing a hole in your boyfriend's head."

"Don't listen to him, Gaia," Will said easily. "We can take them."

No, Gaia thought. *No, no, no.*

Not again.

If there was one lesson she'd learned, and learned harder than anything else she'd learned in her whole, strange, sad, violent life, it was this one.

I won't do it, she told Will with her eyes. She couldn't tell—maybe he understood. *I can't take the chance of losing you, and I won't let you take it either. I can't let you try to be a hero here. That's how I lost Jake, and it nearly killed me.*

Slowly, making no sudden moves, Gaia lowered her suspended leg and placed her hands behind her back.

Giving up.

"What—? Gaia, *no!*"

Will sounded furious as Rossiter roughly pulled him to his feet. Gaia felt the Socorro henchmen roughly pushing her forward and pulling her hands behind her back. She let them do it. She had nearly gone limp.

"Good," Catherine said, looking Gaia in the eye from up close. "Smart move, Gaia. Very smart. I knew you had it in you."

Gaia stared right back at Catherine. She didn't say a word.

"All right—let's get these two locked up," Marsh ordered the henchmen, clapping. "Once you've done that, go back to preparing the weapons."

The henchmen started leading Will and Gaia out of the room toward the metal doors.

"Back to work, people," Catherine called out. "Today we finally see some justice. Today Nino goes free. El Dia has begun. And they don't see it coming."

Here's a sneak peek at the latest book in the thrilling new series

FEARLESS® FBI

NAKED EYE

unquestionably loyal

"Our time is at hand! The liberation is near!"

Winston Marsh was standing at the front of the makeshift bunker three stories below the streets of Philadelphia, speaking to his assembled players. His daughter, Catherine Sanders, stood to his left, her eyes lit up with pride as she gazed at him. Before him stood six henchmen of various shapes, sizes, and ages, all of them well trained in weapons and hand-to-hand combat. And all of them unquestionably loyal.

"Comrades, all of your faith and hard work is about to pay off," Marsh continued. "In a couple of hours our leader will be with us once again!"

A cheer rose up among the group, and Catherine clapped loudly. In all the weeks Gaia had roomed with Catherine at the FBI training facility at Quantico, she had never seen her look quite so happy—or quite so brainwashed.

"I still can't believe Catherine is part of this," Will mumbled.

They sat slouched against a rough-hewn wall in the back of the room, watching Marsh's pep rally. Both were stripped of their guns and their hands were bound tightly behind their backs.

"It's surreal," Will went on. "She and her dad are *terrorists*, Gaia. If she infiltrated the academy, who knows how many more of them there are."

"Who knows if we'll be alive to find out," Gaia said sternly. It was awful, but it was true. Believing her roommate was in danger, Gaia had actually left base without permission, trekked across three states, tangled with FBI agents on her tail, and broke other various laws and regulations in an effort to find her friend. And she found her. Here. With her psycho daddy and his pet gunmen. Ready to carry out an insurgent kidnapping plot they'd been planning for months, and they'd been expecting her to help them out somehow.

And the worst of it was, they might kill her and Will if she refused to cooperate.

"We've got to get out of here," Will whispered.

Gaia could hear the half-cloaked fear in Will's voice. It enraged her that she'd dragged him into this. She'd deserved to fall into their trap, but not him. He'd only been trying to help her. She closed her eyes and remembered the look of stunned terror on his face as he shuffled into the room with Marsh's gun pointed at his head. An all-too-familiar clod of grief welled up in her throat.

It was like Jake all over again. Her worst nightmare, part two.

Jake . . . It was hard to picture her former boyfriend the way he'd usually been: smiling and cocksure. Instead she could only picture him the way he'd looked in his last few minutes of life: gasping and blood soaked, staring at her urgently, his broad chest torn to shreds.

Not again, she thought. It wasn't so much a lamentation as it was an order—to herself. *It will* not *happen again!* She was being given another chance to save someone she cared deeply about. And this time she wouldn't blow it.

"Can you get your hands free?" Will asked.

"No." She'd been trying for the last hour, but it was no use. Marsh's henchmen must have roped cattle in their previous lives.

Her main concern now was to catch them off guard and overpower them.

"What are you guys doing over there?"

It was James Rossiter, Marsh's favorite go-to guy—and Gaia's least favorite of the thugs. She noticed he'd tried desperately to squeeze his paunch into the standard-issue fatigues the others had on, but they looked more like a mottled potato sack on his stocky frame. Yet even though Rossiter wasn't as lean and athletic as the others, he was still a force to be reckoned with. Her throat probably still had marks from their brutal tangle two days earlier.

Rossiter lumbered over and glared down at Gaia. "You know, I'd get some real pleasure from gagging you."

"Is there a problem?" Marsh called from the front of the room. He seemed slightly perturbed that his speech had been interrupted.

"These two were whispering," Rossiter explained.

Marsh smiled slickly. He lifted his gun and stalked over to Gaia and Will. Catherine followed him. "It's okay, Jimmy, I'll handle it. You and your team need to get ready. You leave for the courthouse in a few minutes."

Rossiter grunted his assent and after a final glower at Gaia walked off to join three other thugs in the corner.

"Don't make me use this, Miss Moore," Marsh said, waggling his hand with the gun in it so that the tip of the barrel made a spiraling motion over Will's skull.

"Dad, why are you threatening him?" Catherine asked, staring at Will with conflicted eyes. "There's nothing he can do to stand in our way."

"I disagree," Marsh replied. He paced back and forth in front of Will, looking him over intensely as if he was the target of a stakeout. "He made it this far, didn't he? We may have to neutralize him if we want to ensure our mission gets carried out without further interruption."

"But if keep him alive, we can coerce Gaia into doing what we instruct," Catherine replied.

Suddenly the girl did something really weird, something that Gaia thought she'd imagined. Catherine winked at her, as if to indicate that she was just trying to keep her father from blowing away an innocent person who was only out to save a friend—or, Gaia hoped, more than a friend.

Catherine and I are more alike than I thought, she said to herself, a twinge of empathy running through her. She and Catherine were merely victims of their own upbringing. Instead of recruiting the perfect soldier, Marsh had tried to make one within his own genetic pool. She could only imagine what Catherine's childhood must have been like. The lessons and drills. The repeated methods of indoctrination. To Gaia it represented what her own life would have been like had she been raised by her father. Then again, was she in any less danger now that her life was in her own hands?

"Catherine, keep an eye on these two while I go over the details one last time with Jimmy," Marsh instructed. "When I come back, I'll have found something to shut them up with."

"Yes, sir," Catherine said.

Marsh gave his daughter a peck on the cheek and then stalked across the room to Rossiter.

"I don't know if I should thank you or end you," Gaia grumbled.

"I don't think you're in a position to do much of anything." Catherine pointed her pistol directly at Gaia's nose. Gaia could feel Will stiffen beside her.

"But you are," Gaia went on, ignoring the gun. She needed to appeal to Catherine's good side. To try and make her see the irrationality of her actions. "It's not your fault your dad is a psycho terrorist. You might think you have no choice in the matter, but you do."

"My dad is a great man."

Gaia rolled her eyes. "Then why is he out to hurt people?"

"He's out to *help* people," Catherine said solemnly, and sat down on an overturned crate. "Besides, you and I both know that there are always casualties in war."

"*War?* What war? Just because he declares one doesn't mean it exists. There are other ways he could get his point across. Peaceful, legal ways."

Gaia noticed that her words were flustering Catherine, but her ex-roommate still had a tight grip on the gun. "You don't think we've tried that? We have! And it never works. Those corporate monsters hide behind red tape and politics to get whatever they want. It doesn't do any good to go through proper channels when all those channels are owned or controlled by the people you're fighting."

"That may be, but why become as bad as them? You don't have to become a monster yourself."

Catherine shook her head. "God, you are so naive," she said in a condescending tone that Gaia was sure Marsh had used on his daughter many, many times. "You think if there was any other way, we wouldn't use it? Our people are suffering. We need to do something now, not wait years and years for the international courts to get their acts together. And the only thing those cold, bureaucratic bastards pay attention to is the bottom line. We can't get them to be humanitarian, so we must get them to leave. And the only way they will leave is if it becomes too expensive for them to run their slave operations."

"So you ruin their property and kill personnel," Gaia concluded for her.

"Exactly. Soon they realize they will have to spend billions to secure their enterprises from our liberating forces, making it impossible to turn a profit. So they give up. They turn and run like babies."

Gaia stared at Catherine. There was something familiar about her wild-eyed expression, something that hit very close to home. Suddenly she realized who it reminded her of . . . her uncle Loki. He was always able to rationalize doing horrible acts in the name of a "greater good." Using only words, he could twist the most abhorrent crime into something brave and valiant. In his mind he was prophetic, not psychotic—a harbinger of the future, not doom and despair. Catherine, it seemed, had a similar pair of rose-colored terrorist glasses.

Which gave her an idea . . .

Maybe this could end up working in our favor. If there was one positive thing about Gaia's screwed-up childhood, it was that she got very good at dealing with people with twisted senses of reality. All she had to do was make Catherine think she was winning her over—not too easily, but enough to make her lower her defenses.

It would require an Oscar–winning performance, but Gaia could do it. After all, it might be their only hope.

HOG-TIED, OUTNUMBERED, OUTGUNNED

Will kept staring at Gaia with equal parts awe and annoyance. It was unnerving to see her registering zero fear, despite the fact that they were in a place no one knew about surrounded by a handful of armed brutes. Not only did she seem all la-di-da about the whole trapped-in-terrorist-headquarters aspect of their situation, she was actually using this time to chat with Catherine as if they were at a slumber party.

"Don't mind me, y'all," he said, slouching against the wall. "You gals just keep visiting. I'll probably just take a nap."

He'd meant it half as a joke, to try and quell his rapid pulse, but also as a subtle hint to Gaia that she was wasting valuable time and energy.

It didn't work. After a quick glance in his direction, Gaia bowed her head toward Catherine again. "But there are humanitarian organizations that could help," she said. "Why not go to them instead of taking matters in your own hands?"

Will groaned and bumped his back against the wall. He was hungry, tired, frustrated as hell, and barely keeping his panic in check. And now his partner was more interested in debating world economics than preventing them from meeting a grisly death.

At least the numbers were thinning. Rossiter had left with three of the henchmen, heading up the tunnels toward the courthouse. That left only Marsh, Catherine, and two other lackeys. If Will and Gaia were going to make a break, they should do it before Jimmy's bunch returned.

Of course, there was still the little matter of their industrial-grade rope bindings. Not to mention all the loaded guns.

His mind still couldn't quite grasp the fact that Catherine, his fellow trainee and friend, was pointing a loaded Ruger at his head. Or was it his chest? No, not even that high. As she chewed the fat with Gaia, her aim was slowly relaxing. Now the gun was aimed toward his middle.

So that's what Gaia's doing, he realized. She was distracting Catherine, pretending she was interested in their whole radical movement. She was doing a great job of it, too.

If only he could take advantage of it. If only he could find a weapon or send a distress call or hypnotize one of the gunmen, Mesmer-like, into helping them. Anything that could give him hope.

Damn! It seemed like his FBI training should have prepared him for this. But he must have missed the lecture on how to keep from freaking out when you're hog-tied, outnumbered, outgunned, and dizzy from lack of sleep. Either that or he'd been daydreaming about Gaia that day.

"Catherine? What's going on over there?" Marsh called from the center of the room. He was gathered around two crates with the remaining henchmen, looking over a large piece of paper.

Catherine quickly got to her feet, her face flushing slightly. "I'm explaining to Gaia how her country has been lying to her all these years," she explained.

Marsh held out his hand firmly, as if he was giving an order without using words. Instinctively one of his flunkies handed him a switchblade. Will tried to quell the fear that was rising up into his chest. Then Marsh grabbed a piece of fabric off the floor and cut it into two pieces. He strode over and handed them to Catherine.

Marsh glared at Gaia. "Shove this in their mouths. Then come over here for a briefing."

"Okay." Catherine's gun lifted to head level again. "You two, separate," she ordered as she backed toward her father's workstation. "Taylor," she said to Will. "Scoot to your left."

"You don't have to be so formal," Will said snidely. He inched sideways until he was right up against a metal wall brace. "This far enough?"

Catherine smiled, right before shoving a wad of rag into his mouth. "That's fine. If you move an inch, I'll be forced to—" She didn't finish that thought. Instead she glanced furtively at Gaia and then shoved the fabric into her mouth as well.

Will sat back and leaned his head against the metal joist. *Ow!* he thought as something sharp poked his forearm. Glancing down, he saw a rough, serrated corner where the steel beam disappeared into the concrete floor.

Great. Now not only was he unable to talk to Gaia and chewing on something nasty, he was practically impaling himself against a wall of jagged spikes. If he wasn't careful, he could end up slicing open his skin or dying from whatever cleaning solvent this rag had been in contact with.

A sudden realization swept through him, revving the tempo of his heartbeat. Pushing against the wall, he cautiously rubbed his arm against the rough spot again. Yes, it was sharp. Very sharp.

Sharp enough, in fact, to slice through the thickest rope Socorro could buy.

ALMOST PRIMAL

Kim sat across from Special Agent Malloy, trying to stop his legs from bouncing nervously. It worked—for a few seconds. Then his heel would start tapping against the carpeting again, like Thumper pounding the forest floor.

It didn't help that he'd been escorted to the office by a pair of burly jarheads armed with automatic weapons, one of whom now stood to his left and the other in the hall by the door. Nor did it help that his commanding officer was shooting him a look of such intense fury, Kim wouldn't have been surprised to see steam billow from his nostrils. Malloy was a rough, brutish man to begin with. When angered, he seemed almost primal.

"Agent Lau, is it possible that someone with your intelligence would not grasp the magnitude of the situation you are in?" Malloy paused to take a breath, using it to amp up the volume even more. "Ignoring regulations, circumventing security, accessing top-secret clearance files, and helping a fellow trainee go AWOL! Am I forgetting anything?"

Nope. That just about covers it. Understanding the question was rhetorical, Kim kept his mouth shut and glanced down at his quivering kneecap.

Malloy turned and shared a glance with Special Agent Bishop. She raised her eyebrows and shook her head. Ever since she'd stepped into the office, she'd done nothing but serve as a do-wop girl to Malloy's blustery rants. But Kim knew the base's second in command was just as angry and just as capable of making someone squirm as her louder, coarser superior.

"While you have been sitting in the holding cell, my men have been reviewing security tapes and data records," Malloy restarted. "We know what information was being accessed. We know Agent Taylor called up files on Ramon Niño and his group, Socorro."

Kim stared back at him blankly. At the time he hadn't had any clue what Will was searching for. All he knew was that it involved Gaia and Catherine and that Will was trying to help them. He hadn't been privy to the exact details.

When Catherine had gone missing, Kim had also been frustrated at the bureau's official findings. Their explanation that she'd been abducted and killed just didn't make sense. Who kidnaps someone from a heavily armed base? If it was information they wanted, why not nab Malloy or Bishop, someone actually privy to highly classified files? Then, when an agent as smart and dedicated as Gaia had gone AWOL as part of an apparent quest to find Catherine, he'd realized something even more insidious might be at work. Gaia had either thought that the bureau was too inept to find Catherine or, even worse, that they hadn't *wanted* to find her.

Kim glanced at the clock on the wall. He wondered if Will had made it to Gaia yet with the information. Somehow he was sure he had.

"Agent Lau?" Bishop stepped forward and placed her palms on the desk, leaning toward Kim. "What you might not realize is that Ramon Niño is the head of a particularly dangerous group of terrorists. And what you also might not know is that right this minute, he is being transferred to a Pennsylvania courthouse for his parole hearing. We've been tracking his people for a while now, but we've lost contact with one of our undercover agents. Something is going down—we know it."

Kim's gut clenched. Terrorist cells? He'd had no idea the trail would lead his friends into something like that. A couple of blackmailing, kidnapping thugs they could handle. But a group of deadly fanatics? That was something very different.

Malloy rose to his feet, his figure cutting an enormous shadow out of the sunlight that spilled into the room from the window behind him. "Forget your own future for a moment, Agent Lau. If you think you are somehow helping your friends, you are sorely mistaken. And unless you want their blood on your head, I suggest you start telling me everything that you know. So what's it going to be?"

Kim's mind raced, and his eyes darted around the room as if looking for a sign. *What the hell should I do? If I spill my guts, the FBI may simply haul them in and toss them in the brig beside me before they have a chance to rescue Catherine. But if Malloy's right and I do nothing . . .*

"I don't have time for this nonsense!" Malloy boomed. "Guard, take this man to—"

"Wait!" Kim rose to his feet. "I'll help you. I'll tell you what I know—which, by the way, isn't much. But you have to promise me you won't hurt them."

Malloy and Bishop exchanged a brief, indecipherable look. Then Bishop approached Kim and placed her hand on his arm. "Agent Lau, this loyalty you feel for your fellow trainees . . . what makes you think we don't feel it toward all of you?"